WOODEN STARSHIPS

ALSO BY GORDON EKLUND

Cosmic Fusion

WOODEN STARSHIPS

GORDON EKLUND

WILDSIDE PRESS

To the Nameless Ones

"But ever with us are the dreams of our youth…"

Published by Wildside Press LLC.
wildsidepress.com

ONE: MISSILES

i

I know there's still people out there saying how my father, William Gundy, was batshit gaga right from the start. They claim since nothing's been heard from him since he went away it proves he had a screw loose all the time while repeating the long established scientific principle that the velocity of light in a vacuum cannot be exceeded in an Einsteinian universe.

In other words, don't listen to them. They're haters spouting malicious garbage who wouldn't know the truth if it walked up and bit them on the nose.

I ought to know. I was there. The whole entire time. From day one when Pop first went out behind our house in suburban Lake Delridge and started building his two spaceships—*star*ships as it later turned out—made of wood in the back yard.

This was October, 1962. Smack dab in the middle of what historians now refer to as the Cuban Missile Crisis. Also known as the moment when the human race came within a hair's breadth of blowing itself and the planet we inhabit along with several zillion innocent species of plant, animal, fish and fowl, straight to holy fiery hell.

Now tell me again, please: Who was it who was supposedly the raving lunatic here?

* * * *

I'm Charlie by the way. Charles Gundy. (Originally Gunderson but Great Grandpop Isak changed it upon reaching America's welcoming shore, never having much cared for being named after somebody else's son. His father's name being Ingmar, not "Gunder".) Second of four children of William and Lotus (née Snead) Gundy, born (this is me here) August 6, 1945, and, yep, in case you didn't catch the coincidence, that's the same day a B-29 bomber, the *Enola Gay*, dropped a sixteen-kiloton atomic bomb on top of the bucolic seaport city of Hiroshima, Japan, wiping out in the whisk of an eye 66,000 or so men, women, and children. (Many tens of thousands more would eventually follow, dying from various wounds, burns, radiation poisoning, whatever, in the months and years afterward.) And this is without even mentioning the countless other lifeforms wiped out simultaneously.

So again I ask: who are we calling bonkers around here?

* * * *

Back to the Cuban Missile Crisis.

It was 1962. To be more precise, the twenty-second day of October, 1962, 4:00 p.m. Pacific Time as our duly elected (by the meager, often disputed total of 114,673 votes out of some 69 million cast, though none of them mine, since I was a mere whippet of fifteen on Election Day 1960—and also a dedicated Nixon man to boot, though never mind that part, please) President of the United States of America, John Fitzgerald Kennedy, addressed the nation (including us five Gundys clustered around the living room black-and-white Zenith).

He began:

"Good evening, my fellow citizens. This Government—" a brief pause here "—as promised—" another pause, equally brief "—has maintained the closest surveillance of the Soviet military buildup on the island of Cuba. Within the past week unmistakable evidence has established the fact that a series of offensive missile sites is now in preparation on that imprisoned island. The purpose of these bases can be none other than to provide a nuclear strike capability against the Western hemisphere."

And so on. (*Blah-blah-blah.*)

Me, a fresh-faced lad of seventeen, a high school senior, a proud (if frequently onanistic) virgin, who loved his country and family and liked nothing better on a rainy afternoon than to curl up in bed with a good book—especially if it was science fiction—and who hated no one beyond the various bullies who had plagued and persecuted him throughout his boyhood as they had every other sensitive young man of the period as personified (bullies) by one Ronnie "Hogbreath" Hightower, president of the senior class of Lake Delridge High, and whose one and only thought (this is me again) listening to these stirring presidential words was: *This crazy coot wants to kill me!*

JFK: "It shall be the policy of this nation to regard any nuclear missile launched from Cuba against any nation in the Western Hemisphere as an attack by the Soviet Union on the United States, requiring a full retaliatory strike upon the Soviet Union."

With me, silently praying: Christ Jesus, man, I do not wish to die. Not now. Not any time soon. Not later either but who, at seventeen, was thinking in such long terms? (Well, me maybe. But I was a science fiction fan.)

* * * *

Oh, and by the way, what we found out only later on, there were actually two kinds of Soviet missiles involved here, coded the SS-4 and the SS-5. The former, a medium range missile with a theoretical range of 1,100 (likely exaggerated) miles could reach (theoretically) all of the southeastern United States as far north as Washington itself, D.C. By the time of the president's October 22 speech, three of the four SS-4 sites under construction in Cuba were operational, poised to hurl a dozen or so missiles USA-ward. The SS-5, a longer range intermediate missile capable of soaring some 2,200 miles upon launch, was anticipated to be deployed at another four Cuban sites with an estimated completion date in early December, just in time for the always hectic Christmas buying season. These missiles, given the unofficial estimates, could reach every single significant American city except—

Here's where the punchline comes:

Seacrest, Washington.

Which is where I, yours truly, Charlie Gundy, happened then to dwell. With his loving family.

Not that anybody bothered mentioning any of this at the time. We Americans expected to be all in this thing together. One American city goes up in a mushroom cloud, all other American cities go right up with it—in spirit if not in actual burnt, charred flesh.

But since good old all-out armed nuclear conflict eyeball-to-eyeball with the Rooskies never actually took place—not at this time anyhow—I suppose all this is basically beside the point, though still cheerful to contemplate, the part about me and mine likely being spared, that is.

A number of Soviet leaders, notably including Premier Khrushchev's most intimate advisor, his son-in-law Sergei, later declared that several armed nuclear warheads were already present on Cuba at the time of the crisis and ready to be fired if and when needed.

If true, this would appear to indicate that actual all-out nuclear conflict stood much nearer fruition than anyone realized at the time.

Including, it would seem, the highest officials of the United States government.

But everybody's allowed a few slip-ups per lifetime, right?

It says so in the Bible, does it not?

The way it looks to me now, given an American invasion of Cuba, (the option just about every member of the president's ad hoc Executive Committee supported in their initial deliberations of 18 October and still an actively anticipated event as late as Sunday the 28th), with an invasion tentatively scheduled to occur as early as dawn on the 30th, killing as it no doubt would a significant number of Russian soldiers and scientists, and thus leading in turn to a panicked Soviet army commander ordering a prompt retaliatory missile strike against the continental U.S.

Use them or lose them, so to speak. And no rational Soviet commander worth his weight in salt who wanted to avoid slaving the rest of his life in a Siberian, um, salt mine (joke!) was about to surrender an armed nuclear warhead to a bunch of invading American Marines.

No, siree!

Launch!

So, assuming the presence of nuclear warheads and assuming a Soviet commander thinking rationally, then—*ka-bang!*—there went (at least) Miami Beach.

And here came—*ka-bang, ka-boo!*—World War (*wheee!!*) III.

Only just saying.

But it never happened.

Apocalypse averted! World saved! We the living (note reference here to the writings of Ayn Rand) went right on living!

Hooray for our side!

* * * *

My own pet theory, based on my later somewhat obsessive study of the matter (funny how one tends to get hung up on peripheral kipple—useless stuff—like people trying to kill you) is that the whole "crisis" was pretty much done and over with well before the moment President Kennedy opened his keen Irish mouth on national television that Monday night, that it had in fact ended a number of days earlier at the second top secret Ex-Comm meeting when Robert Kennedy jabbed a finger at the scowling puss of former Secretary of State (1949-53) Dean Acheson, prime architect of the U.S. Cold War containment strategy, and yelped nasally, "My brother will not go down in history as the American Tojo. We Americans do not do sneak attacks."

Acheson referred to this later as "sophomoric drivel."

Which—*chuck-a-muck!*—perhaps it was. There's even, if you peer closely, a certain racist tinge to it. (*Sneaky Orientals*.) But since said sophomoric drivel from the mouth of the younger brother undoubtedly reflected the opinions of the elder president, nobody was going to dismiss them out of hand.

And the proposed invasion (sneak attack) never happened.

"It is *insane* that two men, sitting on opposite sides of the world, should be able to decide to bring an end to civilization," John Kennedy was later heard to remark. (Emphasis mine.)

You can say that again, Jack-o!

* * * *

But, whoops! Getting a little ahead of our story here.

Let's backtrack.

October 22. 1962. 4:17 p.m. Speech over.

Man, was I pissed. Not just mad either. I mean *angry* mad. *Mean* mad. *Outraged!*

For, as I said, the crazy sons-of-a-bitch here and in Russia seemed intent on killing me. How come? I hadn't done anything to them. I was a mere boy. Seventeen years old. A child. A virgin as previously noted. Only kissed one girl in my life, Bonnie Greenberg, back when I was thirteen. It wasn't right, man. It wasn't—stop me if you've heard this one before—*it wasn't fair.*

I sprang to my feet. Tears of rage clouding my vision like rain on a windshield, I spun a pirouette, shifting on the big toe of my left foot, brown penny loafer, sock underneath as white as the snows of Kilimanjaro when…

Guess what?

I couldn't budge an inch.

Because there he hovered right behind me. The whole time too, I'd be willing to bet. Looming back there as motionless as a ghost, never uttering a sound, like a statue carved from marble, and me crouched there in front of him on the fur-encrusted (two dogs, three cats, not to mention three kids) living room carpet.

My father. William Gundy. Pop.

We stood toe-to-toe. At five-eleven I loomed a good four inches above him.

Our eyeballs locked. Three of them. (Bill Gundy, blind in his left eye from a botched kitchen table surgical operation by a drunken doctor back when he was an infant, black piratical patch covering the vacant eye socket.)

We did not speak.

* * * *

Now I know what the whole world wonders at this point, what everyone wants to know. Is this when it happened? Did you see it there in his eye? You were there, Charlie Gundy, at the exact moment of inception—of origin—of creation. Tell us what you saw. Tell us everything, boy—the truth, the whole truth. Speak.

Sorry. I have to be honest here: I didn't have a clue. I looked Bill Gundy square in his one good right eye. He did not blink.

"So, Pop, what do you think?" I could have said. "Sure looks like World War III's on its way, right?"

I could have said that.

But I didn't.

"Goddamn it," I heard him murmur. Breathlessly. All in a single gasp. *Goddamn it.*

That was it though.

Then I noticed that Mom was crying.

Which gave me genuine pause.

It wasn't as if I'd never seen Mom cry before. For instance when her beloved Granny Snead died at age 98, the four-foot nine-inch Texas side-winder who'd raised Mom and her brother Phil down there in the Red River Valley where the Panhandle meets the Comanche Nation following the sui-cide of Mom's natural father J.C. Snead on Christmas Day, 1926, when she was only ten. (Family gossip rumored it had something to do with another woman, a divorcée.)

Mom sat at the dining room table, her regular perch in those years, where you'd likely find her either reading or else playing five-card solitaire, cards spread out in front of her, paperback book turned spine up. Let's call it the Signet 35 cent edition of Isaac Asimov's *The Caves of Steel*. You know, the one with the robot detective and the future city of New York teeming with forty million people jampacked together like kittens in a sack. (Mom always read whatever I was reading and most of what I read was science fiction, though thanks to my friend Tom Powers, a writer himself, I'd begun branching out to Steinbeck, Salinger, and a cool book I found in the town library called *The Dharma Bums* by Jack Kerouac.)

"Mom," I said, hurrying over, "what's wrong?"

She gave her head a shake.

"But you're crying."

Voices could be heard coming from the living room, TV anchors and newsmen blathering blithely on about the president's courageous speech and how the Strategic Air Command was on full alert, bomb bays poised, and the navy steaming full speed ahead and General de Gaulle had the presi-dent's back and the Queen of England and Prime Minister Nehru were danc-ing a frisky jig. (I wasn't really listening all that closely.)

"Russia and Cuba are the same as us," I heard myself saying. "They're only defending themselves. And that crazy Kennedy wants to blow every-body up for no good goddamn reason."

"Charlie, don't curse," said Mom, dabbing at her eyes.

That's when I heard it. For the first time. The sound of hammers and saws. Emanating from the backyard.

Turning my head, I noticed that that Pop was no longer standing where I'd last left him.

I went over and looked out the window.

There he was. Out in the yard. Standing in the rain, a hammer cocked in one fist, crosscut saw at his feet.

"What's your father doing out there?" Mom called over to me.

"It looks like he's building something," I called back.

"I wonder what on earth it could be."

Earth had nothing to do with it, as we soon found out.

ii

The next day, like it or not, was school. It was Tuesday the 23rd of October at Jesus H. Christ Senior High. (As I sometimes liked to think of it.) In reality: Lake Delridge High. Our school nickname: the Fightin' Geoducks. Not that I felt in the least like being there. But federal law stipulated that because we were located in a peak military zone the school district got certain specified federal dollars for every student who showed up daily for class and when one failed to appear it cost everybody where it mattered. In the wallet. And that was bad. Worse than bad—like drowning a newborn puppy.

Or at least that was how Vice Principal Mortimer Washburn (aka *The Prune*—I always had a way with nicknames) phrased it to me when I skipped my early morning PE class one rare sunshiny spring day and went frog hunting in the slime pool near the airport while mentally drafting a letter of comment in response to the latest monthly issue of our local science fiction club fanzine, *The Howl of the Rocketeers*.

My truancy was (big word coming, he non-verbally indicated me in advance, wagging a finger like Leonard Bernstein's baton under my nose) *irresponsible*.

Like washing one's drawers in a public drinking fountain. (My own simile.)

Then he gave me two weeks' cafeteria detention. Worse than the regular afterschool variety, because it was during school hours so every other kid got to snicker and sneer observing your shame as you wiped their spilled crap off the tabletops. Like a dog licking up its own shit on a sidewalk, as my friend Cisco Cordova eloquently pointed out to me.

* * * *

But that was then. This is a different day we're talking about.

It was—in case you've forgotten—October 23, 1962.

I was a senior that year. One of 492 in our Class of '63, Lake Del Hi, a three-story red brick fortress in the shape of the letter 'L', originally erected in (I adore the stiffness of the terminology) 1936 and among the initial seventy-three graduates none other than my great-uncle Adolph Gundy later to die serving his country invading the volcanic isle of Iwo Jima, his name now inscribed on a memorial plaque out by the football field.

My first 8:00 a.m. class of the day was scheduled for the Block. So I headed straight there off the bus, taking my assigned seat in the first row of the right rear quadrant and propping my pee-chee portfolio open strategically in front of me so as to conceal the presence of the latest December 1962 issue of *Serendipity Fact & Science Fiction*, containing among other items the article "Hari Botts's Basement Battery Defies Conventional Science" by the magazine's editor-in-chief Kingsley C.K. Babbitt IV. For usage if and when things turned dull. Which, normally, was right from the start. (The magazine also contained a new Poul Anderson serial I was halfway through.)

The Block, I ought to here explain, was the Big New Experimental Learning System that year, implanted in the old tin barn of an unused metal shop building at the back of the school grounds adjoining the student parking lot where all the greasy wannabe JD rinks hung out between classes smoking unfiltered Pall Malls and receiving furtive hand jobs from their skanky bleached blond girlfriends dressed in black leather jackets.

Within the Block there were crammed this particular autumn morning some ninety-seven students, the cream of the school's intellectually superior senior-class elite, me numbered among them, though less for my actual achievements, which were minimal—2.5 cumulative grade point average—but rather for my tested potential, which remained (in theory at least) as vast as the plains of Jupiter.

The classroom was set up so that it could be partitioned off by heavy blue-black (our school colors) curtains into as many as four smaller groups of approximately twenty-five students each or else you could pull the curtains all the way back to make it into a single big room for the entire hundred or so students. On paper we were supposed to study contemporary problems/psychology for an hour and then advanced English for the second hour. But it seldom worked that way in practice. There were four teachers assigned to the Block: Mr. Larry Lemon, the bald and impassioned one, whose son—a jerk—was also in the class; Mr. Bill Moberg, the younger, vaguely cool one who liked Dave Brubeck records and Broadway show tunes; Miss Edna Mae Hunt with her wooden leg and faintly Southern accent; and Mr. Ken Myerson, the rough, take-no-shit vice-principal wannabe who could recite the entirety of Shakespeare's *Julius Caesar* using a chorus of voices. Mr. Lemon was the chief contemporary affairs guy, the one who told you at the start of the year that all he wanted was to teach you *how* to think, not *what* to think, and if you went through the entire year without ever deducing his own point of view, then his teaching was a grand success.

"Liberal pansy," murmured the soft seductive voice behind my left ear instantly recognizable as Sue Dietz, recording secretary of Lake Delridge's John Galtist Group and the subject of several late night wet dreams in the weeks just past. (Mine, I here confess.)

Today in the shadow of an incipient World War III, I sat huddled as usual between my two all-time best schoolyard buddies, the three of us dating back as an informal team to kindergarten. (Think of us as Curly, Moe, and Larry for short.)

Like patient lambs awaiting slaughter, we sat poised waiting for the clanging of the final bell.

Prior to which event I gave my pencil a gentle shove and watched it topple lazily off the sloping edge of my desk to the floor below and then in reaching down to retrieve it I managed to cock my head at just such a precise angle as to provide me with an unvarnished view of Sue Dietz's exposed left kneecap where it lay crossed like a block of chiseled ivory upon the equally gorgeous, though furtively hidden beneath the folds of the green plaid skirt she wore every Tuesday and Thursday, knob of her right kneecap.

My, um, heart gently throbbed.

"So how come you happen to drop your pencil like that every morning?" quizzed a voice to my nearest left. *Curly's voice*, you might call it. (Actually Cisco Cordova's voice. And his pile of black Spanish hair anything but curly.).

"Stick it," I whispered back. (You may call me *Moe*.)

Returning to a fully upright posture proved more awkward than usual as my, um, heart was not the only bodily part throbbing. As pointed out by Dr. Albert Ellis in one his sexual treatises, several of which I'd read over the summer past, fear and anxiety are major sexual stimulants among the young and vulnerable. (Like for instance, say, me facing the threat of nuclear annihilation while looking at a bare female kneecap.)

"Easy, Charlie," murmured a voice to my right. *Larry*. Actually Nedd Young, who encompassed in his person Lake Del's one and only native-born Negro student—a status he'd proudly maintained for all the dozen years we'd been going to school together. Nedd and his dad happened to make their home in a converted garage turned shotgun shack located directly behind the Gundy family backyard fence.

"Can't help it," I whispered. "Body over mind."

"What mind?" Cisco unhelpfully chipped in.

The bell rang.

At which moment Mr. Lemon and his bald head strode boldly forth to its accustomed spot directly squat center in the middle of the four quadrants, curtains drawn back, and hurling a white-sleeved arm Caesar-like in the air, he began:

"So last night we all sat in front of our TV sets and watched and listened and we all heard the same words. Right? We heard what the president meant for us hear. Right? Ah, but did we? Did we all hear it the same? And did we hear it the way Señor Castro did? Or Premier Khrushchev? And what of our boys manning the attack submarines in the Caribbean? Or the ones in the air flying their B-52's? Or the French? Our allies. And the people of Mexico and Peru? What about the Red Chinese? What's their stake in this? If World War comes, won't they fight too? Who wants to start things off today?"

A dusky figure in the far right corner of my vision rose heroically to his feet. All five foot two inches worth of him.

At my side Cisco groaned.

My own mind immediately reverted to the candid black-and-white image of last year's junior varsity girls gymnastic team as captured on page 202 of the 1961-62 edition of our Lake Delridge annual, *The Clam Shell*, depicting the eleven nubile squad members propped on a balance beam in their skintight black leotards, among them posed, third from the front, the full expanse of her creamy lower limbs revealed, Sue Dietz.

And she was smiling. Beckoning. As if at me.

As a matter of policy, I kept a sheaf of similar mental images conveniently stored at the forefront of my adolescent brain for ready reference in the event of incipient classroom boredom.

Cisco noticed my eyes glazing over. He poked me with an elbow. "Wake up, buddy."

The mental image vanished in a pop.

Oh, and by the way, did I mention earlier that of the 1,867 pupils enrolled in Lake Delridge Senior High in October 1962, a grand total of three could be classified as other than white? One you've already met—my old pal Nedd Young, who'd been around so long we'd mostly forgotten he was black. (Though he hadn't.)

The two others were brand new this school year.

One was our senior class exchange student. From far-off, exotic East Pakistan: Amida Abdul Sirrah. Who thus far, stalking the halls in her weird flowing get-ups, had been overheard not to utter a single word in any known language with the sole exception of the phrase, *Happy to be in America.* With Amida mostly what anyone wanted to know was what she wore underneath those flowing gowns.

Our third non-white was the real problem, now on its feet. Raymond Sung. From Singapore. Whose old man now owned Clem & Clyde's Burgerland at the corner of Delridge Drive and First Avenue South where on Friday nights the cool rinks and grease monkeys hung out in their flashy cars while the lame and meek and mild—me, for example—stayed home reading science fiction books and writing for fanzines and thinking prurient thoughts of creamy white thighs and skin-tight black leotards.

The same Raymond Sung who had already earned a major reputation for never knowing when to shut his moronic mouth.

So now, as pretty much usual this time of day, there he stupidly stood on his tiny Asian feet, orating in the general vicinity of his red tennis sneakers while the rest of us fidgeted and made sickly faces and rolled our eyes and even kindly bald Mr. Lemon had long since given up trying to appear interested.

"...and the president is terribly mistaken if he believes the rest of the world will tolerate his militaristic posture…"

And so on. (*Blah-blah-blah.*)

Though that doesn't really capture the tone or the essence. It was never so much what Raymond Sung said as how he said it: in fits and starts of monotone, like a Guy Lombardo record stuck in a groove playing the same dull keening note over and over again.

After ten or twenty minutes of babble—or so it seemed—Mr. Lemon finally cut Raymond off: "That's, ah, a really interesting point, Raymond. Thanks for sharing your viewpoint. But is that the only viewpoint? Isn't there an alternative? Who wants to give it a try? Yes, Ronnie, you."

A hushed groan. (Mine this time.)

Moi bête noire. Ronnie Hightower. Not that he knew of my loathing. Or even, really, knew much of me. Except, I'd imagine, as a kind of splotchy blur at the far peripheral edge of his vision. For Ronnie Hightower and I resided in different worlds—if not different galaxies. Ronnie and his close-cropped Ivy League hair, his khaki pants with the buckle in the butt. Toss in the white sweat socks, tasseled loafers, and the short-sleeve cotton shirt with the buttons in the collar. Senior class president. Not to mention commander-in-chief of the John Galtist Group. And also voted (at least by me) as the boy most likely to attain carnal knowledge of Sue Dietz before the class of '63 graduated.

As usual, Ronnie spoke with utmost confidence. "I think Kennedy is a coward, Mr. Lemon. This is our one real chance in years to stand tall and show what this country really stands for and instead of doing it and wiping out the Commies in Cuba once and for all he wants to wait and negotiate. The Reds only understand one thing, Mr. Lemon—brute force. I say we hit them hard and hit them now, because then they'll never dare confront us again."

"Because we'll all be dead," Cisco muttered at my elbow, but only loud enough for me to hear.

Actually, to give fair credit, Cisco had been known now and then to rise to his feet and voice a genuine dissent to the prevailing classroom viewpoint (among those who actually spoke up) that Barry Goldwater was an intellectual prince and all Democrats from the president on down groveled in mongrel dog poop.

Unlike, for instance, me—under normal circumstances a total coward when it came to public speaking.

But not this time. No, sir. I'd had enough. This was my moment to shine.

But unfortunately right then—just as I was about to leap to my feet and deliver a righteously withering response that would demolish Ronnie Hightower utterly and result in a standing ovation from the entire class, up to and including a suddenly converted Sue Dietz, her white cotton panties knotted in a bunch, who would then lift up her green plaid skirt to reveal thighs like ivory pinions and would then—

Anyway, this was when the fire siren went off.

Loudly.

We all froze where we sat.

What the—? thought all of us in unison

Now this was not necessarily extraordinary. As a matter of fact each and every day precisely at noon the siren went off on the roof of the local fire station seven blocks from the school grounds and you could hear it everywhere, indoors and out. The noon siren such a regular phenomenon of life in Lake Delridge that nobody hardly noticed it—certainly not consciously.

Except for old Henry Tucker, the half-crazed First World War vet gassed at Chateau-Thierry who lived in a tin shack in the woods below Five Corners, collected junk, which he sometimes resold, and drank fermented grape juice till he puked up his guts and howled like a hound dog whenever the siren went off. Which was every day. At noon.

But this wasn't noon. It wasn't even close.

Then I heard a sudden scream and looked over just in time to see Miss Hunt, our beloved one-legged English teacher, go hopping down the center aisle, head tossed back like it was bobbing on a stick.

Then came a shout: "Everybody get down!" It was Mr. Myerson taking charge. "Duck and cover! Now! Move! *Everybody hit the deck!*"

The deck? What deck? There were only walls and curtains. Like lemmings seeking shelter, we all raced for the curtained walls.

Lord, I thought, huddling with the rest, so this was it. This was war. *World War III.*

And me smack in the middle of it.

The fire siren wailed on: *Wheeoooow!*

The preferred position, as best I could recall from previous drills, consisted of kneeling on the floor with both hands overhead, face buried in arms and elbows to protect the eyeballs and turned away from any exploding windows.

A clamor of slithering knees. A couple of muted whimpers. A sharp intake of breath. Then out of it all came a familiar voice—Raymond Sung—his mumbled words indecipherable—and then cut short by a wordless *snap*. Had somebody just throttled him? I was reasonably certain he'd only been trying to pray.

As for me, no prayers. After all, I'd been raised an agnostic, had I not? So I just lay there. No, knelt. On the bare naked floor. Eyes shut. Hands overhead.

And waited for.... What?

Death? Extinction? Annihilation? Obliteration? The Four Horsemen of the Apocalypse? But didn't I just get through saying I was an agnostic? You see, that was the horror of the battlefield, 1962 style. Because you never knew what to believe till it actually happened and once it did, then you were never likely to know anyhow, on account of being like dead, a burnt bread crust pronged in the electric toaster of life. Or death.

Something smelled. I sniffed the air. Oddly, it smelled rather pleasant. It wafted. A sweet perfume scent that tickled the nostrils and twitched the lower brain. In a way, agnostic or not, I could have been glimpsing heaven. Or at least the gently rolling fields of ancient Greece. The Elysian ones.

I let my eyes slide open. I glanced swiftly around. No, I wasn't in heaven. No Elysian fields here. Just a bunch of scared kids cowering on the floor next to curtained walls.

Then I saw it—saw her.

For there, not an iota distant from where I currently knelt awaiting my final fleeting moments of earthly consciousness, there loomed, as if in mute revelation, the white fluffy ruffles of a young girl's blouse.

An unbuttoned blouse.

Sue Dietz's blouse.

And there, exposed to casual view, where my eye could easily penetrate, the cup of her left breast, as pure and white as mare's milk. As if in answer to an unspoken prayer. (Never mind that Raymond Sung had been the one praying, not me.)

So what to do?

A dilemma.

Not that I could have helped myself. I moved as if in a mystical trance. I edged closer. I slithered. I snaked. Till the skin of my face grazed warm flesh. My lips opened, my tongue slid, and then—that fast—I was doing it.

I was licking the crest of Sue Dietz's naked left breast.

No, really. I was.

Back and forth. Up and down. Back and forth. Up and down.

I heard her gently moan. (Well, didn't I?)

And then I felt it—at the tip of my tongue—like the treasure at the bottom of a crackerjack box—the tawny tautness of her... nipple.

I believe it was at that point that I fainted dead away.

Cisco later claimed he'd found me afterward passed out with my tongue lolling on my chin.

It was further rumored (by him) that I had ejaculated. Though how he could tell that, I preferred not to contemplate. But at some point, while I lay unconscious, the siren stopped.

And Sue Dietz apparently skedaddled.

"Okay, everybody," I heard Mr. Myerson calling, as I snapped awake. "Everybody back to your seats. It was only a drill."

iii

The earliest known Gundersons from whom I trace my descent were residents of Fasta Aland, an autonomous Swedish-speaking region of Finland located at the entrance to the Gulf of Bothnia in the Baltic Sea. After my great-grandfather Isak (renamed) Gundy first arrived in America leaving his wife and two young children behind (a daughter Elise, a son Augustus known as Gus), he rode the Great Northern Railroad across the broad expanse of the continent to northwest Washington state, where several of his Gunderson cousins had earlier settled. Finding the area less than compatible—"too much wet," he growled—he drifted east again, eventually arriving in the gold mining region of central Colorado in the mountains above Adobe, the fabled "Pittsburgh of the West," home to the giant Colorado Iron and Fuel Company steel mill, whose majority stockholder was John D. Rockefeller, Jr. The mill then in the midst of a bitter months-long strike that only ended when the Colorado National Guard opened fire on the line of picketing strikers killing 13 and wounding many others while allowing the several hundred waiting strikebreaking scab workers to enter the plant to go to work. Numbered among these latter was my great-grandfather Isak, whose gold mining endeavors in the mountains near Cripple Creek had come to naught.

Assured of a steady job, Great-Grandpop Isak sent for his wife and two children to join him in Adobe. In time two additional sons were born, Albert and Adolph. The eldest son, Gus, soon joined their father working in the CH & I mill. In March 1913 when the Arkansas River overflowed its banks flooding the city of Adobe, the first born infant son of nineteen-year-old Gus Gundy and his Irish bride Caitlin came down with a swelling of the brain that threatened his life. When the company doctor fetched to perform the surgery needed to save the child turned up blind drunk, it was Gus's elder sister Elise who performed the operation on the family kitchen table while standing in her wading boots knee deep in water. In the end the swelling of the brain was relieved, the child survived, but in the course of the surgery his left eye was severely damaged and had to later be removed.

These ancient family stories and many more were told to me by my parents as I was growing up. They never tried to use them to make any particular point or teach a lesson beyond just one: "Don't trust them," Pop told me over and over. "Don't ever let them fool you again."

The odd part though was that he never told who "they" were supposed to be.

"You'll know them when you meet them," he said, when I asked.

* * * *

When I arrived home from school the afternoon of October 23, 1962, the day following President Kennedy's televised address to the nation concerning the Soviet missile bases in Cuba, I found everything pretty much normal with my thirteen-year-old kid sister Polly, the math genius, sprawled on the living room sofa, working on her own secret form of trigonometry in the notebook diary she kept under lock and key, and my little five-year-old brother, the Dink, curled up on the floor a few inches from the TV showing *Weatherman Willy's Chuckle Cartoon Carnival* featuring Popeye the Sailor Man on channel 11. Mom at the dining room table was reading another of my science fiction paperbacks in between hands of five-card solitaire. The book this time was *Double Star* by Robert A. Heinlein, about an out-of-work actor named the Great Lorenzo who goes to Mars and ends up pretending to be somebody he isn't. *Wish I was there with him,* was my thought at the time.

From the backyard I could hear the sound of rhythmic hammering.

"What's going on with that?" I asked Mom, while making myself a bologna sandwich, four thick slices of meat squeezed between some Wonder bread and mustard.

"It's just your father again."

Puzzled, I went over and looked out the window. There he was all right, once again hammering away at… something.

"Any idea what he's making out there?" I asked.

She didn't look up from her book. "Building spaceships, he says."

"He's building spaceships made out of wood?"

"That's what he told me, yes." She turned the page.

TWO: FOUR COMMANCHEROS

i

Her given name was Daphne Irene Kopplewicz. I know because shortly before graduation I happened to sneak a peek at her official school records while hanging out in the counseling office with Nedd Young, who was trying to find out about scholarships he might qualify for at Oberlin College in Ohio where he'd been accepted for the coming fall semester. Her IQ on the Stanford-Binet Test was listed at 138 and she'd previously attended schools in Vallejo, California and Nampa, Idaho.

None of which jibed with what she'd been telling the rest of us. Even the IQ part was questionable, since she claimed to be a Mensa member and I happened to know because of a man named Warren Wunderly who was supposedly a high muck amuck in the organization that it took an IQ of 140 to qualify.

The name she was using by the time she enrolled at Lake Delridge Senior High was Katy Cross.

Where at first she told everyone who asked that she was a transfer student from New York City.

Me, the first time I set eyes on her, I remember thinking to myself, *Jeez, what a freak.*

This would have been late October 1962 when calling somebody a freak was not regarded as a compliment.

She came striding into the morning Block shortly before class started that fateful Wednesday, October 24, 1962, dressed in a polka-dot pink and green sweater with threads dangling everywhere, some kind of bright purple peasant skirt that drooped to her ankles, white cotton sweat socks barely visible beneath, and black Keds. Her dark hair twisted back from her forehead and braided into twin pigtails. She wore no make-up except for spots of rouge on each cheek and a third at the tip of her chin.

"Hey kids, it's Bozo the Clown," murmured a voice from beside me, which I knew belonged to Cisco Cordova.

"Be quiet," I said.

"Jay P. Patches," murmured the same voice. "Or Gertrude." A reference to a local kids' TV clown personality and his cross-dressing sidekick.

"I said shut up, Cisco."

As I lowered my eyes to the textbook on the armrest of my seat, I heard a *slap, slap, slapping* sound drawing increasingly near.

I didn't want to look up.

The *slap-slap-slapping* stopped. A pregnant silence followed.

I ventured a peek.

There she stood, looming over me like a bird fallen from its nest, the threadbare sweater less than six inches from my chin.

"Is this seat taken?" she asked.

"Well, it's—"

Without awaiting a reply, she spun a twist and plopped down in the empty seat beside me. "Good, because it's now mine."

"That's where my friend usually sits," I said. Meaning Nedd, whose regular seat it indeed was. But he wasn't at school today—something about visiting a sick aunt in the Central (or more popularly "Colored") District in downtown Seacrest. More likely, I figured, his dad was probably just hungover again and needed somebody to cook him breakfast.

"So what?" She was chewing gum. A lot of it. Her cheek bulged. "Where is he?"

"I mean, it's somebody else's regular seat."

"I don't see a name. They're assigned?"

"Well, sort of—yes."

She smirked. "Sort of's not good enough, bud."

"Look," I said, trying another tact, "it's against school rules to chew gum in class. You could get detention."

"No fucking shit." Resting her chin in the palm of her hand, she surveyed the room.

At the time I don't believe I'd ever heard a female utter the word *shit* before. Let alone *fucking* shit.

I swallowed hard.

The entire time she hadn't looked directly at me once beyond the initial quick smirk. Instead her head turned slowly on her shoulders, pausing briefly to meet the gaze of all the other eyes staring back at her, chin lifted, dabs of red rouge shining.

"Sure is a nosey bunch here," she muttered in my direction. "Guess they've never seen a lady before."

"That our new foreign exchange student?" came a loud voice—Ronnie Hightower, I knew—followed by a bray of appreciative giggling.

"You know, this bunch is even dumber than I expected," she said with a plaintive sigh.

Again, she seemed to be talking to me. "Look," I said, deciding to try again, "there's a bunch of us who sit together and we kind of...."

I let my voice drift off, realizing that it no longer seemed to matter. Cisco was staring down the row, trying to catch my eye. I ignored him.

"You don't really mind my company, do you?" she said.

"No... I guess not."

"Good. Wonderful." Suddenly her hand was resting on top of mine. "I needed that, you know."

The strangest electric ripple coursed through my body.

Then the warning bell rang. The shuffle of pee-chees and notebook paper being primed in readiness like gusts of rustling wind.

"You better get rid of that gum," I whispered.

"Right-o, pal. Thanks." She raised a palm to her mouth, made a spitting noise, and the hand whisked down out of sight under her chair.

I stared straight ahead, knowing that Cisco was still trying to catch my eye. But I couldn't be bothered—not then.

"I'm Katy Cross," she said. "From New York."

"New York *City*?" I said, impressed in spite of myself. Like most of the kids I knew, for me anything east of the Rockies was exotic terrain.

"My lord, yes." She dipped a hand into her purse, which might well have been a knapsack as vast as it was, and pulled out a well creased paperbound book. "And do I ever miss it right now."

She bent her head, opening the book.

Right then it was as if God had punched me in the belly.

The book was *Childhood's End.* By Arthur C. Clarke. A Ballantine paperback. Thirty-five cents.

A science fiction novel!

The final bell sounded.

"Good book?" I managed to squeak.

"Great, actually." She was reading now, head down, no longer looking at me.

"Then you must be a... a..." I swallowed so hard my Adam's apple threatened to pop through the skin of my neck. "You mean you're a—you're a science fict—"

Tragically, before I could find the words to fully articulate my thoughts, Mr. Lemon raced to the head of the class, tore off his glasses in a flourish, and said, "So here we are on the third day of the crisis that threatens to put an end to the world as we know it. Or to Western Civilization, I should say. Has anybody heard the latest news?"

For a long moment we all held our collective breath, anticipating the worst.

"The ships have stopped," drawled a voice from behind. Ronnie Hightower again. I was still staring at Katy Cross—and the book she was reading.

"What ships are those, Ronnie?" Mr. Lemon asked.

"The supposed Soviet supply ships. They've stopped dead in the water short of our naval blockade. It was on the news this morning."

"So what do you think that may mean, Ronnie?"

"I say it means we won, sir. We stood up to them—like Senator Goldwater has been saying we should. They threw up their hands like the cowards they are and quit."

"The cowards of Stalingrad," muttered a voice. I cocked my head. It was her, all right—Katy Cross.

"We went eyeball to eyeball with the Reds," Sue Dietz quickly piped up in, from her dutiful perch at Ronnie's elbow, "and they were the ones who blinked."

There was a spontaneous burst of applause. I joined in rather hesitantly, having heard the news myself on the radio just before leaving the house but figuring, *Big deal, so all they have to do is start up their engines again.*

Still, Katy Cross might have been the only student in the room who failed to join in the sustained clapping. Instead, she slipped her book back inside her purse, folded her arms on her chest, and curled her lip in a sneer.

Mr. Lemon said, "Any thoughts from anyone else on the meaning of this morning's events?"

I expected to then hear Raymond Sung prattling on but instead it was the girl beside me—yes, Katy Cross—who rose to her feet, not even bothering with the usual prelude of raising her hand.

"I've got something to say."

"Ah, you do, Miss... Miss...?" His face showed consternation. Who was this girl? "And what—what might that be, young lady?"

"What I think it means—since you asked—what all this absurd charade comes down to—is that we may get to stay alive for a few more hours. So big goddamn deal."

And she sat promptly down again.

I couldn't believe my ears. I mean, this was Lake Delridge Senior High, the morning Block, the fall of 1962, and there were Mr. Lemon and Ronnie Hightower and Sue Dietz and there was...

Anyway, you just didn't ever say *goddamn.*

The ensuing silence dragged on forever. As if we were all frozen in place like terrified seals on a melting ice flow. There weren't even the nervous titters you might have expected.

"And you are?" Mr. Lemon, finally managed. The polished crown of his bald dome beaded with moisture.

"I thought I already signed in," she said, from her chair beside me, not even standing. "I'm Katy Cross."

"The new transfer student from Idaho," Mr. Moberg helpfully put in.

Both he and Mr. Myerson had joined Mr. Lemon at the front of the class in an apparent show of pedagogical solidarity.

"Well, young lady, Miss Cross, let me welcome you to Lake Delridge High School and to the state of Washington. But I do need to remind you that as open as our discussions are we need to monitor our choice of language."

"How come?" she asked.

I thought it wasn't a bad question. But the tittering began.

"Because," said Mr. Lemon, after a pause, "even when disagreeing, we must respect the views of others."

"When the whole world's about to be blown sky high?" she asked. "When we're all scrambling around on the floor, hugging our heads like beanballs?" She hadn't been present at the drill yesterday morning but there'd been two more later in the day, so maybe she'd been there for them. "Don't you think that's rather pathetic of you to say?"

No titters this time—just hushed expectation. Had she really dared to say what we all thought we'd heard her say? As Thomas Paine or somebody similar once put it, a little rebellion is like a dog on fire howling in the middle of the night.

"Well, it may—it may be—" I think this was the first time any of us had ever heard Mr. Lemon at a loss for words. But then he seemed to get hold of himself. "Are you saying I'm pathetic?"

"Not you, no. Not necessarily." Her voice was as smooth as ice cream on a wedding cake. "But it's a matter of perspective. Like in Germany when Hitler killed the Jews, nobody cared what kind of language they were using when they first smelled the gas."

"Ah, so then you're... you're Jewish?" He sounded like a drowning man who'd just spotted a life raft in a raging sea.

"Is that a problem?"

"Of course not. Only... it's not a viewpoint we've had in this group before."

Like the Bantu viewpoint, I thought. Or the Watusi. Or the Martian. There weren't any Jews among the students of Lake Delridge High. None so far as I knew of in Lake Delridge itself. No Bantus, Watusis, or Martians either. (Nedd's family came from Alabama.)

"But I gather you don't care for my viewpoint."

"Oh, no. Not at all." He was near to sputtering. "I didn't say that." Both Mr. Moberg and Mr. Myerson nodded in agreement. Miss Hunt was there too now, wooden leg thrust forward as if brandishing a spear.

"You cursed, young lady," blurted out Miss Hunt. Her unspoken axiom: real ladies do not curse.

"So I guess I must be really pissed off, right?"

"That's no excuse."

"Because what I meant to say is that if people in this country had any courage they'd march on Washington and hang every one of those lunatics from the nearest tree."

"Now that—" Mr. Lemon began.

"That's treason," came a voice. I'd know the cry of the wild Ronnie Hightower anywhere

"No," Katy Cross said firmly. "It's only an idea. Ideas can't be treasonous."

"And now," said Mr. Lemon, his beaded forehead glowing under the hot lights, "maybe this would be the appropriate time to hear some other points of view."

As Raymond Sung lurched to his feet, I leaned over and murmured, "Tell me you really said what I thought I heard you say."

"Sorry about the New York bull."

"What New York bull?"

"Saying I was from back there. It's really Idaho. My mom's latest dead end secretarial job was there. It's not something either of us like to remember."

I forgave her deceit instantly.

And noticed she was chewing gum again. I hoped it wasn't the same wad she'd stuck under her chair.

Oh, and by the way, before I forget, Katy Cross wasn't Jewish either. As far as I ever found out, like most of us, she wasn't much of anything.

By then, though, Raymond Chung had wrapped up his long dissertation on the complexities of Cold War politics and Ronnie Hightower had stumbled to his penny-loafered feet, Sue Dietz beaming luminously beside him like a Christmas ornament on a tree, and was blandly bloviating on the cowardly deficiencies of the Kennedy administration that had so far failed to seize the moment to bomb everything Russian and/or Cuban in sight. From the discussion that ensued over the remaining thirty minutes of class, you'd never have guessed that Katy Cross had uttered a word. One thing about the emerging conservative majority as exemplified by our Lake Delridge High Class of '63 was its ability to act as if reality was a thing that never existed.

"Thanks for the support," she said in a brief quiet moment when Ronnie paused to gasp for air. "I didn't really expect any."

"I never said a word," I had to admit.

"Yes, I know." She patted my hand. "But the thought was there."

It was right then that I fell in love with her. And why not? No one had ever done that before. Read my mind, that is. It was like something from *The Demolished Man*, one of my favorite SF books of all time. (I was a huge telepathy freak.)

Then came the six-minute break between classes as the curtains were hurled back into place, dividing us into quarters and allowing for individual English instruction to begin. I noticed Mr. Myerson adjusting the cravat at his throat. To my surprise, Katy went over and began chatting amiably with him, as if they'd known each other forever.

* * * *

I felt a touch on my arm. I turned and saw Cisco sliding into Katy's chair.

"Don't worry," he said, "I'll move back."

"I'm not worried."

"No, but your girlfriend might be. I don't want to get screeched at."

"She's not my girlfriend. And she doesn't screech"

"Sure sounded like screeching to me."

"It's what I wish I'd had the guts to say myself."

"Me too." he admitted. "But wishes ain't fishes. And I saw you two holding hands by the way. Sweet."

"No, we weren't."

"Want to repeat that denial under oath?"

He hopped back into his own chair as Katy returned in time for the final bell. Mr. Myerson took charge of our group and spent the hour doing much of Act Three of Shakespeare's *Julius Caesar* in a variety of different tones of voice. He'd once been a radio actor and it showed in his performance:

> *Cry 'Havoc!', and let slip the dogs of war,*
> *That this foul deed shall smell above the earth*
> *With carrion men, groaning for burial*

He was just getting into the juicy part where Marc Anthony stands up to the plebian mob and gets them rocking and rolling for poor dead Caesar—I had as usual read ahead on my own and knew what was coming next—when the bell rang and it was time to head up the main building and the dreary assortment of regular classes that composed the rest of the school day.

Before we left, Mr. Lemon popped his head through the curtains to give a summary of latest news. "The Russian ships still haven't moved. The president is said to be reassured and continues to hope the crisis can be resolved peaceably."

In other words, no new news at all.

There were some skeptical snorts from the John Galtist Group but the rest of us figured no news beat getting blown to smithereens hands down.

As I headed for my next class—Algebra III with mostly juniors since I'd skipped math the year before after a bad experience with Plane Geometry as a sophomore—I managed with the cool suave of a drunken penguin to fall into step beside Katy Cross.

"So how do you like Lake Delridge so far?" I babbled, pouncing on the obvious like a lion on a lamb.

She glanced over at me as if she hadn't noticed I was there. "Oh, I guess it's okay. You know, considering."

"Considering what?" I noticed the wad of gum was gone again, which was likely just as well, since discipline tended to be more strictly enforced in the main building, what with a thousand or so additional drippy sophomores—the initial post-war litter of 1947—milling underfoot.

"It's awfully big."

"Two thousand students," I said. "This year anyhow."

"Almost as many people as in all of Nampa. We lived in California too for a while too. Not far from San Francisco."

"Ah, the beat generation."

"So I heard. I never saw any of them. Everybody looked normal where we lived. Vallejo's like a navy town. Lots of dippy sailors all around."

"Plenty around here too."

"Well, if it isn't the red menace," said a voice from behind I identified as Sue Dietz. The sweet scent of her perfume tickled my sensitive nose. "How's your comrade Fidel doing these days?"

"Don't look back," I murmured, "and she'll go away."

She did too. Sweeping around us, cackling, and bustled through the doors.

"We better hurry too," I said.

"Wait." She grabbed hold of my arm. "Let's skip class."

"We can't do that."

"Why not?"

"Because they take attendance. And call your parents if you're not there."

"Nobody home at my place. Mother works."

"Well, mine doesn't." I thought of Pop too, out in the backyard, hammering, chiseling, sawing.

The warning bell rang. She grabbed the door, jerked it open, hurried through. "Hey, what's your name?' she called back over her shoulder.

"Charlie Gundy," I said.

* * * *

I made it to algebra class as out of breath as a halfback after a ninety-yard touchdown sprint as the final bell went off. I'd lost track of Katy somewhere in the second-floor one-way hall.

The teacher, Mr. Bonner, who closely resembled the television actor Wally Cox, turned away from the blackboard he'd been wiping clean, flashed me a puzzled look, and then said, "Everybody else here on time?"

No one said they weren't.

I could predict what was coming next. And it wasn't algebra.

"I know you're all wondering along with me what's going on in Cuba right now." I spotted the plastic shell of a transistor radio perched on the edge of his desk. "So unless somebody objects—" pause for expectant laughter "—we'll listen to the news while you all take a one-period study break. Anybody with any particular questions or problems, come up and see me. Otherwise, your homework's due at the end of the period."

My homework was already finished. Since I'd actually done it at home for a change. So instead I pulled out the book I was reading, *Nine Stories* by J.D. Salinger, and turned to the last and longest piece, "Teddy."

A science fiction story too. Of sorts. And a great one.

The radio news rambled on as I read, visions of Katy Cross—oddly interspersed with Sue Dietz—threatening to interrupt my concentration on Salinger's lilting prose. "White House Press Secretary Pierre Salinger this morning announced...."

Blah-blah-blah.

Well, at least we weren't all dead.

Not yet anyhow.

ii

We called ourselves the Comancheros. Me, Cisco, and Nedd. The name taken from a movie starring John Wayne we'd seen a few months earlier.

We'd been best friends since grade school. After we kept finding ourselves all three sitting together in the same corner of the room year after year. (Don't ask me why. Destiny, fate, kismet, who knows?)

At the time we shared an abiding fascination with playing war games using those cheap plastic toy soldiers sold in grab bags at the five-and-dime for 98 cents and tax. With them we restaged many of the great battles of World War II.

Cisco's dad had fought in that war. With the Marines in the Pacific. Guadalcanal. Tarawa. Okinawa. He had the battle ribbons to prove it. Nedd's father had served in the army, though later on, as part of the occupation force in Japan during the Korean War. Pop had of course missed all of that due to his having only the one eye. Which was perfectly okay with me, since if he'd been off fighting the despicable Nazis or the wily Japs there wouldn't have been any chance of him doing his part in the making of me. For reasons known only to himself, he still had the original draft notice he'd received prior to flunking his physical exam. *Greetings from the President of the United States Franklin Delano Roosevelt.* I came across it while nosing around in a box old junk I found moldering away in the garage along with a somewhat dogeared copy of *Love and Its Physical Aspects* by Leonard Ward Huntington, PhD, MD, wherein thanks to a series of not especially explicit drawings, I learned of the existence of the four basic positions for marital intercourse. (Later in life reading the *Kama Sutra*, I discovered there were a myriad of additional ways as well.)

"The three losers, that's us," Nedd sometimes lamented, when the going got rough.

"The three dorks, you mean," I corrected.

* * * *

The three of us were hunkered down in Cisco's bedroom. It wasn't an official meeting—we Comancheros didn't actually have those—but it was as close as we ever came.

"Now hold on a minute, Charlie," said Cisco, rising to the occasion and fixing me with a savage glare. "I need to get this straight. Are you proposing a girl for membership in the Comancheros or aren't you?"

"God, Cisco, will you knock off?"

"I need to know, Charlie."

"Then the answer's yes," I said.

Earlier in the evening we'd watched the NBC evening news along with Cisco's dad and mom and his three sisters living at home while their two older brothers were off serving in the navy in undisclosed locations overseas. (The most likely place under the present circumstances: somewhere in the Caribbean.)

Huntley (or maybe Brinkley) kicked things off with these chilling words: "At its beginning this day it looked as though it might be one of armed conflict between Soviet vessels and American warships on the sea lanes leading to Cuba."

But it hadn't happened, he went on to add reassuringly.

Well, not yet anyhow.

Down in the basement Cisco's transistor radio dial was permanently set on KPR, channel 99, which meant the lilting whine of pre-Beatles rock 'n' roll—the Four Seasons and Roy Orbison, about as good as it got—and never any news unless it was really bad news. I'd personally given up on rock 'n' roll when Elvis left for the army and Jerry Lee married his thirteen-year-old cousin and at home mostly listened to the jazz LP's my brother Slim had brought home from his army hitch in Alaska and left behind when he went off again in search of what he called the path to righteous living. Brubeck, Miles, Baker and Mulligan, Count Basie, Bird and Diz, the MJQ.

"Look," I said, hoping to break through the stalemate, "I didn't know we had members."

But Cisco held firm. "We're the Three Comancheros, aren't we?"

Reluctantly, I nodded.

"So, are we going to turn into Four Comancheros or not? Besides, a girl would be like a Comanchera, wouldn't she? So that doesn't fit."

"Well..." I started.

"If not, she shouldn't be coming around here."

"Then forget the whole thing. I don't care. Do what you want."

"I can't."

"Why not?"

"Because you already invited her, that's why."

Well, actually, I hadn't. Not really. The fact was, Katy Cross had more or less invited herself. Not that I was about to admit it.

"She doesn't even know about the whole stupid Comancheros thing," I said.

"So what did you tell her about us then?"

"I said we liked to get together after school and study."

"Study? Us?"

"Well, some of us do. Nedd does. You do too. Sometimes anyhow."

In truth Cisco's grades weren't much better than mine. Which meant in my case a sprinkling of low B's and high C's with an infrequent A tossed in in social studies or history when something came up that interested me. In the coming school year yet to unfold, I would suddenly achieve a straight A average in a burst of unanticipated glory that ended up signifying nothing beyond the fact that the public education system and I had finally caught up with one another.

* * * *

Katy had called me at home. I never knew where she got the number. Likely looked it up in the phone book, where there were only the two Gundys listed, the other being Uncle Horace, Pop's younger brother.

Mom answered the phone. The bewildered expression on her face as she turned and said it was a girl calling for me said it all.

"Are you doing anything special tonight?" asked Katy Cross.

"Um, studying, I guess," I lied.

"By yourself—at home?"

"Well, I usually go over to Cisco Cordova's place. Him and me and another kid, Nedd Young, we study together."

"Which one is he?"

"The, uh, the Negro kid. He wasn't there today. You took his chair."

"Then I didn't mean him. I meant Cisco."

"Cisco's the small stocky kid, walks kind of hunched over."

"He's not Cuban, is it?"

"No, his family's from Mexico actually."

"That's got to be a relief to them these days. So where's his house?"

Before I could stop myself, I'd given her the address. And added precise directions.

"So what time?"

"What time what?"

"Do you guys start? This studying of yours."

"We usually get going right after dinner."

"Seven?"

"Around then, sure, but—"

"See you then."

The line went *click*.

* * * *

While Cisco and Nedd continued to debate the formalities of Comanchero membership, I glanced at my watch.

Seven-fifteen.

So maybe she wasn't coming after all.

But even way in the back end of the house we could hear the doorbell when it rang.

"I bet that's your sweetie pie now," Cisco cooed at me.

"She's not my sweetie pie," I said, looking at my watch again. "And she's late."

The three of us sprang to attention as we heard the sound of confident footsteps coming down the hall.

"See?" Cisco said. "I told you guys, didn't I?"

What exactly he was supposed to have told us I never found out. I hurried across and opened the bedroom door. Katy Cross, escorted by Cisco's mother and his two oldest sisters, stepped inside. She looked much the same as I remembered from school, except that her hair now hung loose to her shoulders and the weird peasant dress was happily gone replaced by jeans and a gray sweatshirt with the face of some guy with a beard stitched across the chest.

"Hey, it's Fidel Castro," said Cisco.

"Try Allen Ginsburg," she said, letting the pile of books she was carrying fall to the floor.

She dropped down cross-legged next to them as Cisco's mom and sisters reluctantly withdrew, leaving the door open a wide crack.

Katy was still wearing the black Keds, I noticed.

She smiled. "So this the place," she said, "where the famous Three Comancheros meet to plan their nefarious capers."

Cisco fixed me with a bitter glare. *You blabbed, didn't you?* he seemed to be saying.

"I did not," I said truthfully.

"No, he didn't," Katy confirmed. "Nedd did."

"I thought you didn't know each other."

"We're in sixth period physics together. Nedd was there when I showed up for class. With the Mole—Mr. Dafoe."

"She came right in and sat down next to me," Nedd said. "The Mole was afraid to make her move."

Katy pushed up the sleeves of her sweat shirt and looked around at the three of us. "So," she said, "have you heard the latest?"

She meant Cuba of course.

We told her we'd watched Huntley and Brinkley.

"Corporate hogwash," she said. "You want the truth, listen to KPFA. That's Pacifica Radio from Berkeley. They say the Chinese are about ready to send in their army if Kennedy doesn't back off."

"You mean the *Red* Chinese?" said Cisco.

"I mean the legitimate socialist government of China recognized by everyone in the world except us. Even England."

We were all struck silent in the face of this information. It wasn't something we'd heard before.

"So when does all this studying get started?" she said, with a quick frown. "I brought some of my books but the rest are out in the car."

"You have a... *a car*?" said Cisco. He spoke the word dreamily. For us non-car-owning seniors it might as well have been a dream.

"It's really my mom's car."

"And she lets you drive it?"

"Sure. Why not? I have a license. I'm careful. I don't drink or smoke pot when I'm driving."

We clearly had no idea how to respond to that.

"What make is it?" Cisco asked. "I mean your car."

"It's a Chevy Bel-Air. 1957. With the fishtail fins."

"Wow, cool. And it's really yours?"

"Like I said, my mom's. Her ex-boyfriend, a poet, gave it to her to pay back some money she lent him. We figured he stole it but asking no questions, you don't hear lies."

She stood up then. "I better go get the rest of my stuff then, huh?"

"Hold on," Cisco said, "and I'll go with you. If my sisters were listening in when you said the word pot, they'll lock the door after you."

"And you can carry my books too," she said.

After they'd gone, I looked at Nedd who was pretending to study his calculus text. "So what do you think of her?" I asked.

He considered for a moment without looking up the way he always did, then shrugged. "You mean about all her books?" He nodded at the pile she'd already brought in.

"No, I meant about her in general."

He grinned. "I think she's great. Peachy keen."

We both laughed at that.

* * * *

When the two of them returned, I noticed right away Cisco's eyes looked as if he'd seen the Virgin Mary floating down the middle of the street. "You should see it," he said in an awestruck tone. "It's beautiful."

"Me?" said Katy.

"No, your car."

"My mom's car."

"Yes," he said. "It's absolutely, undeniably gorgeous."

For a time after that the four of us pretended to be studying.

Then Katy leaned back, stretched, looked over at me. "Charlie," she said, "strictly out of curiosity, what's all that stuff going on over at your place?"

"What stuff?" Though I had a pretty fair idea what she was talking about.

"In your backyard. I drove past on my over way here. What's all the hammering about? And the lumber. What are you guys building? An ark? An outhouse?"

"It's something my pop's making," I said.

"Like what?" This time it was Cisco. He seemed curious too. "My sister Gloria told me she heard the noise too and went by to look."

"It's…" I hesitated. "He says it's… spaceships."

"Spaceships made out of wood?"

"That's what he says."

"He's joking, right?"

"I suppose so, sure."

"Or else he's out of his gourd."

"He's not. Pop's as sane as anybody," I added, with perhaps more confidence than I felt.

* * * *

We went back to studying. Supposedly. Though I think Nedd was the only one of us who genuinely focused on the printed page. Cisco, Katy and I spent most of the time furtively looking at one another and then looking away again when the other person noticed.

Finally, Nedd closed his calculus book, tucked it under his arm, and stood up. "I guess I better go," he said.

"Wait and I'll walk with you," I said. Most of the time we walked home together. Since we lived so close.

"Or I can give you both a lift," Katy said.

"Not me." Nedd shook his head. "I'd just as soon walk tonight. There's things I need to think about. Thinking always works best when you're alone."

"You're sure about that?"

"Yes."

Most any other seventeen-year-old you'd figure there had to be something terribly wrong. But Nedd actually liked being alone. He liked thinking too.

On the way out—we split carrying Katy's books between us—Cisco called out about us getting together again later in the week.

"If there is a later in the week," Katy murmured at my side.

* * * *

On the drive to my place Katy wanted to talk about school. She asked about various people, kids and teachers both. "Who's the tall Nazi-looking creep with all the answers?"

"That's Ronnie Hightower. Senior class president."

"You know him pretty well?"

"Not really, no. My pop's a dental technician and Ronnie's father is a dentist, a prosthodontist. Sometimes Pop makes false teeth for him."

"Rich?"

"The Hightowers? They're pretty well off. They live at the Point. Have a boat. Ronnie has a car too. A Triumph."

"Cool car but they break down a lot."

"I suppose."

"What's with all the Ayn Rand baloney he and that dark-haired douche keep spouting?"

I assumed she meant Sue Dietz. "It's just a craze around school with some of the kids. They call themselves the John Galtist Group. It's an official school club. They get together after class in Mr. Lemon's home room and read *Atlas Shrugged* out loud."

"Is he a fascist too?"

"Mr. Lemon? I don't think so. He just wants to encourage all points of view. That's what he says anyhow."

She parked in front of my place. Despite it being ten o'clock, we could hear the hammering coming from the back like the beat of tribal drums.

To my relief, Katy didn't mention it.

"So this Ronnie Hightower," she said, "he's not a pal of yours or anything?"

"Not at all, no."

"He seems to know you though."

That came as a surprise. "He does? When did you talk to Ronnie about me?"

"At lunch today. I was eating alone since I didn't know anybody and he came over and sat down across from me."

There were three lunch periods at Lake Del. Before, during, and after fourth period. I ate with the middle group—the B lunch. Katy was in the C group.

"What did he want?"

"He asked me to join his club."

"You're kidding me."

"First he asked if I'd read *Atlas Shrugged*. I told him I didn't have time for a book that ridiculously long. But I had read *The Fountainhead*."

"You did? Really?"

"Sure. It's not bad. Not good either. Heinlein would have done it way better. I told Ronnie that too. He said he'd never heard of Heinlein. Then he asked me again if I wanted to join his study group."

"And you told him no."

"I told him I might fall by sometime. Just to listen. And argue. He seemed okay with that."

"And will you?"

"I don't know yet. I guess we'll have to see. How boring my life here turns out to be."

She turned the key and restarted the engine. I took that as a signal and got out, taking my books with me.

With the car door open the noise from the backyard seemed even louder.

"Tell your dad good luck with his spaceships," she called, as she leaned over to shut the door.

She drove off into the night.

iii

The next morning, Thursday, October 25, 1962, as I gulped down my usual morning breakfast—bowl of Wheaties, canned peaches, three scrambled eggs, cup of coffee with plenty of cream and lots of sugar—half-listening to the latest radio news from the Cuba, I could hear Pop in the backyard, hammering relentlessly away. Mom didn't say a word but I could tell she was worried, and when I finally looked up and asked her if he'd been out there all night, she just blinked her eyes, went over to the stove, and fetched me the coffee pot for a refill. I decided to let it ride. When you've been married to the same man for twenty-seven years, you have to know when to ask questions and when not to, and Mom never asked Pop much of anything at all.

The aggressive designs of United States imperialists must be foiled!
Peace on Earth must be defended and strengthened!
Hands off Cuba!

So, according to the radio, read the headline in the morning edition of *Pravda*.

I reached across the kitchen table and grabbed up today's *Seacrest Times-Post*. The front-page banner headline read:

Kennedy Stands Firm!
Red Ships Test Quarantine!
Crisis Unsettled!

Overnight two Soviet ships had passed over the quarantine line, with neither being stopped. One was believed to be the oil tanker *Bucharest* and the other an East German passenger ship. That last sounded a bit peculiar but I figured for an East German maybe a vacation cruise to Cuba with World War III about to break out didn't necessarily sound as half-crazy as it did to me.

Still, my scrambled eggs seemed especially tasty this morning, which likely meant nothing more than Mom using store-bought chicken eggs instead of raiding the mother duck's nest to cover the gap in her food budget.

While I spooned up the last of my Wheaties and drained my coffee, the clock over the stove read 6:42. The bus for school didn't leave from the Chevron filling station on Delridge Drive until 7:15.

Which meant there was still time. If I wanted it.

I could feel Mom's eyes on me. "Why don't you go talk to your father?" she finally said.

I felt myself nod.

As I headed for the door, I went past the radio as it was reporting a United Nations Security Council meeting scheduled for later in the day. A critical crisis meeting, it was being called.

"That might settle something," Mom said optimistically, as I swept past.

I had a feeling we'd be listening on the radio in the Block today to find out more.

* * * *

The yard out back of the house was huge and green, though much of the romance it had held for me when we'd first moved in ten years earlier had gone. Originally, the entire back portion of the yard had been fenced off for a vegetable garden but Pop had run out of time and patience by our third summer and plowed the whole thing under, planting grass instead. We Gundys weren't dirt farmers, he said. We were craftsmen—artisans. Pop had gone to work straight from school while still a boy. His first job at fourteen was working in an Adobe mortuary cleaning and washing the dead bodies as they were brought in. For a time before I was born he'd earned a good living making artificial eyes for the military. Odd in that he never wore a glass eye himself. When the war ended he turned to making false teeth instead. The first dentist he worked for, Dr. Benjamin Simon in downtown Seacrest, helped steer others his way. Now most of the work he did was for local Lake Delridge dentists, using the lab he'd built in our basement. One dentist he did a lot of work for was Dr. Clayton Hightower, Ronnie's father, a leading prosthodontist. I had the impression the two of them had known each other for years but didn't know the details.

The only part of the old vegetable garden Pop hadn't plowed under were the raspberry and loganberry bushes staked to posts in neat rows near the back fence. And the fruit trees had been left standing too. Six of them in total: three apple, one pear, one plum, one quince. The red delicious apple tree next to the rabbit hutches—my sister Polly's domain—was the only one still with fruit this late in the year.

The early dawn sky carried a rosy pink tint this morning, hinting at what I wasn't sure. A gentle wind whipped through the trees, scattering madrona leaves and pine needles.

I came down off the porch steps and stood there a long moment, gazing at the amazing sight in front of me.

Pop's spaceships. There were two of them. They were starting to resemble—incredibly—the real thing.

Pop had jammed two extension ladders together and looped wires around the ends to give him enough length to reach the top of the ships. How he'd got so much done in such a brief time—just a few days—I found hard to believe. But the proof was right there in front of me.

I walked on out into the yard and looked up to where I could see him way up at the top where he seemed to be hammering additional sheets of plywood into place.

I cupped my hands around my mouth and called up to him.

He looked down and saw me standing below. "Hey there, Charlie," he called back. "What's up?"

"Pop, I want to talk to you!" I shouted.

"What about?"

"About these—these things of yours!" I didn't want to say *spaceships*. Not yet. Not aloud. It sounded nonsensical. "What are they supposed to be?"

"Can't you tell? I figured if anybody could it'd be you."

I assumed this was a reference to my reading so much science fiction.

I heard him chuckle. "Hold on!" he called back down. "I'm on my way."

I grabbed the ladder and held it fast, feeling the rhythmic vibrations as he made his way down.

"Well, what is it, Charlie?" he said, once he joined me on the ground. Perspiration trickled down his forehead past his good right eye and over top of the black patch that covered the empty socket of the left. He was forty-nine years old. Fifty come December. As ancient as the proverbial mariner to me at my youthful seventeen.

"I was just wondering what you were up to out here, Pop," I said, as casually as I could. "I've been worried about you."

"You have, have you? How so?"

"It's just strange, that's all. What you say you're doing. I mean, we're all afraid of war right now. Everybody is. But this... I don't see how it helps. Even some of the kids at school are talking about it. People drive by and they see all this and they just stop and stare."

"They do, do they?" He gave me a narrow look. "What people are those?"

"Like I said, some of the kids at school. This girl I know for one. She drove by last night and said you were out here working in the dark, hammering."

He wiped his forehead with a sleeve. "Who's this girl? I didn't know you knew any."

"She's new. Just moved here. From New York. Or Idaho. One or the other."

"New York people are a nosy bunch. You sure it wasn't your colored friend from across the back fence?"

"No, it wasn't Nedd." Pop rarely called Nedd by name. Or Nedd's father either. His name was Earl Young. Twelve years we'd lived here and for Pop Nedd was still the colored kid from across the back fence. But try and understand. This was 1962. Pop had grown up in Colorado—in Adobe, a city where the only "colored" people who weren't either Mexican or Indians were the red caps at the train depot.

"Nedd's never mentioned it."

"Couldn't very well miss it though, could he?" He spat in the grass. "Do me a favor, would you? Run into the house and fetch me a lemonade. Then come back out with it. I want to talk to you too."

I made a point of looking at my watch. "I can't miss the bus. I'll be late."

"Don't worry about it. I'll give you a lift."

That wasn't exactly what I wanted to hear. A ride to school with Pop in his car was not among my favorite moments. It was because of the car he drove. A Hillman Minx. Baby blue. If you want to talk about old cars that were dorky, the Hillman Minx was the king of all dorkiness.

I hurried into the house and got him his glass of lemonade from the fridge.

"What did your father have to say?" Mom asked, from the sink where she was washing my breakfast dishes.

"Not much really."

"He wouldn't talk to you either?"

"He asked me to bring him some lemonade."

She looked at the glass in my hand. "Well, that's a start anyhow."

I raced back out. Pop was waiting on the porch, sitting on the bottom step. I handed him the lemonade and dropped down beside him. He took two long deep swallows, gulping it down.

The chickens had come out of their coop in back of the garage now. Six plump hens and a foul-tempered bantam roster. The ducks were out too, foraging underneath the rhododendron bush, hunting their favorite food, live slugs, which by now, mid-October, were starting to appear in mass.

Pop pointed at the big wood framework looming over us. "So what do you think so far?" he asked me.

"I... well—I mean, they're very impressive."

"But you don't think they'll fly?"

"Pop, I mean, come on. They're made out of wood." Plywood for the most part, it looked like, two by four inch supporting beams underneath.

"What's that got to do with it?"

"Why, because they'll blow up. They'll catch fire. You can't build rocket ships out of wood."

"Then I guess we'll have to try something else. A different form of propulsion. If we want to reach escape velocity and leave the Earth behind." He shook his head, took another long swallow of lemonade, emptying the glass. He set it down on the porch step beside me. "Have I ever told you how I lost this eye of mine?"

"Uh, yeah, sure," I said. Where had this come from? Maybe the others were right. Maybe Pop had gone bonkers. He didn't look it though. Not to me. He looked the same as always. "Somebody did anyhow. Told me the story, I mean. It might have been Mom or Aunt Elise."

"Elise would know. She was there. When the company doctor my old man fetched turned out to be blind drunk, she was the one who took the scalpel out of his hand and finished the operation. Otherwise I would have died there on the kitchen table for sure. Elise saved my life, no question about it. I lost an eye but like they say that's why God gave you two."

"That's the way I heard it, yes," I agreed.

"I was only a year old at the time. They forced brandy down my throat to deaden the pain. Don't know if it worked or not. I've got no memory of it. The whole town was flooded that day. The Arkansas River spilling its banks the way it did every few years."

"You were lucky you lived through it."

"Maybe. But I still had to get through life with only one eye. Not as easy as it may look." He reached up and touched the eyepatch covering the empty left socket. "People always stare. The other kids called me names too. Captain Kidd. Blackbeard. Long John. I'd get into fights. The nuns and priests would beat hell out of me, then call home and the old man would be ready with the strap as soon as I walked in the door. You want to know why I quit school as soon I could and left home when I was fourteen. That's why. There was no love in that house. None at all. I got tired of living that way. Got tired of the kids at school too."

"Kids aren't like that now. They're not as mean."

"You think not?" He laughed. "Give them a chance. Human nature takes forever to change. You may not see the meanness right away. But it's there. All the old ugliness, it's hidden down underneath, festering. But it won't take much for it to come pouring out again. How old are you anyhow, Charlie?"

He'd done it again. Caught me by surprise. Not the most supportive of parents in the world, no—he was no *Father Knows Best* Robert Young—but he had to know that much. He was there the day I was born. "Count the candles on my birthday cake," I said, feeling hurt.

"Damn it, Charlie, how old?"

"Seventeen," I said, sullenly.

"You know where I was when I was seventeen?"

I shrugged my shoulders. "Home in Adobe, I suppose. Working at the mortuary." There were stories about that too. A hotel fire. Forty people burned alive. Pop's job was to put what was left back together again. His father and grandfather both worked at the steel mill. Pop said he'd starve to death rather than work there.

"I came close too. The starving part, I mean. For a while I lived at the city dump. Built myself a shelter out of cardboard and old lumber. Warmed myself with a makeshift fire. Food was whatever scraps I could find. Grandpop Isak used to sneak stuff off the table for me when he could. He was the only one I let know where I was. The rest of them could go to hell as far as I was concerned. It was a miserable life."

"Sounds like it," I agreed.

He looked up at the sky. "A better life up there, I bet. It's what I'm counting on anyway. The stars."

"But, Pop," I said, my voice catching in my throat, "how can you think—?"

Bur he wasn't listening anymore. There was a distant look on his face. "Come on," he said, standing up. He slapped at his pants, scattering sawdust to the wind. "We better get you off to school before it's too late."

I looked at my watch. The bus was long gone.

He gave me a light slap on the bony part of my shoulder. "Run in and get your books. Time for me to crank the old jalopy up. I'll meet you on the street."

I suppressed a groan. The family car, the jalopy. The Hillman Minx.

It was enough to make having a father who was building spaceships out of wood in the backyard seem not so horrible after all.

iv

I slipped into the Block just as the warning bell went off.

As I dropped into my usual seat, I noticed the chair to my right was empty. When I did, I experienced a sinking sensation in the pit of my stomach that caused my head to spin furiously on its axis.

"Jesus, Charlie," Cisco said, from his seat on my left. "You look like you just swallowed a frog."

"Pop gave me a ride in," I tried explaining, hoping that would prove sufficient.

He didn't seem convinced.

But Katy Cross, I thought desperately, where was she? What if she wasn't coming in at all today?

Was it my fault?

Something I'd said? Or done?

"You really don't look so hot, Charlie," Cisco went on. "Maybe you better go see the school nurse."

Fortunately for me, just then the final bell clanged.

At which precise point, emerging from the crowd gathered around Ronnie Hightower and sliding into the seat next to me with the grace of a ballerina, here came Katy Cross. Today she was wearing what looked like a pair of laced army brogans under her peasant skirt.

"Hi, boys," she called out in a singsong voice. Then she looked right at me. "Jeez, Charlie, you okay?"

"Fine," I somehow managed.

"You look awful. You sure it's not the flu?"

Before I could try and explain, Cisco broke in excitedly. "It said on the radio this morning Khrushchev isn't backing down after all."

"I know." Katy nodded glumly across at him. "He said his missiles might soon fly."

"And that means ours will too," Cisco agreed, making a zooming noise with his hand.

At that moment the rattle of wheels on linoleum swung our heads back to the front of the room as Mr. Lemon and Mr. Moberg came bustling down the center aisle followed by Mr. Myerson and Miss Hunt pushing a dolly containing a rabbit-eared television set.

The four of them looked as solemn as mourners at a preacher's funeral.

"The four horsemen," whispered a voice in my ear. I glanced back. It was Nedd sitting behind me today, having given up his regular seat to Katy.

Mr. Moberg took charge of the unraveling of the extension cord, shoulders hunched as he raced toward the wall socket nearest us.

Mr. Lemon marched briskly to his usual perch at the front of the room and when he got there gave his hands several brisk claps.

With our attention riveted, he intoned: "Young ladies and gentlemen, today marks a day that may turn out to be the single most critical in the lives of every human being on this planet. For that reason, the four of us have chosen to dispense with our regular lesson plan and instead bring live television into the classroom for the first time in school history. In a few short moments the United Nations Security Council is scheduled to begin debate on the current situation in Cuba. We will be there as a group to watch and learn and listen."

"Not necessarily in that order," murmured Katy.

Darting a hand, Mr. Lemon clicked on the TV with a flourish. At first there was only silence. But after Mr. Myerson fiddled with the dials a low whining noise erupted followed by a frantic burst of dizzying patterns racing randomly across the screen.

"One moment, please," Mr. Lemon said. "It's warming up now."

While they struggled with the picture and sound, I could hear Ronnie Hightower several rows back lecturing his minions: "The United Nations is as useless as the fifth leg on a dead mule. My father fought against the Chinese Reds in Korea and he can tell you how—"

"Your father's a dentist," I muttered. "He pulls rotten teeth."

"Now, people," Mr. Moberg called out from the wall outlet. "Let's have no talking here."

"Liberal pansy," hissed Ronnie Hightower.

"Pinko fairy," murmured Sue Dietz at his side.

Mr. Moberg had earned their permanent ire earlier in the semester when he'd spoken in favor of school integration in the South.

In the meantime, under Mr. Myerson's ministering touch, a blurry black-and-white picture was emerging into focus

"Hey, look, it's Eric Sevareid." Katy said.

"With a crooked haircut," said Cisco.

"Liberal," muttered Ronnie.

"Pinko," murmured Sue.

At which point Mr. Myerson shut everyone up with one of his patented loud clearings of the throat.

Mr. Lemon turned up the volume. The moment he did, as if in response,

Eric Sevareid's crooked haircut vanished to be replaced by the fluttering black-and-gray image of a circular table, around which huddled an assortment of well-dressed men with nameplates announcing the countries each represented: United States, United Kingdom, China, France, Soviet Union, Ceylon, Mexico, Norway.

The show was on.

The American ambassador, Adlai Stevenson, a paunchy bald-headed man in a saggy suit who had twice run for president back in the fifties, losing badly both times to President Eisenhower, was already on his feet, addressing the assembly.

As he spoke, he used an easel to display a series of aerial photographs rendered even blurrier than they were by the poor television reception. These photos, Stevenson claimed, showed the Soviet missile sites currently under construction in Cuba.

Across the table from him, the Soviet ambassador, who looked like a twin brother of Broderick Crawford from the TV show *Highway Patrol*, methodically denied every charge. "There are no Soviet offensive weapons in Cuba," he asserted.

But Stevenson pressed his point, hands waving. *Then what do these photographs show?* he demanded.

Again, the Soviet Ambassador demurred. *They could be anything.*

"Then do you, Ambassador Zorin," Stevenson said, "deny that the USSR has placed and is placing medium- and intermediate-range missiles and sites in Cuba? Yes or no—don't wait for the translation—yes or no?"

The ambassador remained unflustered. "I am not in an American courtroom sir, and therefore I do not wish to answer. In due course you will have your reply."

"You are in the courtroom of world opinion right now," Stevenson said, "and you can answer yes or no."

"You will have your answer in due course," the Ambassador reiterated.

"I am prepared to wait for my answer until hell freezes over," said Stevenson.

His big moment.

The classroom exploded into spontaneous cheers. I could imagine something similar happening all over America at that moment. Even Ronnie Hightower and Sue Dietz looked smugly pleased.

"You know, we're still going to get blown to smithereens any moment," Katy leaned over and whispered in my ear.

"*Ka-blooey,*" agreed Cisco.

* * * *

It wasn't till later in the day—during fifth period Chemistry and yet another air raid drill—that I understood their point.

Because there I knelt, head burrowed beneath arms and elbows, eyes squeezed shut, huddled like a bug awaiting a squashing shoe beside the wall farthest from the windows.

The funny part, I could have sworn I could smell Katy Cross's sweet perfume wafting past my twitching nostrils.

Even funnier though, she wasn't in the class.

And I was pretty sure she didn't wear perfume either.

As mentioned earlier, it was one damned strange time in which to be alive.

v

That following Sunday, October 28, 1962, the crisis broke.

The world—and all of us in it—was saved!

Though peculiarly the first thought I had when word came through was an old memory of mine from back in the ninth grade. Miss Hefner's home room English class—the same class where we'd been required to read *Great Expectations* by Charles Dickens over Christmas vacation and I'd stubbornly read all three *Foundation* books by Isaac Asimov instead.

Bet I had the better time though. (And ended up the semester with a C- in English.)

Though looking back from today's perspective, I'd need to note that Miss Hefner was undoubtedly the best teacher I had in my three full years of junior high school. She was young, recently graduated from the university, bright, enthusiastic, articulate, acutely fond of books and reading. And also a bit on the hot side in a dark-hair-cropped-short sort of early-twenties-in-1959 kind of way. I still recall her shocked delight when I did my book report on *Brave New World* by Aldous Huxley. And why not? To me it was just another science fiction story. Then our class beatnik Bob Collins did his report on *Peyton Place* and stole my thunder.

But so far as this particular memory goes, sweet little Miss Hefner in her white blouse and black knee-length skirt and high-heeled red pumps—and who married the summer afterward and failed to come back for a second year of teaching—ranks as a mere side player.

The real action takes place at the table in the corner nearest the radiator.

There were four of us there—seated alphabetically by last name—two girls and another boy. The girls were Cindy Federman and JoAnn Hines.

The boy was Brian Jones.

JoAnn was best known around school for possessing the second biggest pair of breasts in the ninth grade. (The acknowledged champion was a trailer park inhabitant sneeringly referred to as "Falsie," who was supposed to have been caught giving her cousin, an eighth-grade cretin named Dale Wiggins, a blow job in the boy's second floor bathroom. Likely yet another junior high school myth.) JoAnn was also the sweetest, most soft spoken girl I knew, though, admittedly, not terribly bright.

The other girl at the table—Cindy—budding breasts aside—was JoAnn's polar opposite. Sharp as a razor, built like a hydrant, raven haired, with black eyebrows that swooped above narrow brown eyes and a wide mouth like a goblet that contained the meanest tongue in the entire ninth grade.

Much of it aimed at poor sad sack Brian Jones.

A dolt. A moron. Sap, geek, loser. Six feet tall already at fourteen, skinny as a tree limb, with a nest of festering red pimples splattered across his cheeks and chin. He lived in the Gardens with his ma and pa from Carolina and his unwed sister, a prostitute. (More myth, I'm sure.)

Brian never spoke a word.

Cindy did all the talking. To Brian. As she had all semester long.

She never let up on him.

From the first warning bell, she spewed venom like an Australian viper. She had a way of talking through both corners of her mouth simultaneously so that while every word could be heard at our table, nobody more than two feet away—like for instance Miss Hefner—would know she was even speaking.

Brian heard every word though.

Cindy told him all about his ugly face, his scrawny neck, his pimples, his cheap Wigwam clothing, his smell (bad), his hair (greasy), his complexion (terrible), his brains (few), his brawn (non-existent.)

She never let up. From the first bell onward.

And me? Me, I laughed. No, make that chuckled. I smiled. I grinned. I snickered appreciatively.

Oh, forget the justifications: I *laughed*.

Out loud when I could. (Silently when I couldn't.)

I was Cindy's primary audience. (Since JoAnn, with her innate sweetness, pretended not to hear a word.)

After all, why not? At least she wasn't picking on me.

The day it happened was like any other day with Miss Hefner lecturing and JoAnn listening and Cynthia spewing and Brian gulping and me laughing.

"You ever try squeezing those pimples, Brian, to see if you could get enough puss for a soup and your old ma could fix it for you in between your slut sister turning tricks with her nigger—"

At which point I stopped laughing too.

Then it happened.

Brian snapped. He cracked.

His head jerked like the nozzle on a hose, his eyes clicked shut, then burst open, bulging like a pair of ripe tomatoes. He sprang halfway out of his chair.

And he punched me in the side of the head.

It really wasn't much of a blow. There was no blood. It stung a little—but not much.

Still, I knew what I had to do in response. As a man. I leaped up out of my chair and gave him a hard shove, which knocked him back over his own chair and sent it—and him—tumbling to the floor.

I stood there with my fists cocked in the classic Marquis of Queensbury pose and waited for the shit to hit the radiator, so to speak. (It was winter—and chilly.)

JoAnn picked that moment to emit a startled scream.

But I was looking at Cindy, at the angelic expression of wide-eyed innocence on her face, saying better than mere words how she had absolutely no inkling whatsoever of how any of this dreadful physical violence could possibly be occurring anywhere in the vicinity of her purely angelic self.

It has nothing to do with me, radiated her sweet charming face.

By then I was hearing a sobbing sound. I looked down.

Poor sappy Brian, stretched out flat on his back on the floor, his fists still furiously clenched at his sides, crying like a baby.

Miss Hefner then came scampering over, legs pumping furiously under her maybe-a-little-too-tight-around-the-butt skirt, bare knees flashing in and out of view like a magician's rabbit, and placed herself between the fallen Brian and me.

* * * *

In the end both of us—though not angelic Cindy of course—ended up in the vice-principal's office and for a while he was going to suspend us both till Miss Hefner intervened, saying that at least we'd stopped when she'd told us, and she crossed and uncrossed her legs a few times nervously, and the kindly drooling V-P relented and gave us each two weeks' lunch room detention instead.

(And, no, we didn't thereafter become the best of friends. That happens only in storybooks. I still regarded Brian as one dumb cluck moron likely fated to die under fire in Vietnam some ten years later.)

My point here? In terms of the Cuban missile crisis, how it ended?

You figure it out.

* * * *

It goes something like this: on Sunday, October 28, 1962, precisely at nine a.m. Washington time—noon on the West Coast—the following letter from Chairman Nikita Khrushchev addressed to President John Kennedy was received at the White House:

"In order to complete with greater speed the liquidation of the conflict dangerous to the cause of peace, to give confidence to all people longing for peace, and to calm the American people, who, I am certain, want peace as much as the people of the Soviet Union, the Soviet government, in addition to previously issued instructions on the cessation of further work at building sites for the weapons, has issued a new order on the dismantling of the weapons which you describe as 'offensive' and their crating and return to the Soviet Union.

"I regard with respect and trust your statement in your message of October 27, 1962, that no attack will be made on Cuba—that no invasion will take place—not only by the United States, but also by other countries of the Western Hemisphere, as your message pointed out."

In other words, in return for Kennedy's promise not to invade Cuba and to thus let the Castro regime remain in power, Khrushchev would withdraw his missiles and destroy their launching sites.

So it was over!

The world would live to breathe and sing and whine and wail and curse and crap and scream and rut yet another day!

Talk about your letdowns.

The end of the whole world impending and it pops with a couple goofy letters back and forth.

Kennedy responded in kind: "I welcome Chairman Khrushchev's statesmanlike decision. We shall be in touch with the Secretary General of the United Nations with respect to reciprocal measures to assure peace in the Caribbean area."

One day they're talking about missiles flying and the next it's down to "reciprocal measures."

Oh, well.

So was I disappointed? As a matter of fact, God, no, of course not. I was as rightly relieved as pretty much everyone else on the planet. I was *gratified*—like a lobster having avoided the pot of boiling water. Oh, except for a tiny handful of dug-in right wingers who figured why not get the whole thing over with now when we have more bombs and missiles than they do. Like Air Force Chief of Staff General Curtis LeMay, who angrily spurned Kennedy's offer of congratulations with a snarled, "Hell, we lost! We ought to just go in there today and knock them off!" Or a fellow Air Force general who on his own authority had placed his squadrons of B-52's on DEFCON II alert in the first hours of the crisis in the plain hope of sparking a belligerent response from the USSR.

But for most of the rest of us that Sunday was a day of national relief. (Prayer, under the First Amendment separation of church and state, purely optional.)

Only later on did it come out that the deal also included an additional (whispered) promise by the president to remove the U.S. Atlas missiles from Turkey at the earliest possible opportunity. Less than a year later they were gone.

Which only goes to show.

* * * *

Later that cheery Sunday I slipped away from the television news and wandered out into the backyard. It was a pleasantly clear and warm Indian summer late October day and for a long pregnant moment I stood there, letting the sun caress my skin and feeling the cooling breeze as a breath of joy and hearing the humming of crickets and the chirping of sparrows and sniffing the sweet pine scent of peeling bark and fallen cones.

Then I heard the hammering.

Rap-tap-rap.

I cocked my head, looked up, and saw him working.

On his spaceships. His wooden spaceships. Two of them. Towering above everything else.

I bit my lip.

Heck, I thought, maybe it's not over after all. Maybe nothing has changed one bit.

Rap-tap-rap.

Pop saw me looking. He waved down at me.

I waved back.

Then I turned around and went into the house and climbed the stairs to my bedroom.

I grabbed the first book off the shelf where I kept the ones I hadn't had a chance to read yet and flopped down on the bed.

Wouldn't you know it?

The Long Loud Silence by Wilson Tucker.

A masterpiece.

About what it might be like after World War III. After the missiles flew and the H-bombs went off.

With the few survivors hunting down one another to cook for dinner.

Not a happy tale. No siree bob.

vi

After dinner that night when I was about to hurry up to my bedroom to find out how *The Long Loud Silence* came out, Mom called me back to inform me it was my turn to take out the garbage.

I was toting the last of three huge bags when I happened to notice a strange car parked across the street.

It didn't look as if it belonged there. It was Cadillac. A new one. A long black limousine.

Seeing it sitting there in the dark gave me the instant creeps.

I couldn't say for sure why.

But it did.

As I dropped the last of the bags into the garbage and turned to go, I heard a noise coming from the car and saw the driver's front window slide slowly open. A hand reached out and a finger beckoned to me. "Hey, son, come over here for a moment, would you please?"

Naturally, I hesitated. Maybe I was a bit too old to be overly concerned about talking to strangers. But you never could tell. There were perverts everywhere, right?

Then the rear window rolled open too and a way too familiar face peered out at me.

"Hey, snotface, get your butt over here when a grown-up tells you to."

Ronnie Hightower. Here. On the street where I lived. I considered giving him a flip of the old bird but curiosity won out.

I crossed the street.

A steely-eyed man with a trim Clark Gable moustache wearing a broad-brimmed Stetson hat sat behind the wheel. He was the one who'd beckoned me over.

Since my pop sometimes worked for him, I was polite: "Good evening, Dr. Hightower. What can I do for you, sir?"

"We were just wondering, son." He pointed past me at the house. "What exactly is going on over there? What are those things your dad's building in the backyard?"

I looked over myself. The uppermost portions of the two unfinished spaceships could be seen rising above the roof of the house.

"I don't know," I lied. "Just something he started the other day."

"To me they look like missiles. Rockets." A smaller man in a tweed suit and thick eyeglasses sitting in the passenger seat had spoken up. He reminded me of the actor Peter Lorre. A favorite of mine from the movie *20,000 Leagues Under the Sea*. The man's accent sounded foreign—Russian perhaps or Hungarian. Foreign anyhow.

"That's screwy," I said. "They're made out of wood. They couldn't possibly—"

"No," Clayton Hightower broke in. "They certainly could not. But they're still quite impressive nevertheless. Like something from a Chesley

Bonestell painting. Or Morris Scott Dollens. You're familiar with the work of these gentlemen, I believe."

Oddly enough I was. Both Bonestell and Dollens had done cover paintings for some of my favorite science fiction magazines. But how did Dr. Hightower know about them?

From the back seat Ronnie Hightower snorted. "Don't waste your time on this little loser, Dad. He's about as smart as a toilet seat. You want to know something, talk to his old man."

"I suppose I'll have to do that, Ron. Thanks for your help though, son," he added, speaking to me.

He let the window roll back up.

The car drove off.

Through the rear window I could see Ronnie Hightower wagging both his middle fingers at me as he went down the street.

I returned the gesture in kind and went back inside.

THREE: SCIENCE FICTION STORIES

i

Before getting on with rest of our story, a few background details to be sketched in first.

Science fiction. What is it? Where the heck did it come from? What's it all about?

Even now so many years later you could stack the days in piles, call them silver dollars, and feel rich just counting them, controversy swirls like water down the drain when it comes to the (seminal) origins of what we now call "science fiction." Or for short "SF." ("Sci-fi" is the preferred term *du jour* only among Hollywood poseurs; may their tongues rot in the putrescent cavities of their mouths, as my friend the writer Tom Powers puts it.)

Some academic theorists maintain that the literary genre now known as science fiction dates back in history as far as the second century A.D. when the Grecian writer Lucian of Samosata in his *True History* wrote of voyaging to the moon, engaging in a bit of colonial warfare with the non-Grecian inhabitants there, and then returning home in an entirely happier frame of mind. Others favor starting with the renaissance figure of Cyrano "the Beak" de Bergerac (as depicted on screen by actor Jose Ferrer, winner of the 1950 Oscar for his performance, as ably assisted by a brilliantly rendered prosthetic nosepiece). De Bergerac wrote circa 1687 not only of a trip to the moon but also of a second, presumably more heated voyage to the sun.

All commentators agree, however, on the crucial date of 1818 when the novel *Frankenstein or a Modern Prometheus* by the teen phenome Mary Wollstonecraft Shelley first appeared. Those of us who've read the actual text—me in the seventh grade—strongly urge you to rent the not terribly faithful 1931 movie version instead. You'll have a way better time, trust me.

The French novelist Jules Verne loomed leviathan in the nineteenth century, managing in the course of a long career to hit most of the science fictional basics: not only another journey to the Moon—propelled via cannon this time—but a trip to the center of the earth, five long dull weeks in a runaway balloon (but how do you pee?), and of course Captain Nemo and his luxurious submarine the *Nautilus*.

Again, those of us who've actually plowed through the original tomes agree that Walt Disney did the whole thing better. (*20,000 Leagues Under the Sea*, Richard Fleischer, 1955). Not only does Kirk Douglas get to sing a sea chantey accompanying himself on acoustic ukulele while Peter Lorre lisps background vocals but he also develops an odd romantic relationship with a (presumably) female harbor seal. (Check it out, bestiality buffs.)

Which brings us to the chinless ex-shopkeeping figure of Herbert George Wells—or "Bertie" to his intimates. Devout atheist, Fabian socialist, one time apprentice draper, self-proclaimed scientific humanist and expert in nearly every known field of knowledge in his time. (He would have ruled on *Jeopardy*.) His early novels of scientific romance written before he turned thirty-five include *The Time Machine* (1895), *The Island of Dr. Moreau* (1896), *The Invisible Man* (1897), *The War of the Worlds* (1898) and *First Men in the Moon* (1901). If you haven't read any of these—or better yet, all—do so right now. Immediately. No cheating either. Texts only. No movie versions. No Classic Comix allowed either. I know that old ploy. See as an example my notorious seventh grade book report on Melville's *Moby Dick*, which didn't fool Miss Colfax one minute; she awarded me a D-. (Presumably for the sheer nerve of it all.)

While we're paused here waiting for everybody to come back from doing their homework, let me ease any remaining tension by assuring those who've come this far with the story that a certain amount of explicit sex is projected to intrude on the narrative at key points in the future. In other words, voyageurs, do hang on.

* * * *

Everybody back now? Feeling better? Pretty good books, eh? (Better than this crap here, says the plucky lad in the back row.)

So Herbert George Wells. (1864-1946.) It doesn't get any better than that—science fiction, that is.

Which, alas, also constitutes the grim news: *Science fiction reached its zenith as a literary genre before it even acquired its name.*

A huge popular success, Wells naturally attracted imitators like flies to cow patties. A few more adept than most. I particularly commend to your attention Garrett P. Serviss, an American journalist whose *Edison's Conquest of Mars* depicts the heroic inventor bringing it all back home to Wells's invasive alien horde, finishing off the whole slimy godless lot by melting the Martian polar caps and drowning the no good bug-eyed bastards under a genocidal deluge. (Thus foreshadowing much of American foreign and military policy in the latter half of twentieth century right up to and including the Cuban Missile Crisis of October 1962.)

In addition to such relatively respectable luminaries as Verne, Wells, and Serviss, science fiction in the early years of the new century, though still lacking a formal name, came to flourish in the ragged pages of various cheap wood pulp magazines aimed at the mass of newly literate readers, many of them immigrants not long on the American shore, such as, to give one example, my own Grandfather Gus Gundy, though so far as I know the man never read a book from cover to cover in his life.

Among the more successful of these pulp writers was a failed door-to-door ladies intimate undergarment salesman by the name of Edgar Rice Burroughs, who first gained literary fame with a series of tales concerning the prosaically named John Carter, a Confederate Civil War veteran, who found himself miraculously transported to the planet Mars, upon which dwelled a host of various humanoid races—copper red, uppity black, superior white, six-limbed green—all but the latter no doubt reminding Carter of his native Virginia before the fall at Appomattox. (Burroughs, though a Midwesterner, tended like many poor white men of his day to romanticize the slave-owning Old South.) The initial entry in this long running saga, *A Princess of Mars*, written under the penname "Normal Bean," concludes with the titular heroine—the red-skinned Dejah Thoris—impregnated by Carter in a process left frustratingly undetailed—nesting forlornly atop a huge (though white) egg which, in the sequel to come, will disgorge her and Carter's love child, Catharsis.

Miscegenation anyone? (Illegal in all forty-eight states at the time.) I mean, even apart from the whole weird egg thing, you gotta let your jaw drop through the floor just thinking about it.

Yet the formula worked. Brilliantly. *Argosy* and *All-Story* magazines, where most of Burroughs's tales appeared, sold hundreds of thousands of copies weekly. Sex and its big muscled brother, violence—Carter is quite the swordsman in more ways than one—with a taste of exotic racism tossed in. And it would work even more brilliantly in Burroughs's most famous work, *Tarzan of the Apes*, which tosses rampaging gorillas and spear-chucking natives into the already heady brew.

Which brings us to the crucial year of 1926. Pause to envision the moment suspended in time: Verne long dead, Wells gone on to writing social tracts, egg-laying red-skinned Martian damsels cavorting with sword-thrusting racists on a Mars equipped with a breathable atmosphere, semi-Mediterranean climate, and canals awash in crystalline blue water.

Science fiction, no freaking way. If that's science, call me a nutcase.

At which point —*ka-ding, ka-ching, glory glory hallelujah!*—enters one Hugo Gernsback.

Soon to be crowned the father of science fiction.

(Which he at first called "scientifiction" before wiser heads prevailed.)

Our hero!

For it was Gernsback who in April 1926 launched upon the newsstands of America the first issue of the first all science fiction magazine, *Amazing Stories*.

The cost: twenty-five cents. (Hardly more than the price of a pack of Fatima cigarettes.)

Hugo (I repeat) Gernsback.

Who was this guy?

Briefly: a forty-two-year-old bird-beaked native of far-off exotic Luxembourg, with a slick-backed pompadour, detachable collar, and the air of a demoted schoolmaster. Who boldly immigrates across the raging Atlantic in the year of Theodore Roosevelt's election, 1904—Roosevelt being America's youngest president before the advent of John Kennedy, who in October 1962 will instigate the Cuban missile crisis threatening my then seventeen-year-old existence—and settles amid the dizzyingly phallic cityscape of greater Manhattan.

Years slip by like ham sliced from a bone. Young Gernsback eventually achieves some moderate financial success as the editor/publisher of a series of popular science magazines: *Practical Electrics*, *Radio Amateur News*, *Science and Invention*, *Sexology* (oops, how did that get in there?).

Among dense pages of prose detailing how to build one's own crystal radio from things found in your mother's kitchen or launch a submersible naval vessel in your neighborhood duck pond, Gernsback sprinkles in the occasional piece of what he quaintly calls scientifiction—stories with a scientific slant designed to teach and instruct. Among the resonant titles: "Marriage and the Wireless Companion"; "Chemicals Grow Hair"; "The Earth as Viewed from the Moon"; and (sure to gratify any Burroughs fan in the audience) "How the Martian Canals Came to be Built." The majority of these "stories" Gernsback pens himself under a variety of quirky pseudonyms including (my favorite) "Baron von Saddomann." In one long story, *Ralph 124C41+* (you have to speak the syllables aloud to achieve the full effect), Gernsback predicted such fabulous futurist inventions as the awesome wonder of something he called "tele-vision." (Through which medium, I pause to note, President Kennedy will one future day address the nation in order to clue them in that there's a pretty fair chance they're all going to be blown to bits in a few days' time.)

Which leads one to wonder: was Hugo Gernsback himself, in 1962 still very much alive, a spry seventy-eight-year-old, watching President Kennedy on his "tele-vision" receiver that fateful night? And if so how did he take the news?

Since, after all, atomic annihilation was yet another science fictional prophecy. Not Gernsback's alone this time. At least one other had preceded him. Our old friend Bertie Wells in his 1911 opus *The World Set Free*. (Look it up.)

But—to untangle the digressions—Gernsback's tales of scientific wonderment prove such a hit with his readers—mostly bright young urban adolescent boys—that he comes up idea of a new magazine containing only such fiction all the time.

That first April 1926 *Amazing Stories* featured a beautiful full color cover by the Viennese-trained former architect turned painter Frank R. Paul, illustrating a scene from Verne's *Off on a Comet*—ice skating astronauts no less. Among the other stories (all reprints) were works by Wells, Edgar Allan Poe, and George Alan England. (Three names split down the middle inexplicitly popular among writers of the day.)

From the start the new magazine sold like cinnamon hot cakes. No, better. Like Henry Ford's Model T automobiles.

By 1929, Gernsback had developed his own stable of writers including A. Hyatt Verrill, G. Peyton Wertenbaker, Claire Winger Harris, Dr. David H. Keller MD, and Colonel S. P. Meek, USA Retired.

Far and away the best of these was Edward Elmer Smith, PhD, a chemist who first appeared in *Amazing Stories* with his serialized novel *The Skylark of Space*. Not content with such simple wonders as a jaunt to the moon or a flight to a passing comet, "Doc" Smith (as he came to be known) sent his heroes and heroines (and accompanying evil villains led by the one "Blackie" Duquesne) soaring across the starlanes to the far corners of the expanding multi-galactic universe as recently propounded by astronomer Dr. Edwin Hubble of the Mount Wilson and Carnegie Observatories.

Unfortunately for Gernsback and the burgeoning field of scientifiction, soon thereafter the first stirrings of the economic disaster known as the Great Depression came slithering serpent-like from under the slimy rock of corporate America to confront a still blithely innocent populace with a vision of future rack and ruin, of hunger and deprivation, of dispossession and despair.

By the late 1930's Gernsback was out of the science fiction publishing business and the few remaining venues attempting to interest a distracted public in possible futurist marvels struggled to survive under such unpromising titles as *Astounding Stories of Super Science* and *Thrilling Wonder Stories*.

That was when a twenty-seven-year-old, bespectacled, bullet-headed MIT graduate and occasional science fiction wunderkind named Kingsley C. K. Babbitt IV assumed the editorship of one of these failing magazines,

Flabbergasting Tales of Wonder and Mystery.

In the history of science fiction this event was tantamount to the moment when Napoleon Bonaparte seized the reins of power in revolutionary France.

But more—much more—on that later.

For now I want to scotch an ugly rumor. Namely that the only way to explain Hugo Gernsback and his achievement of 1926 is that Gernsback was not in fact born in Luxembourg in 1884 as his biography insists, but rather sometime in the late twenty-second century. Or perhaps the twenty-third.

In other words, Hugo Gernsback was a man from the future. A time traveler. Who journeyed to early twentieth century New York and in his struggle to survive hit on the notion of using his knowledge of the future to invent the literary genre eventually known as "science fiction."

Horse pucky, I say. Poor myth.

A few years back I personally spent some forty days traipsing across continental Europe, specifically the rolling pastures and spiraling mountaintops of the Principality of Luxemburg, and in that time I not only pursued and perused all available local documentation concerning the life and ancestry of Hugo Gernsback but had the great honor of meeting the nonagenarian Franz Gernsback, sole surviving nephew of the great Hugo.

Franz claimed to remember his uncle well.

"He sent us much stray kipple from America," he told me.

"Kipple such as what?" I prodded, in my halting German.

"Better yet, I show you."

And he does—producing one dusty object after another from crates and boxes piled in the basement of his chalet. Gadgets. Devices. American curios. A miniature tea kettle that whistles "Yankee Doodle Dandy" when heated. A bottle opener in the shape of a Coney Island hot dog. And, lastly— most potently—a six-inch model rocketship. Made of tin. Painted a soft pastel pink.

A tear dampens my eye. I recognize this as one of the early examples of a science fiction achievement award—the Hugo—now given out annually at World Science Fiction Conventions.

This one is inscribed to Hugo Gernsback—*The Man Who Invented Science Fiction*, it says.

* * * *

It's at this pregnant moment that the front door of the elderly Gernsback's chalet bangs open and a blonde apparition in Nordic pigtails, snugly zippered ski pants, and a long trailing neck scarf bursts through the gap.

I melt as I stand.

"My grand-niece," introduces old Franz, with a leering glint in his eye.

"Our Hilda. She knows your American—" his tongue seems to stick to the roof his mouth "—your persuasions."

"But does she know that she's related to Hugo Gernsback, the Father of Science Fiction?" I ask avidly.

"Ah, naturally," she answers, speaking up for herself. "The great Hugo was my dear ancestor."

"You speak excellent English," I point out.

"I learned it while studying at UCLA," she says.

"Our Hilda, she lived in the Hollywood Hills," explains Franz.

"At college?" I say.

"Some." She shyly lowers her gaze. "I also… I worked in the art cinema industry."

"The private movies!" cries Franz, beaming proudly.

At Franz and Hilda's gracious invitation—as darkness wraps the Alpine slopes in its benighted grip—I consent to spend the night in their rustic home. Huddled beneath a mountain of blankets and quilts, I lie poised in wait, naked and supine. Soon enough Hilda joins me. Shortly after midnight. And in my arms she—I—well… *enough*!

I can say no more.

Let the veil of time descend.

But, yes, it's true what you may have heard: I banged Hugo Gernsback's last living descendant. (Several times actually. Afterward together we'd watched one of her old movies.)

Talk about your seminal moments!

ii

In the meantime, before getting on with the story, one other thing needs to be settled.

What's all this literary history stuff got to do with two wooden spaceships being built in somebody's backyard?

Well, I'll tell you. It's got plenty to do with it. Because in the end it's all just science fiction.

And science fiction is what we're all about here.

For me, personally, it started in 1957. In October of that year. (Coincidentally, the same month as humankind's first halting step into the void of infinite space. Sputnik One launched into orbit—October 4, 1957.)

I was in the seventh grade—twelve years old. And if you've ever been in the seventh grade, twelve years old, you'll understand me when I say that humankind's first halting step into the void rolled past me like rain off a duck's wet butt.

I had troubles of my own.

For me—at age twelve, remember, the seventh grade, when everything awful and ugly looms way huger than it will before or ever after—it was the worst of times. My cozy secure this boy's life had suddenly and without warning turned into veritable dog-doo.

Let me explain. (Or at least summarize.)

The first six grades of school you had one room, one teacher. You also had a long lunch period smack in the middle of the day during which in winter when the weather turned nasty, they put you in the gym and let you watch movies like *Last of the Mohicans* with Randy Scott or *Lusty Men* with Bob Mitchum or else frolic at basketball with the other keen lads—shirts versus skins!—and you also had two long recesses in which to frolic and play games like dodgeball with all your many, all quite wonderful pals. You knew everyone in your class. Even the girls like fat Dorothy Dow and tiny dark Isabel Avila who smelled like an old clothes closet. They were the same kids every day too, boys and girls alike. You swapped cards with them all come St. Valentine's Day. It was a sheltered world, cocooned, wrapped in velvet as fluffy and gentle as Mary and her little white wooly lamb.

Then you turned twelve. Seventh grade. Junior high school. A new environment. A change. Like a nail driven through the center of your eye.

I attended six different classes in six different rooms with six different teachers with six minutes between class to get from one to the other. There were also thirty minutes in the middle of fourth period for lunch where, if fortunate, you found a back table where you could eat your bologna sandwich and carrot sticks in peace without either getting the holy crap beat out of you by a bully or, worse, your Hostess cream-filled cupcake dessert swiped out of hand by that same bully. (Think Ronnie Hightower.)

Or both.

My classes that year consisted in daily order of social studies—with an odd emphasis on Latin America—English, both grammar and literature, basic mathematics, basic science, physical so-called education, and some kind of shop, probably dealing with metals. Or tin.

In other words, *pure hot red hell.*

I loathed every class.

I—let's be honest here—*I hated school.*

Never the case before. Throughout my first years of schooling I was not only a top student, a budding genius, but more crucially—this was the 1950's, after all—a Good Citizen.

Certified.

I still have in my possession the now tattered document presented to me in the fifth grade:

Lake Delridge Elementary School
District Good Citizenship Award

Charles Gundy
Nineteen Hundred Fifty-five

How many others out there have one of these? Tell me that.

But come seventh grade everything changed. Good citizenship went rocketing out the window. The iron spike pierced the gooey eyeball. My grades plummeted instantly into the nebulous world of the C- and the D+. A classic underachiever I became, though not yet a "discipline" problem. (That would come later.)

I raged with the burning fury of rebellion.

Looking back, I now blame four things for this change, three obvious, one not.

The obvious: (1) puberty, (2) rock 'n' roll, (3) the movies.

The fourth and less obvious: (4) drawing bananas.

The puberty part is easily explained. I was twelve years. And a boy. Dare I mention wet dreams? Onanism? Say no more

The rock 'n' roll part involved Elvis Presley, Gene Vincent, Jerry Lee Lewis, Chuck Berry, Little Richard. It was 1957. The movies included *Blackboard Jungle, Rock Around the Clock, Teenage Doll, The Wild One*, and of course *Rebel Without a Cause*. In some of these pictures you clearly were meant to root for the wise teachers, the benevolent cops. Not me, baby. Not in my peer group. We all cheered the hoods, the rinks, the JD's and thugs. See, for example, Vic Morrow in *Blackboard Jungle* flying high on Sneaky Pete wine. Whatever that was. (And where can I get hold of some?)

* * * *

Now the part about drawing bananas.

Yet another flashback. To me again. At age five this time. Kindergarten. The windowless basement of the Sacred Palsy Presbyterian Church of Lake Delridge. Even though my parents were no more Presbyterian than I was the love child of Mahatma Gandhi and Joan of Arc. (As Pop put it when he heard where Mom had enrolled me.)

Then I missed the first two weeks. I had the mumps.

One thing about starting school the first time is no matter what you do, don't miss the first two weeks.

Trust me. I should know. It'll follow you like a curse the rest of your life. You'll never get over the feeling that you're ten steps behind everybody else.

By the time Mom nudged me forward into the big ugly room for my first day of school in the chair held open for me by my best pal Cisco Cordova, the class had already zipped past the simple lessons in drawing the apple, the orange, and the red ripe red tomato.

The easy stuff was past. Now the going got rough.

"Today," chimed our teacher, Mrs. Autry, "we're going to learn to draw a banana!"

Oh my sweet Jesus in heaven!

Because I could not do it.

No, really.

As hard as I tried. Whatever I came up with always ended up looking like everything else except an actual banana. (Feel free to use your imagination here.)

For the first time in my sheltered existence I knew the meaning of *failure*.

How it felt to be laughed at.

As a result I became what I'd never been before.

I was *self-conscious*.

Like the green monkey in the zoo.

Resentment builds early. Many respected authorities in child development confirm his. It's likely what happened with little Adolph Hitler as a young boy. With Ivan the Terrible, Jack the Ripper, Mack the Knife, Louie the Finger.

Resentment, brewing, bubbling, festering in the black cauldron of the unconscious, and then exploding, spewing forth into—well, as the above list of names attests some pretty bad shit.

But also: Picasso, Beethoven, Johnny Cash. The line between madness and genius as thin as the webbing between a baby duckling's toes.

Plus, one other factor worth noting, I had always been drawn to science. I don't mean the practical kind of science that my friend Nedd Young pursued in the cell-like bedroom of the shotgun shack he shared with his father on the other side of our backyard fence. Things like building a crystal radio set (hey there, Hugo Gernsback), performing chemistry experiments, entering the soapbox derby year after year. (Nedd always seemed to finish second. His old man watching from the sidelines always shrugged and laughed: "It only goes to show, kid," he said to me.)

I was more into theory than practice.

Not the Einstein or Darwin kind of theory, you understand. More the Isaac Asimov or Edward E. Smith kind.

I'm talking science fiction here.

Science fiction saved my life.

* * * *

Cut to the seventh grade again. My first day at my new school. Marcus Whitman Junior High. As I tread the narrow dark corridors, fighting to find sufficient air to breathe.

Rebellion ripples around me like a red tide.

I see heavy black engineer boots, silver belt buckles flashing. I smell pompadours piled high with pomade and brilliantine. I hear the crinkle of leather jackets. Switchblade knives swish. Zip guns click.

The soul of Elvis Presley holds sway, the world clasped in his tight hillbilly fist.

Soon enough I conformed. Or tried to. I let my own hair grow longer. I bought Vaseline petroleum jelly and smeared the medicinal goop on my head till it lathered my comb like foam from a rabid dog's mouth. I tried growing sideburns, not realizing they were actually whiskers. My grades tumbled like loaded dice. I made the other kids laugh, doing my class clown routine. By January I'd paid two visits to the vice-principal's cozy office with the moose head on the wall and his fat counseling finger wagging in my face.

Somewhere around in here—my original point—I started reading science fiction.

Soon enough I was going through a book a day. (They were almost all 192 paperback pages in length. I was a quick study.)

I'd always liked monster movies. My older brother Slim, before he went off to seek his own path to enlightenment among the native peoples of the far north, took me to see the George Pal version of *War of the Worlds*. I was only eight. On the walk home in the gathering darkness afterward, Slim kept waving a hand at the sky crying out that the Martians were up there, they were landing, they were coming for us, we were all going to die.

He was testing me of course.

The movie was frightening enough without that. But Slim brought it all back home.

Scared the holy bejesus out of me.

I loved every minute of it.

After that I saw them all: *The Beast from 20,000 Fathoms*; *The Thing from Another World*; *The Creature from the Black Lagoon*; *Tarantula!*; *Them!*

Monsters everywhere! Up in the sky! Out in the garden! (Giant slugs.) Right in your own home. (*Invasion of the Body Snatchers*.)

Fear, horror, and dread everywhere you looked.

And that's without even getting into the part about the Communist Menace.

Some definite scary shit going on there.

* * * *

But I may be getting slightly ahead of myself again.

Let's backtrack.

I first started reading serious science fiction when I was twelve years old. In October 1957. In the seventh grade.

What it was was you had to read something. In second period English class when they took us all down the library and said find a book, check it out, write a report.

I grabbed the first book I could. No, really. I reached out blind as a bat on a hot date, took hold of the first book at hand, and raised it to the light.

It was called *Red Planet*. The author's name was Robert A. Heinlein.

It looked good to me.

I wandered over into the corner where my friends Cisco and Nedd were already thoroughly immersed in books of their choosing—Cisco with *Thirty Seconds Over Tokyo* by Captain Ted Lawson as told to Bob Considine and Nedd *The Kid from Tomkinsville* by John R. Tunis.

I sat down and started reading *Red Planet*.

I didn't stop till hours later back home in my bedroom. By then I was hooked.

The cover of the book said *science fiction*. Which kind of confused me. My assumption going in inspired by all those dumb scary movies I'd seen was that science fiction was all about monsters, creatures, and beasts.

Red Planet contained none of the above.

It was a story about a bright teenage boy, kind of like guess who else, who happened to be living on the planet Mars sometime in the future and had most of the same growing up problems I had plus having a Martian pet named Willis shaped like a basketball with legs and arms but which turned out at the end to be something else altogether. (*Wow!* I said, dazzled with wonder when I found out the secret.)

As soon as I finished *Red Planet* around nine that evening night, I turned back to page one and started over again. I read until my eyes burned and refused to stay open a moment longer.

In the morning, as soon as I woke up, I picked up the book and went back to reading.

* * * *

So, yes indeed. Science fiction saved my life. (With all due apologies to the sublime poetry of Mr. Lou Reed and his sweet sweet Jane.)

Let me explain further.

There was a program on TV back then I rarely missed called *I Led Three Lives*. It was a stupid show, starring the bland refugee from a zillion monster movies Richard Carlson as an undercover FBI agent named Herbert Philbrick, who had infiltrated the American Communist Party.

Me, I was soon leading not three but two lives of my own as well.

Life number one was my normal regular miserable rotten life as a junior high school student and prospective teenage rebel.

In my second life though, I drifted free, lost in the clouds. No, farther up than that. In outer space. The dominions of the far galaxies. The outer reaches. The infinite depths.

I was a science fiction fan.

After *Red Planet* followed a batch of other Heinleins from the school library with titles like *Starman Jones* and *Between Planets* and *Farmer in the Sky*. Then I stumbled on the work of the great Arthur C. Clarke—*Prelude to Space*, *Childhood's End*, *Expedition to Earth*, *The City and the Stars*. There was Isaac Asimov of course and *The Caves of Steel*, *The End of Eternity*, and the utterly mind blowing *Foundation* trilogy. I read books by Frederic Brown and William Tenn; Phillip K. Dick and Frederick Pohl; Harlan Ellison and Robert Silverberg. A few were maybe still a bit over my head—Sturgeon and von Vogt in particular—but I was only thirteen and fourteen and I figured I'd eventually catch on. My favorite—after Heinlein—was Ray Bradbury. *The Martian Chronicles* dazzled me, *Fahrenheit 451*, which I recall finishing at 2 a.m. huddled under the bedcovers by flashlight, made me feel like crying. (Maybe I did.)

It was propitious time to be first reading SF as the late 1950's and early 60's were heralded as the years when science fiction was fast becoming science fact. That Sputnik thing again. Earth satellites, the space race, NASA, and the International Geophysical Year (you can look it up). Most of the heralding being done by people who'd clearly never read much if any actual science fiction. But still…

* * * *

Soon enough I also discovered besides the paperbacks and library books an entire wire rack of digest sized magazines in the newsstand at Holmes Drugstore on Chelsea Way. Some of the titles: *Galaxy*, *Infinity*, *Astounding Science Fiction*, *Amazing Stories* (yes!—still going years after Gernsback), *Fantastic Universe*, *Other Worlds*, *Imagination*, *Imaginative Tales*.

And what soon became my favorite, the reigning prince of the field, *Flabbergasting Science Fiction*.

Edited by Kingsley C.K. Babbitt IV. I read every word of every monthly issue. (Even the editorials and a few of the science fact articles.).

The December 1960 issue of *Flabbergasting Science Fiction* contained my first ever published words. In a letter to the editor I wrote (quoted here in full):

Dear Mr. Babbitt IV.:

In the course of Calvin M. Ellsworth's "Blazing Through Infinity" in the May *Flabbergasting* he describes a fifth dimensional magna-system that allows his characters to travel simultaneously backwards and forwards and sideways through time and space. I'm only a high school senior but know of only four dimensions known to science. The other stories in the issue were also fine. Please more Mark Phillips and less Randall Garrett.

Yours cordially,

Charles J. Gundy
Seacrest, Washington

Editor Babbitt's response filled three pages of tiny italicized type, incorporating a veritable history of the science of multi-dimensional theory, including what still strikes me as the most insightful summary I've ever seen of Einstein's relativity theories.

The day the issue hit the local drugstores, I put down my thirty-five cents and tax and rushed home to show Mom her son's first published literary endeavor. (Secretly, I was already harboring an ambition to become a science fiction writer myself when I grew up.)

When she finished reading my letter and Mr. Babbitt's response, Mom looked up with a disappointed expression. "But you told a lie."

"I did?"

"You said you were a high school senior."

Senior, sophomore, who cares? I thought. What difference did that make? I was an author, wasn't I?

* * * *

Two nights later. The family—all except Pop, who was down in his basement lab polishing somebody's dental bridgework for Dr. Hightower—gathered in the living room to watch *Bonanza* on TV. I couldn't stomach the show myself but hung around so that during commercials I could flip over to Ed Sullivan and Steve Allen to see if either had anyone cool on his show tonight. Like Chuck Berry or Bo Diddley or the Platters. So far, though, it was just the usual gaggle of juggling chimpanzees and gargling ventriloquists.

Ring, ding, ring. (That's the telephone.)

Polly raced to answer. As always. Even at age eleven she seemed to live in a strange parallel universe where people were forever calling her on the phone.

Not this time.

"It's for you, Stupid Face," she said.

"Who's Stupid Face?" said Mom, her gaze riveted on Little Joe and his horse. Or maybe his Hoss. (Gad, I hated that show.)

"Stupid Charlie Face," she said, holding out the receiver.

"Who is it?" I asked.

"Some man."

"Cisco?"

"I said man, not boy."

No man had ever called me on the phone before.

I answered. "Hello," I said.

"Is this Charles J. Gundy?"

"It is, yes."

"My name's Budd Champion. I just finished reading your letter in the new *Flabbergasting*. The reason I'm calling, I noticed you live in the area and I wondered if you might be interested. We've got a little club of local fans, SF fans, and call ourselves the Rocketeers. Though don't hold that part against us. We meet every other Thursday night. I could send you some details if you're interested."

"You mean a science fiction club? For people who read science fiction?" The prospect overwhelmed me, I admit.

"Started back in 1950 by a bunch of us going to the UW at the time. Nothing formal, nothing serious, we mostly sit around and shoot the breeze. What we're reading, what we're thinking. Whatever comes up. We can always use new blood. What do you say?"

"I... I... well, gee, sure. I could..."

"I'll send you a meeting notice."

"You have my address?"

"It's in the book."

"No, I want—I think I do want to go."

"Well, great. I'll be seeing you."

His voice had sounded old. Well, older anyhow. He'd never asked my age.

My life had just changed.

Utterly, totally, dramatically.

iii

I attended my first meeting of the Seacrest Rocketeers a week and a half later, the first Thursday of the new month, October 1960. An-older-than-petrified-dog-poop Ike still hanging on in the White House while the young Nixon and the younger Kennedy traded tepid verbal blows competing to see who would replace him.

In the meantime the perennially mighty New York Yankees faced off against the upstart Pittsburgh Pirates in the World Series. The Pirates would eventually stun the baseball world by taking the Series in seven thanks to Bill Mazeroski's bloop home run in the bottom of the ninth inning in the final game. (A harbinger, perhaps, of other great upheavals to come.)

At the time the Rocketeers met in a dusty rented room on the fourth floor of the venerable Arcadia Building on Second Avenue in downtown Seacrest. That first time I was able to get there by talking Pop into giving me a lift in and dropping me off while he went on up to Dr. Simon's office in the Carson Building on Fourth Avenue and put in a little unpaid overtime, grinding dentures.

The meeting was supposed to start at seven-thirty. I arrived five minutes before and went in past the security guard, who didn't give me a second glance, and stepped into the waiting elevator.

There already were two people on board.

They both glanced at me curiously, looked back at one another, and grinned. Then one of them shot out a hand, which I grabbed hold of and shook before I could think. He was a tall, gangly, uncoordinated-looking man of around thirty wearing wire-rimmed eyeglasses and a flannel shirt with a load of ballpoint pens jammed in the pocket. "A prospective Rocketeer?" he asked, through his grin.

I managed a nervous nod. "The science fiction club, yes."

"I can always tell a fan by the glint in the eyes," he said. "I'm Yul Borensen, secretary-treasurer of our august organization, and this lovely lady is Mrs. Eva Jones. She's our president in charge of vice."

The president in charge of vice was a short chubby woman with at least three chins who wore white gloves on dainty hands, a flowing Hawaiian mu-mu that reached past her ankles, and brown-and-white saddle shoes on tiny feet. She waddled as she walked and looked to be somewhere on the far side of fifty—hard to be more precise when you were only fifteen and all old people looked the same.

"Pleased to meet you both," I said, in my best winsomely polite manner.

"You must be the bright young fellow who had the letter in the last *Flabbergasting SF*," Yul Borensen said.

"That was me, yes."

The elevator seemed to be taking an awful long time to rise a mere four floors.

As if reading my mind, Yul Borensen reached out and thumbed a bright red button at the top of the instrument panel. The elevator shook, groaned, quivered, and then started to rise.

"So what masochistic motive inspired you to write a letter to the formidable Kingsley C.K. Babbitt IV?"

"Well, one of the stories...."

"Wait." He held up a hand as the elevator ground to a halt. The door grudgingly slid open. "Don't tell me you actually read the stories? I just like to look at the funny pictures."

"Don't listen to a word he says," Mrs. Eva Jones put in as we headed down the hallway. "Yul has been reading SF since he was a boy no older than you. He never misses an issue of *Flabbergasting*."

"But I much preferred *Thrilling Wonder*. Or poor dead *Planet Stories*."

I'd never heard of either magazine.

"Then you missed the Golden Age of Science Fiction," he said. "It was when I turned twelve."

"That's when I first started reading SF too," I said.

"Then you had your own Golden Age."

The meeting room was located at the far end of the corridor next to a well-stocked janitorial closet. Wafting ammonia fumes scented the air as we stepped past, stinging the eyes. During the day the room served as a health food distribution center. Crates of wheat germ were piled in every corner.

"Mrs. Jones found the room for us," Yul explained as we went inside. "She's old friends with the owner."

"At last!" cried a voice from within. "The man who makes the coffee!"

"That's me," said Yul, holding up a paper bag. "Ready, willing, and unable."

There was maybe a half-dozen people in the room. Most were seated around a long conference-type table. One couple—a man and woman in their middle to late thirties—stood apart from the rest against the far wall.

Mrs. Eva Jones waved a dainty white-gloved hand in my direction. "This is Charles, the young man who had the letter in the last *Flabbergasting*. He seems to be a very enthusiastic fan."

While he made coffee, Yul introduced me to the others present. Looking back on these events from today's perspective, it's hard recalling exactly what it was I'd anticipated. Maybe some sort of literary society, a group rather like Herbert Philbrick's Communist Party cell where everyone sat around puffing on pipes and talking excitedly while waving their hands.

The Rocketeers weren't like that. A couple of the men smoked cigarettes, true, and while everyone talked—often all at once—there wasn't much waving of hands. If anything it seemed more like one joke after another. Most of which I didn't understand. The people all seemed to have known each other for a long time.

I was by far the youngest person in the room. The others were all adults. But they didn't seem to hold that against me. Whenever I spoke up—admittedly not often—it was my first meeting, after all—they listened attentively and responded in kind. There was no looking down their noses at me. They treated me as if I were an equal.

* * * *

Eventually, there was a sort of official meeting called to order. Old business, new business, the reading of minutes. The president turned out to be the man who'd called me on the phone, Budd Champion. He was the male half of the couple who'd been standing by the wall when I first came in. A brisk, stocky man with lively eyes and a neat chin beard. (Something not often seen in those days.) He reminded me a bit of my uncle Phil Snead,

Mom's brother, mostly in the way he talked in flat declarative sentences that seemed to pile one on top of another like building blocks.

His wife Melanie sat beside him. She had a gentle musical voice you had to bend your ear to catch and, like almost everybody else there, she wore glasses.

Which was definitely one other thing that made me feel at home. The glasses. I wore them too. Since the beginning of the ninth grade. Though only when I absolutely had to. Which meant only when I was with my family, Cisco, or Nedd. Or when I was alone. Or at the movies.

And we all read science fiction.

Though as Budd Champion had cautioned me in advance there wasn't all that much talk directly concerning SF during the meeting.

Instead, in between jokes and a lot of punning, everyone tried explaining fandom to me. Science fiction fandom, that is. Though that's not how they put it. They just said "fandom." As if it were the only kind of fandom there was, a unique phenomenon. Which at the time happened to be basically accurate. If not the only fandom, science fiction was certainly the first fandom.

The Champions, it seemed, had just returned from attending the World Science Fiction Convention in Pittsburgh, where they had won a Hugo Award (named after Hugo Gernsback) for publishing the best fanzine of 1959, *Howl of the Rocketeer.*

"So what's a fanzine?" I innocently asked.

That meant it was time for everybody to explain that one to me as well.

Again, they all tried to speak at once.

Much of it didn't make immediate sense to me. But enough did that I found myself… well, intrigued anyhow.

A fanzine was an amateur journal produced by fans, written by fans, and designed to be read by fans. A *fan* magazine.

But not in the sense of as, say, a movie fan magazine. In fact, there was no rule saying that a fanzine had to have anything in it about science fiction at all. "Some of them do," Budd Champion explained. "But not all. The contents of a typical fanzine might include pretty much anything you can think of under the sun."

"That's not illegal, illegible, or fattening," Yul Borensen added.

"There are fans all over the world," Mrs. Eva Jones said. "Many in England, in France, Australia, Argentina, everywhere."

"Except maybe Cuba," Yul Borensen said.

"So far as we know," Budd said.

"Though Castro does resemble some of the fans I know."

"Just because he has a beard."

"Lincoln had a beard too."

"Not to mention Jesus."

"Or Allen Ginsburg."

"Or yours truly," Budd Champion finished up. "And if the rest of you don't like it, you can all go saw Courtney's boat."

As I mentioned there were a great many humorous references being tossed around that went soaring right over my teenaged head. (As far as Courtney and his boat, you can look that one up too.)

"I thought we were supposed to be telling poor Charles here about fandom," Mrs. Eva Jones said, letting her annoyance show. "You men keep straying from the point."

"Hear, hear," Melanie Champion said. Apart from Eva she was the only woman in the room

"Well, it all started in 1926," Budd said.

"With Uncle Hugo," Yul explained.

"Gernsback."

"Yes, I know about him," I said. There'd been a profile in a recent issue of *Amazing Stories*. Also, I'd once tried to read Gernsback's *Ralph 124C41+* in paperback. It was incredibly dull. Worse than Jules Verne's *From the Earth to the Moon*. Oddly, Verne's *Journey to the Center of the Earth* was a favorite of mine.

"The first true fan," Budd said, "was a fellow named Milton J Arbogast. He had a letter printed in the fourth issue of Gernsback's *Amazing Stories* calling on readers everywhere—he lived in San Francisco—and asking them to write to him. Apparently, several dozen did and it all sprang from there."

"Like Topsy," Yul put in. (Whoever that was.) "It just sorts of growed."

The way it was explained to me, Milton J Arbogast, a young teenager at the time, soon found himself corresponding back and forth with as many as a hundred regular readers of *Amazing Stories*. Eventually, in late 1929—after Gernsback had lost control of *Amazing* and started two new competing magazines, *Science Wonder* and *Air Wonder Stories*—Arbogast published the first ever science fiction fan magazine—later dubbed *fanzines*—on a $1.98 hectograph his parents bought for him at an army surplus store.

The total initial of the circulation of *The Planetary Digest* (as he dubbed it) was fewer than fifty. That being the most copies a hectograph could reproduce legibly.

"And from there it didn't just growed," Budd said, nodding at Yul as he did. "It exploded. Today's fandom—I don't know—what do you guys think? Five hundred, a thousand, two thousand? Prozines like *Flabbergasting* and *Galaxy* sell upward of a hundred thousand copies a month. But only a small percentage of SF readers are fans."

"And that depends upon one's definition of what makes a fan a fan," Melanie said.

"Which we could argue about till the end of time."

"Or eternity," said Yul. An apparent reference here—which I caught!—to the Isaac Asimov time travel novel *The End of Eternity*. "Whichever comes first."

"Because there's almost as many different types of fans as there are breeds of dog. There's club fans, con fans, fanzine fans, fannish fans, sercon fans—"

"Fringe fans," said Yul.

"And fake fans," Budd finished up. "Most of us are a combination of several different types. Melanie and I are fanzine fans—we publish one of our own and belong to three different apas—amateur press associations. We're club fans too—obviously. And we're con fans. We went to the World-Con in Pittsburgh, the one before that in Detroit, and we'll be putting on one of our own right here in Seacrest next Labor Day weekend."

Which was news to me. Exciting news though. If nothing else, a chance to meet and talk with some of my favorite writers.

"We're going to invite Heinlein to be our Guest of Honor," Melanie said.

"And if he turns us down, then King Babbitt is our second choice."

Budd meant Kingsley C.K. Babbitt IV, the longtime editor of *Flabbergasting Science Fiction*, the leading magazine in the field—and my own favorite—which would soon be changing its title to the more dignified—and perhaps accurate—*Serendipity Fact & Science Fiction*.

"Assuming he's not locked up in the looney bin by then." This remark coming from a man at the table who'd been quiet until then. He was a bit younger than any of the others. Closer to my age. Twenty-five or so, I thought. Tall, thin, with a pronounced Adam's apple and two big front teeth that stuck out of his mouth when he grinned.

Budd cocked a thumb at him. "Tom here doesn't think much of King Babbitt's latest hobby horse."

"His version of a perpetual motion machine."

"The Botts Battery."

I only vaguely knew what they were talking about since I'd barely skimmed the science article in the magazine this month. That was an odd thing I'd noticed. After discovering SF I gradually lost my former all- consuming interest in science itself. A pity maybe. I might have made a good scientist. The science we were taught in school tended toward the dry, the dull, and the boring. While science fiction in contrast—the marvels of the universe as depicted by Heinlein, Asimov, and Arthur C. Clarke—that was where the excitement came in. The sense of wonder.

Later on Budd and Yul showed me copies of some recent issues of *Howl of the Rocketeers*, their monthly fanzine. While the meeting went on around me, I leafed through the mimeographed pages. After cute cartoon covers, each issue contained several short articles, a pair of regular outside columns by people I hadn't heard of named Carr and Berry, some editorial notes and comments from Budd, Melanie, and Yul, and a long letter section that took the remainder of the forty or so pages. I glanced at some the names and addresses on the letters. They came from all over the country and the rest of the world too. England, Japan, Germany, Australia, even Brazil.

Around nine-thirty, the meeting started to break up. Which was a relief to me because I was worried Pop might be getting impatient. As I was saying good-bye to the Champions and promising to attend the next meeting —without really being sure how I was going to manage it—a voice spoke up behind me.

"From what I understand you don't live far from me. I could offer you a lift here and back if you're interested."

I turned and saw Tom Powers,

"Sure," I said. "That'd be great."

"I'll pick you up at a quarter till six."

"Fine. I'll be there. I mean, I'll be waiting."

"And if you change your mind, too bad. I don't have a phone and I refuse to accept collect telegrams."

* * * *

Which meant that two weeks after my first Rocketeer meeting there I was again at the health food distribution store on the fourth floor of the Arcadia Building thanks to Tom Powers and his baby blue Volkswagen bug with the New York license plates and the *Support Your Local Police* bumper sticker pasted to the back. "Helps avoid speeding tickets," Tom explained.

Tom, I found out, was currently employed at the Cantrell Air main plant in Seacrest as an engineer. He'd graduated from college at Cornell the year before with a degree in physics.

"But what he really is is a writer," Yul said. "Tom's working on his first novel even as we speak."

"Actually, I'm drinking coffee and trying not to spill it," he said.

"This novel of yours, Tom," Budd said, "I don't think you've ever told us. Is it SF or not?"

"Then depends on your definition."

"And not yours?"

"I don't have one," he said. "I'm not that crazy."

Everyone laughed then. Arguments over the specific definition of science fiction having been ongoing and endless ever since Hugo Gernsback first invented the term.

As for me, let me just say that if science fiction gave me a new identity, if it saved my life, then SF fandom changed it—transformed it utterly. If I started out leading two separate lives, it wasn't long before the second of the two—the science fiction part—became the more real one. I felt I'd found my home at last. The place where I belonged.

For the moment anyway, I wanted to be nowhere else.

iv

For as long as I was a member I remained the one and only teenage Rocketeer. I didn't really mind. In most every respect the others treated me as if I were another adult. An equal. Sometimes more so—say, when compared to the often addled Mrs. Eva Jones. They listened to what I had to say with interest and respect. They never talked down to me. How rare that was—how unique—ask any teenager you know. Some things never change and that's one. When you're grown up and have kids of your own, you immediately forget what it was like being one yourself.

Of the Rocketeers Tom Powers was the closest to my age. He turned out to be even younger than I'd first thought. Only twenty-two.

"An old and wise twenty-two though," he pointed out, when I mentioned our comparative ages. "With the pure innocent heart of a young boy."

"Which Tom keeps in a jar on his desk," Yul said, as he went past on his way to the coffee maker.

There were no female Rocketeers. Apart from the older married women like Melanie Champion and Mrs. Eva Jones, whose husband—despite always introducing herself as *Mrs.* Jones—was never otherwise referred to. Separated, divorced, deceased, non-existent? I never found out.

"I think it's the science in science fiction that scares the ladies off," Tom theorized as we chugged and rattled up the steep Miller's Way Hill on our way back to Lake Delridge after one meeting night. "You tell me, Charlie. You're a man of experience. Have you ever known a woman who could tell a logarithm from a log boom?"

"Well, sure," I had to admit. "At least one anyhow."

"Really? Pray tell, who?"

"A girl at school I know. She's great at both science and math. Better than me, which isn't saying a whole lot. But she's getting A's in both chemistry and trig."

"Sounds like a real blue ribbon prize. She doesn't happen to be a voracious reader of the crazy Buck Rogers stuff too, does she?"

"Well, sure. Some anyway." I'd lent Katy a couple of my favorite recent SF novels when she'd asked me about them, saying she'd read both *Brave New World* and *Fahrenheit 451* as well as Clarke's *Childhood's End* and wondered if there were more good SF like that. The books I gave her—*Rogue Moon* by Algis Budrys and *A Canticle for Leibowitz* by Walter Miller—she'd read and liked both. Especially *Canticle*. "And me a devout atheist," she said, when she returned the books. "But it made me so sad at the end I almost cried."

"You ought to bring her to a meeting," Tom said. "She and Mrs. Jones could share a good cry together."

I said I'd ask her. But I didn't. Not right away. For the time being anyhow I was keeping my involvement with the Rocketeers—and SF fandom as a whole—secret. Not even Cisco and Nedd—my fellow Comancheros—knew anything about it.

It was part of my leading two separate lives.

The first few times Tom came by to pick me up I waited for him in the street out front. I wasn't quite ready to introduce him to the family yet.

"You know something, Charlie my boy," he said as we drove into town for one of my early meetings, "I have to give you credit. You're not like the others."

"What others?"

"Most neos never come back for a second Rocketeers meeting."

"I wonder why that is."

"Who can tell?" He laughed. "They never come back to tell us."

* * * *

Eventually I relaxed sufficiently to make myself wait in the living room long enough for Tom to come up on the front porch and ring the doorbell. It seemed safe enough. Pop was usually down in the basement working on teeth in his lab while Mom was in the kitchen washing dinner dishes and the kids upstairs watching something undoubtedly dumb on the used TV Pop had got for them.

Though one time just as I was slipping on my jacket preparing to go, Mom wandered in from the kitchen and saw Tom standing there.

"Charlie tells me you read science fiction too," Tom said to her, causing me to instantly curse my own big fat mouth.

"Well, some of his books, I do, yes. I like the ones taking place in the near future here on Earth. Some of the others—like E.E. Smith for instance —are just too far out for me."

"You ought to come to our meetings then."

"Oh, no," she said. (To my instant and immense relief.) "Not me. I don't want to spoil the fun for you boys."

Later on during the drive into town I told Tom: "Please don't ever do that again."

"Don't do what?"

"Ask my mother to go to a meeting."

He threw back his head and laughed.

But he never asked her again either. Thank goodness for that. There was always a chance she might say yes.

* * * *

It was nearing the end of my first year attending meetings of the Rock-eteers when Warren Wunderly showed up one hot night in late August. It was early enough in the Kennedy administration that the jokes were still good natured. "Jack, Bobby, and Teddy went for a sailboat ride," said one of our Republican members, a schoolteacher named Gary Farnham. "The boat struck a reef and sank to the bottom. Who do you think was saved?"

"The country!" all of us hollered in unison. (The jokes were getting a bit stale though.)

Right then was when the door opened and in strode one of the weirdest looking people I'd seen in my admittedly sheltered life up until that time.

It was Warren Wunderly.

He wore a curly black beard as dense as anything Santa Claus ever grew and his long greasy hair fell well past his shoulders. He had on a loose fit-ting blue denim suit, opened-toed sandals, and a red-white-and-blue Uncle Sam top hat. He reeked of what I instantly recognized as Old Spice cologne. (Pop's favorite too.)

An immediate hush fell over the room.

Budd, who was sitting closest to me, let out a groan. "Oh, good lord," he muttered. "If it isn't Warren Goddamn Wunderly."

"Budd, be nice," Melanie murmured from across the table

Mrs. Eva Jones broke into a welcoming smile and stumbled to her tiny feet. "Why, Warren dear," she said, waddling over to greet him with a hug, "I've been so dreadfully worried what's happened to you."

"And hoping," muttered Budd. "Dreaming and praying."

"Budd, please," Melanie said.

Surveying the room from over top of Mrs. Jones's head, Warren Wun-derly broke into a smile. Pushing Eva gently aside, he marched over to where I was sitting and laid a hand on my shoulder.

"Young man," he said, "I've only one question to ask."

"What's that, sir?" I mean, what else could I say?

"Warren, leave the kid alone," growled Budd, half rising from his chair.

"No, Budd, no," Melanie said, grabbing at his arm.

"Do you," said Warren Wunderly, ignoring everyone else and fixing me with a fierce gaze, "do you believe in the Cosmic Kingdom or do you not?"

* * * *

To be honest long before that night I'd heard a great many stories about

Warren Wunderly. If there was a more talked about figure in science fiction fandom in the early 1960's, I don't know who it could have been. Warren had once been among the biggest of Big Name Fans. (BNF's, they were called.) The bi-weekly fannish newsletter he'd produced while living in Berkeley, California and attending the university there—*Fanacdotes*, it was titled—had twice been nominated for the Hugo Award as best fanzine. (It finished second to *Howl of the Rocketeers* at the 1960 WorldCon.)

Then he disappeared. A farewell final issue of *Fanacdotes* announced that he was leaving on a personal journey, a spiritual quest. "Like Frodo and Sam in *The Lord of the Rings*," he wrote, "I have a mission. Theirs was to destroy the power of evil in the One Ring That Binds Them All. Mine is to found a Cosmic Kingdom where all fans and slans can live in peace and harmony without fear, guilt, or retribution."

In the months that followed Warren was occasionally reported having been seen at various fan centers around the country. He'd already visited Seacrest briefly, staying with Yul, even though Budd swore to have him tossed in jail if made one single wrong move. After Warren left, Yul reported missing his copy of the extremely rare first Arkham House edition of H.P. Lovecraft's *The Outsider and Others*.

Years later a diligent researcher revealed that Walter Wunderly's real name was Daniel Cassius Dunkleberger. He was a native of Muncie, Indiana, who had served nine months in the Air Force during the Korean War before being discharged "under less than honorable conditions." He had also spent a year and a half confined under sealed court order at the California State Hospital for the mentally ill in Napa.

How he'd found science fiction fandom nobody was entirely sure. There was no question, however, that he was an avid reader of SF and fantasy. His detailed monographs on the works of Tolkien and Lovecraft are highly regarded in academic circles even today.

"Do you believe in the Cosmic Kingdom?" he asked me again.

I gave the question my utmost concentrated thought before finally responding the best I could: "The—the *what*?"

"The Cosmic Kingdom, Charlie." *He knew my name. How?* "The country of the mind where all fans are slans who can live free of guilt and shame. Do you at least acknowledge its possibility?"

I nodded. "Sure. I suppose. Anything's possible, right?" It was a pretty weak response, I admit. But the only part of what he'd said that made any sense to me was about fans being slans. Slans were the name of a superior form of human mutant in a novel by A.E. van Vogt. They could read minds and do other things with their superior intelligence. The way you could tell them apart from normal humans were the two golden tendrils growing out of the tops of their heads

"Damn it, Warren," Budd said, up on his feet now. "I'm not warning you again. Keep your hands off that boy or I'm knocking your block off."

Warren threw his hands up in the air and backed off immediately. "Don't misunderstand my intentions, Budd. I was merely recognizing the young man as a fellow slan. As are you, my friend. As are all of us here. We are all slans. For all fans are slans."

"That's right, Budd," piped up a wide-eyed Mrs. Eva Jones back at the table now. "Warren has always been forthright in his belief in fans as a superior breed."

"Horsecrap," said Budd. "*Slan* was just a story and fandom is just another goddamned hobby. Most people who read are smarter than the average knucklehead. SF readers are no different."

I wasn't so sure about that myself. For me at the time—let's face it— fandom was not simply a hobby. It was a way of life.

Melanie reached up and pulled Budd back down into his chair. Glowering, he said, "Damn it, Warren, we're trying to have a meeting here. How about letting us get on with it?"

"Sorry, Budd. I meant no harm. Please proceed with your meeting."

With his hands still raised, Warren retreated into a far corner, hopped up on a counter piled with packets of dry yeast and bottles of prune juice, and sat there, legs hanging over the side, humming gently to himself.

The meeting, such as it was, resumed. Yul told us about the "amazing, astounding, astonishing" hat he'd found in the bargain bin of a West Seacrest Salvation Army store near his house: a green and gold beanie with a propeller mounted on top.

To demonstrate, he slipped it on and gave the propeller a spin.

From his corner Warren Wunderly gave an appreciative chuckle but said nothing. When he noticed me looking his way, he gave me a wink and a smile.

Soon enough the conversation was flowing freely again. It wasn't so much that everyone was ignoring Warren Wunderly. It was more as if he occupied his own private space separate from the rest of us. But it was hard forgetting he was there. Like it or not, Warren was one of those people you couldn't ignore.

By nine-thirty the meeting was winding down. In ones and twos people were leaving. Mrs. Eva Jones went over and began talking to Warren in hushed tones. To my surprise Tom Powers joined them briefly before coming back to where I was sitting and saying it was time to go.

"Warren's totally bonkers of course," Tom told me on the drive home. "Least sane man I know who's running around loose. But he's fascinating too. Make a great character in a novel. Just don't let him get too close though. Budd's absolutely right about that. Don't ever go off anywhere alone with him."

I wasn't planning to of course. Just because I was still a high school kid didn't mean I was stupid. Some things you sense on your own.

"What this Cosmic Kingdom thing of his all about?" I asked.

"Who knows? What makes you ask?"

"I don't know. It just sounds kind of interesting."

"That's the trouble with people like Warren. They always manage to make whatever crazy things they think up sound kind of interesting."

* * * *

The next meeting I was expecting Warren Wunderly to be there again but he never showed up. Yul admitted that he'd let Warren sleep on his couch again for a few days. "But he got up early the other morning, even before I did—and I had to be at work—packed his knapsack, and disappeared. I haven't seen him since."

"Did you do a full inventory to see what else disappeared?"

"Only my first edition of *The Skylark of Space*. But I probably just misfiled it. I'm always rereading Doc Smith, you know."

"I wonder if he's going to be at our WorldCon?" Mrs. Eva Jones piped up to ask.

"He bought a membership," Budd said. "With that deep an investment—three dollars—he wouldn't be apt to miss it."

* * * *

Which is a good lead in to something else I definitely need to mention here. Yet another momentous event in the life of young Charlie Gundy. Over Labor Day weekend that year the World Science Fiction Convention took place in downtown Seacrest. For three days and nights I was there every minute I could. It really ought to have a chapter of its own and it would too, except that it was all so dazzling, amazing, and wonderful that it went past me all in a haze. Specific details are impossible to remember. As hoped, Robert A. Heinlein did agree to be Guest of Honor. He held open house in his hotel suite the whole entire time. Anybody who wanted to talk to him could. Even a youngster like me. And I did—if only briefly, telling him how much his books—especially my first one, *Red Planet*—had meant to me. He thanked me, adding that compliments like that from readers like me was what made the whole often tedious work of writing a book worth it in the end.

There were other major SF writers of the day there too. I remember Frederick Pohl, Robert Silverberg, Poul Anderson, Harlan Ellison, and, yes, A.E. van Vogt, the author of *Slan*, among the attendees. Van Vogt in fact autographed my paperbound edition of his novel *Slan*. Besides the pro writers, just about every known active fan within a five-hundred-mile radius was there along with many from as far away as New York and Boston. Even Milton J Arbogast himself, the original fan, was there all three days along with his longtime friend Forrest Ackerman. And all us Rocketeers of course. We all pitched to help keep things running smoothly. I spent the first two days at the registration desk welcoming people as they arrived.

Total attendance topped three hundred by the time it was over. Not bad for a distant corner of the science fictional universe like Seacrest, we all thought. One person who wasn't there was Warren Wunderly. Though I kept an eye peeled for him. Nobody seemed to have any idea what had happened to him. One rumor said he was in Mexico. Another said he'd been arrested there and was being held in a Tijuana jail. One fan claimed he'd seen someone who looked like him from a distance in San Francisco recently and he was wearing a neat double-breasted business suit and tie.

"And no red-white-and-blue Uncle Sam top hat?" Budd asked

"No, he was wearing a fedora."

"Then it wasn't Warren Wunderly."

* * * *

Right after the convention it was back to high school for me. My junior year at Lake Delridge High. The Yankees bounced back from their defeat the previous year and won the World Series with ease in five games over the outmatched Cincinnati Reds. In April of the following year Soviet cosmonaut Yuri Gagarin became the first person to orbit the globe.

Science fact was catching up with science fiction yet again, the newspapers declared.

We fans all laughed at their ignorance.

Then the summer streaked past with the speed of gazelle as it always seemed to and the next thing I knew school was back in session again.

My last year!

It was October.

Time for the Cuban Missile Crisis.

FOUR: HIGHTOWER

i

Pop sat me down on a stool in a corner of his basement lab and said, "Charlie, you've probably wondered how it was I ever got to know that no-good rotten son of a bitch Clay Hightower."

"Well," I admitted, "sometimes I do wonder, yeah."

It was late at night—early in the morning, actually, a few minutes past midnight. I'd been up in my room cutting (that is, typing on the wax surface of) mimeograph stencils for the first issue of my soon-to-be-coming first ever fanzine, *Briar Patch #1*. An article by veteran fan writer Harry Warner Jr. about his early days as a cub newspaper reporter in Hagerstown, Maryland in the 1930's. (And, no nothing to do with science fiction. But I warned you about that part, right?)

Then Pop came up to my room and asked if I wanted to give him a hand down in the lab with some bridgework he had to have done by morning. With all of the time he was spending building wooden spaceships in the backyard, it wasn't a surprise he was falling behind in his denture work. I said sure, even if I couldn't figure out what it was I was supposed to do to help. Making false teeth not being one of my strong points.

But when we got down there to the lab he just went to work at the polishing wheel with a set of dentures and pointed me to a stool and said, "Have yourself a sit."

When he was done polishing, he put the teeth in a cotton-lined box and then came over to where I was. That was when he brought up the subject of Dr. Clayton Hightower.

"It goes back a ways," he said. "Hightower and I do. Back to when there was a war going on and he was pretending to be Lieutenant Commander Hightower of the United States Navy. The man's worn more titles and different suits and hats in a lifetime than Emperor Hailie Selassie and he's likely not done yet."

"I didn't know that," I said.

"Lots you didn't know. Lots more you still don't. Maybe too much. I shared things with your brother Slim more than with you, Slim being my first. We two were always close. Maybe too close. Might be part of why he took off when he did to the North Pole to live with his Eskimos. He needed to exert his independence."

"They're actually called Aleuts," I said, "not Eskimos. And Slim's in Alaska, not the North Pole." I'd had a letter from Slim two weeks earlier which so far I hadn't let anyone else read. That was how Slim wanted it. The letter was full of personal details. Slim was now married. To an Aleut woman with eight children of her own by different fathers. He said not to tell Mom because she wouldn't understand. He said he'd found the path he'd long been seeking and had never been happier.

"Same difference," Pop grunted. "But that's not what I wanted to talk to you about." He grabbed a can of what had to be some awfully warm beer off the workbench and took a swallow. Brew 76—his favorite brand. You could buy a six pack of 12-ounce cans at the IGA for 99 cents.

He wiped his mouth with the back of his hand, the skin coated with hardened chunks of the pinkish wax he used in making gums for dentures. "It was your mother's brother, Phil Snead, who started it all. This was during the big war. 1944, it must've been. You wouldn't have known anything about it."

"I couldn't have." Since I wasn't born until the year after, 1945. Again, I figured he had to know that.

He continued in a reflective tone: "Your mother and I and Slim had been out here less than a year at the time. Staying with Aunt Elise to begin with. She's the one who operated on my eye and saved my life back when I was a baby."

I told him I knew that story.

He went on: "I'd just started working for Dr. Simon downtown and we'd moved into our first little house here in Lake Delridge when the cable arrived saying that Adolph Gundy was reported killed in battle. We weren't nearly over that yet when one day out of the blue Phil Snead showed up and said the Navy had given him a month's shore leave. He had a woman with him too, a chubby Polynesian named Mimi, who could hardly speak three words of English in a row. She said she was a nurse. If that was true, then I was Mahatma Gandhi. And I wasn't."

"So what was going on?" I said.

"You really need me to draw a picture? Phil had been out there in the South Pacific on a destroyer ever since he enlisted the Monday after Pearl Harbor. And he was sick to death of it. He'd been in the Coral Sea, Midway, Leyte Gulf. Every damn naval battle there'd been. Came out of them all unscathed. They never laid a Jap bullet on him. But he wanted to come home. He wanted to see his sister. Hell, maybe he even wanted to see me. As for Mimi, no idea where she came from. But she was nice enough. Maybe he loved her."

"Are you saying that Uncle Phil—" who I'd never cared for, I have to admit "—are you saying he was a deserter?" All the time as I was growing up, Phil Snead would show up at the house maybe once every two years with a new woman in tow we kids were always told was his wife. Sometimes also a couple or three children to boot. They'd sponge off the folks for a few months before sneaking off in the middle of the night usually taking Pop's latest car with them leaving behind whatever old heap had brought them in the first place. The fact that this happened over and over again might seem strange to some but you never knew my parents.

"AWOL was the officially preferred term," Pop said. "Meaning Absent Without Official Leave. Deserters, they either shot or hanged them. AWOLers they tossed in the brig for a couple months and then discharged them. Phil was AWOL. He'd even lugged a couple of his uniforms along with him so if they tried to hang a desertion rap on him he could claim the uniforms proved he was intending to come back."

"Would it have worked?" I asked.

"Who knows? It never came to that. Not after Lieutenant Commander Clayton Hightower came to the door with a warrant for Phil's arrest. For AWOL. Not desertion. So I let him in."

"Phil wasn't there?" I asked.

"No, he was working. Driving a taxi downtown. I imagine that's how they traced him. Anyhow, he wasn't alone. Hightower, I mean. He'd brought a Marine detachment along with him. When I stepped back out of the way, they all came pouring in. Shouting at the top of their lungs for Able Bodied Seaman Philip Snead. Saying he was under martial arrest. How they were going to search the place from top to bottom—it wasn't that big to begin with—until they found him. I told Hightower to call off his dogs. Phil wasn't there. I didn't tell them where though. None of their business that I could see. That's when I grabbed this Lieutenant Commander Hightower by the lapels and told him to get out of my house because he was violating the Third Amendment to the Constitution of the United States. That stopped him cold in his tracks."

"I don't know that one," I had to admit. "I don't think we studied it in class yet."

Pop of course knew it by heart: "'No soldier shall, in time of peace, be quartered in any house without the consent of the owner, nor in time of war, but in a manner to be prescribed by law.'"

I laughed in spite of myself. I could picture Pop standing up to Clayton Hightower by quoting something that, no matter how you looked at it, had absolutely nothing whatever to do to with the case at hand

"So did it work?" I said.

"Well…" He laughed too. "Because right then Phil Snead walked in the door dressed in his Navy dungarees and Donald Duck cap and said, 'Guess I must have got on the wrong boat by accident and ended up here.' They put him in handcuffs, hauled him away, and gave him six months in the brig. They let him out after two for good behavior and sent him back to Saipan just in time for the Atom Bomb to blow hell out of the Japs and end the war."

"So what about the Polynesian girl?"

"The what?"

"The nurse Phil brought home with him."

"Oh, the usual with Phil and his women. After a while they all went away. This one did too. Probably walking the streets for cab fare in some no-account town in Oregon. Or maybe she's the Polynesian ambassador to Spain. How should I know?"

I thought it was a good story. Bits and pieces of it I'd heard before. This was the first time I'd ever had the whole thing laid out neatly in front of me in one big slice. It was also the first time I'd heard that Clayton Hightower was involved, if only peripherally.

There was only one thing I didn't get. Why was Pop telling me this now? Why had he come all the way up to my bedroom in the middle of the night and dragged me down here to hear him tell it while he worked on a set of false teeth?

So I asked him.

He said, "Because I figured it was time you knew what this was really about."

"You mean about Uncle Phil being a deserter?" I shrugged. "It doesn't matter to me, Pop. That was all a long time ago. The war's over. We won."

"No, not about Phil. Phil doesn't matter a whit. It's Clay Hightower I wanted you to know about."

"What about him? That he was in the Navy?"

"He wasn't. That was a disguise. Let me tell you what happened next. After the Marines took Phil away in their jeep and after I got your mother calmed down, Hightower and me stepped outside for a chat. He told me how in civilian life he was a dentist, a prosthodontist, and he intended to go back to it when the war was over. I told him that was a bit of a coincidence because I'd just started working part time as a dental technician downtown with Dr. Ben Simon. He said there was no such thing as a coincidence and leaned over and took the hat off the top of his head."

I took a while before that sank in. Then I realized I'd never seen Clay Hightower without a hat on his head. Often just a cloth golf cap. Unless it was a formal occasion. Then he'd wear a fedora or maybe a Stetson. It was odd in that hats were then very much on their way out of style. Thanks to President Kennedy.

"So was he bald?" I said, figuring that had to be the punchline.

"Nope." Pop wasn't smiling. "Underneath the hat, when he leaned over, where there should have been hair, instead there were these two fleshy curlicue things like corn stalks growing out of his head."

I stared. "You're saying Clayton Hightower has tendrils growing out of his head?"

"That seems to be about the size of it, yes."

When he said it, he still wasn't smiling.

ii

Christmas Day 1962 fell on a Tuesday. Which meant they had to let us out of school earlier than normal on Friday the 21st. But with the holiday excitement and everything else going on—as always we Gundys traipsed on over to Uncle Horace's nearby place and waited around for Horace and Pop to get enough liquid cheer under their belts to fly off into another of their regular annual head-to-heads over some dumb thing that happened so long ago none of the rest of us cared one holy fig about it one way or the other. Except this year, oddly, nothing like that happened. Pop limited himself to exactly one Brew 76 right after he came in the door and whenever Horace started goading him about something he'd said or done back in 1927 when both of them were boys all he'd do was grin and shrug and mutter, "Don't remember nothing like that, Horace—must be getting senile, I guess."

And neither of them brought up the matter of the wooden spaceships being built in our backyard either. A relief to everyone involved.

So in the end our Christmas Day ended up almost as peaceable as the first one 1,958 years ago (according to the best historical projections) in the little town of Bethlehem.

It wasn't until the day after, Wednesday, that we Comancheros were able to get together in Cisco's bedroom for another one of our "study sessions."

A wet slushy snow was falling as I trudged on over. Katy had offered to give me a lift in her mom's Chevy but with Polly and the Dink both hanging around I decided to avoid the sibling snickering about my supposed "girlfriend" and hoofed it on over instead.

The others were already waiting when I walked in. I shook the snowflakes off my jacket, unwound the scarf Mom had knitted from my neck, said, "Jeez, Cisco, it's freezing cold in here. How do you get through the night?"

"Flannel sheets and a quilt from Granny down home in Durango."

"Try an American-made electric blanket next time," Katy said, from where she sitting curled up in a chair. "Keeps me warm as toast all night long."

"And your pink polka-dot wool jammies help too," Cisco said.

"What jammies? I sleep in the nude. Don't you boys?"

While the three of us stammered through variations of "I— I— I—" Katy sat there, looking smug.

Then she threw back her head and laughed. "Gotcha, fellows!" she cried out.

"Very funny." I flopped down on Cisco's bed, rubbing my hands together to try and get the blood flowing. I looked over at Nedd propped on an elbow on the rug below.

"What's that you're reading?" I asked, indicating the library book open in front of him.

He held up the book and showed me the cover. *Another Country*. "James Baldwin," he said.

I'd heard the name. "Any good?" I asked.

"Great. Tremendous."

"The library actually let you check *Another Country* out?" Katy asked, peering at us over top of her chemistry text. I remembered reading in a recent fanzine review column that the new Baldwin novel was full of explicit interracial and homosexual sex scenes.

"My dad went along to the library and told them it was fine with him for me to have it."

"How did you get him to do that?" I doubted Pop had been to a library in years.

"It was his idea. He'd already read it and wanted me to."

Despite the years we'd lived side by side, I barely knew Nedd's father except to say hello to. I remembered he'd been in the Army and that he now worked at Cantrell Air in the main plant. From the olive green uniform he wore around at home, I gathered he was some kind of maintenance worker. Or maybe a custodian.

"Good for him," Katy said. "My mom does that for me too."

"Have you read *Another Country*?" I asked.

"Not yet. But I intend to. I loved *Giovanni's Room*. I bawled my eyes out at the end. It all seemed such a terrible waste."

"And *The Fire Next Time*?" Nedd said.

"Scared holy crap out of me. And made me mad as hell at the same time."

They both went back to studying then. Cisco had his English text open too. We were studying Tennyson and Robert Burns in the Block with Mr. Myerson. I didn't like either one. The only poets I really cared for were the English Romantics. Mostly, I suppose, because they all died so young. (Except for Wordsworth and he was the only one I didn't much like.)

I gave it another five minutes before I broke the silence. I cleared my throat. Loudly. Like a jet plane revving up.

They all stopped whatever they were doing and looked at me.

"I need to tell you guys something," I said. "It's important."

"Oh my God, you're pregnant," Cisco said.

I glared at him. "No, it's my dad. I think he might be losing his mind."

"Because of those wooden spaceships he's building?" Cisco said. "I wouldn't let that worry you. We all have our quirks. Nedd over there, he thinks his morning milk comes from cats. I know better. It comes from goats."

"It's not just the spaceships," I said. "It's more than that." I then told them the story Pop had told me. About Uncle Phil and the war. It came out all in a rush, me just getting the words out before they stuck in my throat. About Lieutenant Commander Hightower and his hat. And what lay beneath.

I had no reason to think any of them had ever read van Vogt's *Slan*. For that reason I didn't bring it up. About the golden tendrils. As far as I knew Pop had never read it either.

They listened to me politely, without interrupting. Nobody laughed. Or snickered. (Not even Cisco.) Nobody accused me of making the whole thing up.

By the time I finished, I was sitting up straight on the edge of the bed. I folded my hands in my lap and waited for their response.

Katy spoke first: "Did you— do you— do you believe him or not?"

It wasn't the reaction I'd expected.

"Well, do you?" she prodded.

I had think about it. The idea that Pop might have been telling the truth wasn't something I'd even considered. "Do you think I should?"

"I can't answer that, Charlie. I don't know him. You do. He's your dad. Is he somebody who makes up wild stories? Is he somebody who likes to see how people react when he says something crazy? There are people like that."

I shook my head, wishing it were that simple. "No," I said. "Never. That's not something Pop would do."

"Good. So we don't have to worry about that part of it. So either it's what you're afraid of and he's crazy or else he's telling the truth. It's one or the other, right?"

I thought about it. "I guess that sums it up, yes."

"So now let me tell you something you don't know about me."

"Your Mom's got a third eye in the back of her head?" Cisco said.

"No, worse. I've joined the John Galtist Group."

The three of us looked equally shocked and dismayed. "You're kidding," I managed.

"I've been going to their regular meetings two days a week after school. Tuesdays and Thursdays. Ronnie Hightower and I, we've become… well, not friends. Not really. All we do is argue. But I've been over to his house. Once for dinner. I met his dad."

All I could do was stare. I felt… *betrayed* is the word that came to mind. By the John Galtist thing, yes. But worse than that was the thought of her and Ronnie Hightower. She'd been to his house. Where in his house? His room? His *bed*room? And what did they—?

"Charlie, I'm sorry." She got up and came over to where I was sitting. She looked down at me. "But I was interested. Intrigued. The *Fountainhead* really isn't that bad a book. It has its good parts. And Howard Roark is absolutely right. A real artist can't—"

"Oh, fuck Howard Roark," I said. Okay, I didn't say it. I kind of yelled it. Way louder than I ever should have with Cisco's mom and sisters not that far away. Fortunately for me, they must have had the TV on loud because they didn't immediately burst in to find out what was going on and who this Howard Roark character was.

Doing her best to ignore my outburst, Katy spoke to Cisco and Nedd rather than to me. "One thing I noticed when I was over there. I never saw Ronnie's dad, Dr. Hightower, when he wasn't wearing his hat. Even at the dinner table. I thought it kind of odd at the time and said something to Ronnie. He told me to mind my own business."

"That sounds like dear Ronnie all right," Cisco said. He turned to me. "Remember in eighth grade gym when him and his gang tried to pants you and I had to—"

"Cisco, shut up," I said. I turned to Katy. "Are you sure about that? He never took his hat off even once?" I'd never seen him without a hat either. Not that I could recall.

She nodded. "I'm sure of it, yes."

"But you didn't see any golden tendrils either, did you?" Cisco had to ask.

"No," she admitted. "But that doesn't mean they weren't there."

"So what are we going to do about it?" Cisco finally said. "Shouldn't we let somebody know? The government or the army or somebody? If it's really—"

"Whoa, Silver," I said. "Slow down. Let's not get carried away. This has to stay with the four of us for the time being. Till we know more."

"Just us Comancheros," Cisco said.

"I don't want my pop to end up in Steilacoom." The site of the state mental hospital. Where actress Frances Farmer had famously been lobotomized.

"I've got an idea," Katy said. "I'm pretty sure I could wrangle another dinner invitation out of Ronnie. He seems to, um, like me."

"More than Sue Dietz?" I heard myself asking.

"I doubt that. Ronnie just thinks I'm different. Exotic. I scare him a little too."

"That's hard to believe," Cisco said.

We all got a good chuckle out of that one.

"So when I get over there—whether it's dinner or just to study or what-ever—I'll try and arrange it so that I get close to Dr. Hightower. He and I had a talk the last time I was over there. About the election next year. About Senator Goldwater's chances. Oh, and Charlie?" She turned to me again. "I don't know if you already knew but he's a huge science fiction fan."

"Barry Goldwater is?"

"No, Dr. Hightower. An entire wall in his library is full of nothing but science fiction books and magazines."

I hadn't known that.

"Anyhow, if I can get close to him, then maybe I can like accidentally—accidentally on purpose, I mean—I can brush up against him and knock the hat off his head."

"And if they're there?" said Nedd.

"If what's there?"

"The tendrils—what then?"

Katy looked at me. "What do you think, Charlie? What should I do then?"

I had to be honest. "I haven't thought that far ahead yet."

"No," said Katy, "I don't imagine any of us have."

* * * *

We stayed down there the rest of the evening talking, arguing, coming up with this plan or that, even doing a little actual studying in between. Cisco wanted to know how come if Clayton Hightower was a mutant alien from outer space—I bit down hard on my tongue—why Ronnie Hightower wasn't. We'd all seen the top of his head—the only hat Ronnie ever wore was his football helmet—and there were no tendrils there.

I then told them about van Vogt's book *Slan* and how the mutant super humans in the story had tendrils that let them read normal people's minds.

"But this isn't some wild science fiction story, Charlie," Cisco said. "This is real life. This is happening right here in Lake Delridge."

I had to admit that was true.

Or at least hoped it was. Not a story, I mean. Both hoped and didn't hope. Either way it was scary.

* * * *

Come ten o'clock Mrs. Cordova rapped on the bedroom door and told Cisco it was time for his friends to go home.

Katy offered to give Nedd and me a lift. This time we both accepted. It was still snowing out and starting to look more serious.

Having come from Idaho, Katy proved to be more adept at driving through snow than most of us locals. "You just have to do everything in slow motion," she said. "That's how my mom taught me. Never jerk the wheel or slam the brakes. Do that and you'll end up in a ditch every time."

Katy went by my place first and let me off before swinging around the corner to drop off Nedd. I had a feeling she didn't want to be alone with me. I don't suppose you could blame her. Not after my outburst back there. I wondered if I should apologize, tell her I was sorry for the way I'd acted. In the end I decided against it. After all, I *wasn't* sorry. It had actually felt pretty darn good letting it all hang out like that. So why should I apologize?

I knew to be extra careful crossing the front yard in the snow because Pop had been digging trenches and holes out here most of the last year in an effort to locate a plugged-up section of underground pipe that was causing the toilet to back up into the bathtub every now and then. Pop refused to call a plumber unless it was a dire emergency. He said they were all thieves and besides he could fix almost anything on his own anyhow. Most of the time he was right.

As it was, I nearly stepped on top of him, mistaking the dark shape on the ground in front of me for another mound of dirt. But the mound emitted a low moan just as I was about step down.

I froze with my foot hanging in the air. "Pop," I said, crouching down beside where he lay. "Pop, what are you doing out here?"

As he turned on his side to look at me, the smell of his breath hit me like a mustard gas attack. (I'd been reading *All Quiet on the Western Front* borrowed from the school library and revising all my earlier feelings about the glory of war.) In this case the gas attack was only the smell of cheap fortified wine.

I turned my head aside so that I could breathe more easily. "Jesus, Pop, you can't lay out here in the snow like this. You'll freeze to death."

"Charlie?" His voice was a wheeze. "Charlie, my boy. Son. What are you doing out here?"

"Pop, you're drunk."

"I am?" It was a question.

"Yes. You have to get up." I tried lifting him up in my arms but it was like trying to raise the dead. "Pop, what's wrong with you?" I said, giving it up. "Are you trying to kill yourself on purpose?"

"I— I'm just tired is all." His breathing came slowly, his eyes half-closed. "Give me a minute, will you?"

"You'll freeze."

"No, I'm fine."

"No, you're not. Come on." He was wearing a light jacket over his usual work clothes. I tried again to budge him. Somehow I managed to get him sitting up. His head lolled on his shoulders.

"Now let me alone, damn it," he said.

"No. Let's go inside where it's warm. I'm cold too, you know."

For some reason that seemed to work where nothing else had. He stood up. On his own. He wavered for a moment, then took a step toward the house. His knees buckled under him.

I reached out and caught hold of him before he could fall. I held him steady.

After a minute he pushed me away. "It's okay, Charlie. I can make it on my own now."

And he did. Walking straight. With his head held high. He knew where to put his feet down too. He remembered where the holes and trenches he'd dug were.

I followed at his heels with my hands outstretched. To catch him in case he fell.

But he didn't. The warm air inside was like a burst of summer sunshine. Almost at once I stopped shivering.

"I thought I heard a car drive up," Pop said as he stood in front of the heater with me beside him.

"That was me. Katy gave us a lift home from Cisco's."

"Who's Katy?"

"Katy Cross. The girl from school. You met her once."

"The funny looking one with the hair?"

"That's her."

"She's a good one. A keeper, I can tell. I picked your mother out of the crowd, didn't I? Don't tell me I didn't know what I was doing."

"It's not like that with us. We're just friends."

"Your mother and I are friends too. Now get off to bed. It's late, kiddo. School tomorrow."

There wasn't any school. It was still Christmas vacation. Would be until the day after New Year's.

But I did what he said. I went upstairs and went to bed. I didn't even slow down to put the cover back on the big black typewriter on my desk with the half-finished mimeograph stencil still in it.

There would be plenty of time for that tomorrow.

iii

I suppose I should go into more detail on the subject of fanzines. How they came about, what they were, what they had to do with science fiction and/or SF fandom.

In the beginning—we're back to 1926 again—there was Hugo Gernsback and *Amazing Stories.* Like most magazines of its day, *Amazing* included a lengthy section of letters from readers in its back pages. For the most part these letters were concerned with the quality—or lack of same—of the stories contained in previous issues. Readers wrote in to praise a certain novelette by Harl Vincent—"a brilliant thought variant!"—or to condemn a short story by David H. Keller, MD—"too much science, not enough fiction!" Most who wrote in strongly agreed that *Amazing* really ought to avoid stories containing any significant "love interest" because, as one reader put it referring to the romance in Edward E. Smith's *Skylark of Space* between inventor Dick Seaton and his fiancée Dorothy Vaneman, "smut of this type has no place in a serious, scientifically oriented publication like *Amazing Stories.*"

Along with the letters, *Amazing* also printed the return mailing addresses of the writers.

Making use of this information, a young teenage San Francisco *Amazing Stories* reader named Milton J Arbogast made a habit of sending brief letters to the authors of published letters declaring his own enthusiasm for the new literary genre of "scientifiction" and encouraging all those who shared his feelings to celebrate and promote their favorite literature in all ways possible.

Many of those contacted wrote young Arbogast back to express their own enthusiasm in turn.

Come October of 1930, by which time there were three separate magazines exclusively devoted to publishing science fiction (as it was now called), Milton J Arbogast, overwhelmed by the growing size of his correspondence, mailed out forty-nine copies of a twelve-page hectographed publication he called *The Planetary Digest.*

Historians of the field now deem this to have been the first ever fanzine.

Three more issues followed at scattered intervals throughout 1930 and 1931.

By the early 1940's estimates were that as many as fifty fanzine titles were appearing annually. The majority of these were now printed on mimeograph or ditto machines capable of producing several hundred identical copies. As science fiction fandom itself continued to grow, fanzines played a central role in allowing fans from all over the world to remain in contact despite often vast geographical distances.

By the time another twenty-plus years had passed when yours truly, Charlie Gundy, hove on the fanzine scene, there were literally hundreds of fanzines pouring from the mimeographs and ditto machines of fandom every year. As ever, most of these zines were short lived. My own *Briar Patch*, for instance, never made it to a second issue. Others though showed no signs of slowing down let alone stopping publication. The 1961 Hugo winning *Howl of the Rocketeers* passed its 150th monthly number two years after while the Indiana-based *Yandro*, another Hugo-winning monthly, also numbered in the triple digits.

Pretty much any generally circulated any fanzine could be obtained in return for a publishable letter of comment, as a trade for a fanzine of one's own, or in desperate circumstances, money. The price of a single issue rarely exceeded twenty-five cents. Long term subscriptions were normally frowned upon as well as being unwise, since only a tiny few fanzines lasted more than a dozen issues total.

As for the typical contents of a 1962 fanzine, that was hard to say. Apart from such common items as editorials and letter columns, a fanzine might contain articles and essays concerning almost any subject under the sun. Serious, academic-style articles about science fiction, book and magazine reviews, these still appeared with some frequency even in the top zines. But the one thing you almost never saw in a fanzine was amateur fiction. SF or otherwise. The general attitude among zine publishers was that if a story was good enough to be worth reading, then it would have sold for real dollars (though likely not many) to a real magazine like *Galaxy*, *Flabbergasting SF*, or *Amazing Stories*. While a fair number of the leading SF writers of the day had started out as fans, sometimes as actual fanzine publishers— Bradbury, Clarke, Pohl, Knight, Silverberg, and Ellison among them—few had published much if any fiction during their youthful days.

In a lot of ways fanzines were an early version of an underground press before the self-styled version came into being in the late sixties. (See for examples of the latter, the *East Village Other*, the *Los Angeles Free Press*, the *Berkeley Barb*.)

Among the Rocketeers of Seacrest, apart from myself, the ones most involved with fanzine fandom were the three editors of *Howl of the Rocketeers*: Budd Champion, his wife Melanie, and Yul Borensen. The rest were mainly in the club for social reasons, the chance to meet and talk with other people with similar interests.

For myself, once I discovered them, fanzines became the main focus of my involvement in fandom. I subscribed to several of the leading titles in the field including *Howl of the Rocketeers*, responded by writing letters of comment on all those I received, and within a few months found two or three new zines showing up in the family mailbox every week.

For my birthday in the summer of 1962 I asked for and received a bright, shiny, gleaming, brand new Sears & Roebuck Tower brand hand-cranked mimeograph.

In the months after, I put out a pair of limited edition test zines designed to see if I could manage to get my new mimeo to print something that was at least legible.

I was soon diligently at work putting together the material I needed for a fanzine of my own. I solicited and received articles from Harry Warner Jr. in Maryland and Alan Dodd in England. William Rotsler in California and Steve Stiles in New York sent me small cartoons I could trace onto stencil and sprinkle throughout the text. I wrote and rewrote a three-page editorial introducing myself and giving a quick recitation of my fan history. As for its title, why I called it *Briar Patch*, I couldn't really tell you. I just liked the way it sounded. As with the names of rock garage bands in the 1970's, fanzine titles seemed to spring from almost anywhere. Some like the Hugo winners *Yandro* and *Warhoon* took their names from specific SF stories. (Manly Wade Wellman and Edgar Rice Burroughs respectively.) Other titles like *Void*, *Steller*, and *Orion* were more science fictionally generic. *Xero*, *Habakkuk*, *Viper*, *Hyphen*, *Axe*, *Fanac*—these were the titles of other leading zines of the period.

Briar Patch seemed to fit right in.

* * * *

So there I sat in my bedroom one chilly winter afternoon with traces of yesterday's snowfall lingering on the ground outside hunched over my Royal standard manual typewriter copying onto mimeograph stencil an article by veteran fan Harry Warner Jr. when I heard the distant ringing of the telephone downstairs.

As usual my sister Polly rushed to answer, deserting whatever dumb horsey TV show she was watching on the family black-and-white Zenith— *Fury*, *My Friend Flicka*, *Rin Tin Tin* (whoops, that's a dog), one of those. Even at thirteen Polly assumed all phone calls must be for her.

I heard heavy footsteps trudging up the stairs and anticipated what was coming next. The door flew open. Polly stuck her pony-tailed head inside, made a face at the chaos and clutter, and said, "The phone's for you. Ape-face."

Which was me. Apeface. Another of my nine billion names.

"Who is it?"

"Some girl."

"What girl?"

"You think I should ask? Your girl*friend* maybe!" And then, cackling, she raced off to her own room.

* * * *

I picked up the phone, expecting to hear Katy Cross on the other end since it wasn't as if I had a million various girls calling me all hours of the day and night.

But it wasn't Katy.

It was Melanie Champion. She'd never called me on the phone before. "Happy New Year, Charlie," she wished me.

"Oh, hi, Melanie, yes, thanks."

"We thought you'd be home for sure watching football."

Since I loathed the USC Trojans worse than vomit-flavored ice cream, I'd been studiously avoiding this year's Rose Bowl. "Actually, I was cutting stencils," I bragged. "For *Briar Patch*. My fanzine."

"Good for you."

"It should be out by the middle of the month." (I didn't say which month. As it turned it was April, 1963.) "I've got fourteen pages done already."

"Splendid. Just be careful not go past twenty-four pages or you'll have to pay for another stamp."

"I know." Twelve sheets of paper marked the three-cent weight limit for third-class postage. After that it was another penny-and-a-half per piece. All fanzine fans knew stuff like this as a matter of course. It explained why so many of the fanzines of the period ran exactly twenty-four pages.

"Did you get Tom Powers's article yet?"

Tom had indeed promised me something for my first issue. An article concerning a supposed theory of his regarding the mass of a slice of Swiss cheese in a time-space vacuum. At least that's what he told me it was going to be about. It would mark Tom's first ever appearance in a fanzine. Always before whenever anyone tried coaxing an article out of him, he had some phony excuse to explain why it was impossible. Besides, he said, he was waiting for somebody to agree to pay him some real cash money for something he'd written before inflicting it on an innocent public for free.

I'd talked him into writing a piece for me by claiming I was too shy to ask anyone else for a contribution until I'd proven my ability to put out something that was not only legible but readable as well.

"You should get him to let you run an excerpt from that novel he's supposedly writing," Melanie said. "That's something we'd all love to see."

Rumor had it Tom had been working on this novel since his arrival in Seacrest to go to work for Cantrell Air. So far he'd remained tight lipped about the whole thing. Only Yul claimed to have seen any firm evidence to support the existence of this novel. Having once spotted a stack of neatly typewritten pages more than six inches deep underneath Tom's desk. "When I tried getting a closer look," Yul said, "Tom threatened to put me in a headlock if I didn't immediately desist."

The novel's working title was supposed to be *QZ*. Just that—the two capital letters. When I asked Tom to explain the meaning, he shook his head. "That would be telling." He denied the book was science fiction. "More like fiction science," he said.

Whatever that might mean.

"But, look, why I called, Charlie," Melanie said, "is we're having a small party tonight. A spur of the moment gathering. To celebrate 1963 before it has a chance to turn as awful as last year nearly did. We'd like you to come. I'm sure if you were to call Tom he'd be delighted to give you a lift."

A New Year's party. I'd never been to one before. Then I had a spur of the moment thought of my own: "Would it be okay if I brought a mundane friend?"

"I don't see why not. Someone from your school?"

"A girl I know," I said.

"Oh. A science fiction reader?"

"Sure." Well, there was *Childhood's End*. And *Canticle for Leibowitz*.

"Sounds fine to me," Melanie said. "Ghu knows we Rocketeers could use some new blood." *Ghu* was a mythical fannish god. Silly, yes, but nobody in fandom took it seriously either. "Especially female blood."

* * * *

After hanging up with Melanie, I called Katy Cross right away. Before my nerve gave out.

Her mom answered on the second ring. Katy and I hadn't spoken since the gathering of the Comancheros the day after Christmas. Every day thereafter, I kept expecting her to call. So far not a word though.

This was my opportunity to launch a first strike.

Katy's mom had one of the oddest accents I'd ever heard. It sounded New Englandish—almost Kennedy like—but softer, without the nasal tone. Katy later told me her mom had grown up in Canada—Nova Scotia. Maybe that explained it.

"I'm sorry to say she's not at home, Charlie."

"Oh. Then where is she?" I blurted out. Not that it was any of my business. But you know how it is.

"I believe she went somewhere with that other boy from school. The one whose father is a dentist."

Ronnie Hightower, I thought, struggling to suppress the surge of anger that threatened to overwhelm me. *Jealousy* I think is the other word for it. Katy was only doing what she was supposed to be doing—gathering intelligence. At least that's what I tried telling myself.

"If she comes back in the next couple hours, could you ask her to call me, please?"

"Certainly, Charlie. I'll be most glad to."

* * * *

It was after six before Katy called back. By then I was about ready to surrender all hope, smear my face with fruit jelly, and bury it in the red ant hill in the wild grass out back behind the garage.

This time I beat Polly to the phone by a full length and a quarter.

"Sorry I'm late calling back," Katy said. "I was watching the Rose Bowl on TV and lost track of the time. Great game, wasn't it?"

I had no idea what she was talking about and told her so. (In one of most renowned games in Rose Bowl history, the USC Trojans had hung on to defeat the surging underdog Wisconsin Badgers 42-37. If you're interested in the details, consult your *World Almanac*.)

I told Katy about the party at the Champions and asked if she wanted to go.

"These are like your science fiction friends, right?"

"Yes. They're all adults too. Except me. But I think you'd like them."

She said she'd come by and pick me up at seven.

I promised I'd be ready.

"But remember," she added before hanging up, "you missed the best Rose Bowl in history."

* * * *

When Katy drove up in her mom's Chevy at seven exactly, I was out front waiting.

"I hear your dad's still hard at work," she said over the hum of the sanding machine from the backyard.

"Yes, he is," I admitted.

"They really do look beautiful. Almost like the real thing. Not that I've ever seen a real rocket up close except on television or the movies."

"Neither has Pop," I said.

As she drove off, she said: "You'll have to give me directions."

"It's not hard to find."

I'd only been to the Champions' house one or two times before. It was halfway up Queen Jane Hill above the site of the World's Fair of last summer when for a brief time Seacrest had seemed like the center of the universe. (Even Elvis had filmed a movie there while the fair was on.)

"You know," she said as she drove, "I've never been to a real New Year's party before. I hope it's going to be fun."

"I hope so too," I said, fingers crossed.

* * * *

On the way into town I asked Katy what she'd found out so far about Dr. Clayton Hightower.

"Nothing new to report, I'm sorry to say."

"I thought you were going to keep an eye on him, see if you could figure out what was under his hat."

"That was the plan, yes."

"So weren't you over there today watching the Rose Bowl on TV?"

She let out a sigh, shaking her head. "My mom's a big blabbermouth. I was over there, yes. With Ronnie. But I never saw Dr. Hightower the whole time. I guess he doesn't care much for football. Ronnie said he was in his den with some friends from back east."

"Any idea who?"

"Ronnie didn't say. I didn't ask."

"You should have."

"Don't be a prick, Charlie."

"I'm not."

"You're sure giving a good impression of one."

For a while after that our ride was quiet. We drove up onto the viaduct's scary top deck, whizzing past the empty downtown office buildings on the east side away from the water. Katy drove the same way she talked. As if a part of her mind were someplace else. She jumped back and forth between lanes, cut in and out traffic, making me even more nervous than I already was.

"You don't have to go sullen on me," she said.

"I'm not."

"Then why the silent treatment?"

"Sorry. I was just thinking."

"What about?"

"Nothing in particular." We dropped back into city traffic again. By necessity she had to slow down.

"So tell me something about the people I'm going to be meeting at this party," she said.

I did. Trying to sum up each of the Rocketeers in the best way possible. I tried to make them sound as normal as I could.

"Then they won't be upset because I'm not much of a science fiction reader."

"You've read some. Arthur C. Clarke, right? *Childhood's End.*"

"And *City and the Stars* too. I started it anyhow but never finished. It was good—beautifully written—but hard to get into. If you know what I mean."

"No real characters," I said.

"A lot of science fiction is like that."

I didn't argue. "It doesn't matter how much SF you've read anyhow. Most of the men there will just be happy having a girl around for a change. There's only a couple in the club and they're older and both married."

"I noticed that when you were filling me in. Why is that do you think?"

I went with the most common explanation. "Girls don't like science."

"I do."

"I know. But you're different—you're unusual."

"Well, thanks for noticing. I think.'

We were almost there by then. Climbing the steep hill that wound past the front door of the Champions' snug little house.

"For noticing what?"

"That I'm a girl."

Katy parked in between two cars—one was Tom's yellow VW Bug—beside a wedge of blackberry bushes.

"Sounds like a party's going on all right," Katy remarked, as we went up the front walk.

From inside the house the rumble of laughter and the hum of conversation could be heard.

I gave two quick knocks, turned the knob, and stepped inside. It seemed as if everybody who was there was already jammed inside the tiny kitchen. Drawing Katy behind, I went in to join them.

* * * *

There were way more people here than I'd anticipated. Certainly more than could be accounted for by the Rocketeers alone. I assumed the many strange faces belonged to mundane friends of the Champions. Or neighbors perhaps. The strangers all stood off by themselves in a small cluster, chatting amiably. The Rocketeers held court around the fridge. Here was where the laughter was coming from.

With Katy in tow, I headed that way.

Tom and Yul were standing together as I came up.

"Keeping an eye on the beer?" I said, nodding at the unlabeled bottles of Budd's home brew they were each holding.

"Intergalactic Security Force, at your service, sir," said Yul, giving me a quick salute. "Go ahead and help yourself to the nuclear fizz."

I took out two bottles of beer and handed one to Katy. Yul passed me the church key opener.

I introduced Katy Cross to the two of them, explaining she was a friend of mine from school who'd read a little SF.

"You don't happen to have a brother named True?" Yul asked, deadpan.

She looked confused. "I don't, no. I'm an only child."

"Then your brother isn't a twin either," Tom said.

"You mean Double Cross?" said Yul.

By then we'd both got the puns involved. Katy gave an appreciative chuckle but frowned at her beer. "I'm afraid this is a little strong for me," she said.

"It's designed to grow hair on an alien's chest," Yul agreed, taking the bottle from her and passing it to Tom who took a long swallow. "A special fannish recipe."

"Is there anything else?"

"Punch bowl in the living room."

I looked at the group of mundanes on the other side of the room. They were all drinking something that looked pinkish out of small paper cups. I told Katy I'd be right back and headed for the living room.

When I returned, I found Tom, Yul, and Katy still standing in the same place, laughing uproariously.

"What's so funny?" I asked, handing Katy her punch.

"These two," she said. She took a tentative sip and grimaced but then took another. Her lips—she wasn't wearing lipstick—were coated pink. "They're both wacky. Where'd you dig them up from? Steilacoom?"

"You have us confused with Warren Wunderly," Yul said.

"Who?"

"An old fannish friend we keep locked upstairs in a closet," Tom said. "But never mind him. Tell us something about yourself. When did you discover you were not only beautiful but also a genius?"

"I am?"

"Definitely. As you can see from the crowd around here, we're all great authorities on the subject of female beauty."

Since Mrs. Eva Jones was the only woman within a ten-foot radius—Melanie had gone off to chat with the mundanes—Katy didn't look sure how to react to that remark. Instead, she asked the two of them what they did for a living.

Yul said he was a longtime galley slave at the Cantrell Aircraft manufacturing plant. "Tom works there too. But higher up. In the crow's nest."

"Technically, I'm an engineer," he said. "But what I really want to do is write."

"You're a science fiction writer?" she said.

"Close. Technically, I'm what's termed an unpublished writer. The pay's only marginally better than what SF writers get."

"Tom's writing a novel," I put in. "But he says it's not science fiction."

"Then what is it?" she said.

"It's what I said. Unpublished. But I'll tell you what, mademoiselle." He draped a lanky arm around her shoulders. "Tell me more about yourself and I'll write you in as a character. You can even pick your name as long as it's not Emma Bovary, Anna Karenina, or anything from Jane Austen."

"How about Scarlet O'Hara?"

"Perfect," said Tom.

At this point Budd Champion appeared at my elbow. He frowned at the bottle of beer in my hand. "Watch that stuff if you're driving. It can be wicked. One's the limit around here."

I told him it was safe with me. I wasn't the driver. I nodded at Katy. "She is and she says your beer's too strong. She went for the punch bowl."

"Smart lady. That punch is a neighbor's wicked concoction by the way. If there's anything in it stronger than Welch's fruit juice nobody's found it yet."

I introduced the two of them.

From that point on we just drifted. Like errant bits of wooden debris floating down the river of life. (Maybe I had had too much to drink after all.) Inside of ten minutes I lost track of Katy. I didn't let it worry me. I knew by now she was going to be fine. I ended up on the fringe of a clutch of people, only half of them Rocketeers, discussing the open housing initiative currently before Seacrest City Council. Half were in favor—Rocketeers mostly, led by Melanie—half were not. As an obvious non-voter I kept my mouth shut and listened. Everything else aside, I wasn't yet up to debating serious subjects like politics. Not in public—not with adults.

Looking around the room—most of us were out of the kitchen now as the beer began to run low—I spotted Katy by the dining room table in conversation with Tom Powers. Both their mouths were going a mile a minute. I could have been jealous, I suppose, but Tom was so much older—twenty-two to her eighteen—that I refused to let it worry me.

Melanie Champion crept up on me from behind, slipped an arm through mine, and steered me away from the political back-and-forth. "Tell me more about your friend," she said. "She told Budd she adores science fiction. You don't know how fortunate that makes you. Budd and I only met by pure happenstance when a roommate of mine dragged me to a Rocketeers meeting because she had a crush on one of the other members. Poor girl had never read a word of SF in her life. Needless to say, it didn't work out for her but it did for me."

"I wouldn't exactly call her my girlfriend."

Melanie gave me a searching look. "She's a girl, Charlie. She's a friend."

"Well, sure."

"And so…?"

"We just go to school together."

"And she's an avid SF reader."

"Well, sort of. She's read some Arthur C. Clarke and a couple others. She reads other things too. She's read *The Fountainhead*."

"That's not science fiction. That's lunacy."

I couldn't help laughing.

"But I can certainly understand its appeal to any intelligent teenager. I read it too when I was your age—her age."

"I didn't know that."

"Neither does Budd. Keep it to yourself. So what have you told her about the Rocketeers?"

"Not much. Just that—"

That was when the doorbell rang. I looked at my watch. It was already going on eleven.

"Who in the bloody blazes could that be at this hour?" Budd said, hurrying past us. "Bells ringing in the gloom of night."

Melanie flashed him an anxious look as he went to answer the door.

"I only hope it's not the boys in blue," muttered a voice in my ear. I turned and saw Tom and Katy standing behind me. Katy was making the effort to conceal the beer bottle she was holding in the folds of her long skirt. I hoped it was Tom's beer. She was still the one driving us home.

"We weren't making nearly enough racket for that," Melanie said. "Not for New Year's Night. Besides, our neighbors are all here. That's why we invited them."

Budd threw open the door. It wasn't the police. It was worse. Budd's head snapped back on his shoulders in surprise. "Jesus Harlan Christ!" he exclaimed. "What are you doing here?"

It was Warren Wunderly. As bizarre looking as ever. Along with his denim suit, star-spangled top hat, and sandals, he was now wearing a white satin shirt and a bolo tie. "A fan in need is a fan indeed," he said, and stepped inside. "Mrs. Jones mentioned to me you were having a small gathering tonight."

The room turned quiet as Warren Wunderly made his way through the crowd headed for the kitchen. Since he was a notorious teetotaler, it came as no surprise as he sped past the punch bowl.

"We're fresh out of goddamn deviled eggs," Budd called after him.

"I think he's looking for the bathroom," Melanie said.

As the conversation gradually resumed, I glanced at Katy standing beside Tom. As she handed him back his beer, I saw that the eyes in her head were as big and around as a pair of flying saucers.

Puzzled, I went over and asked her what was wrong.

"That man who just came in," she said. "Who is he?"

"He's a fan of sorts," I said. "His name is Warren Wunderly. Why? Do you know him?"

She nodded slowly. "I think I've seen him before, yes."

"Where? In Idaho?"

"No. Here. I saw him at the Hightowers' house. I think he was one of the men with Dr. Hightower in his den."

iv

The morning after the New Year's party, once I finally succeeded in dragging my aching carcass up and out of the cozy cocoon of bed, I decided since I'd made it this far I might as well go the rest of the way and wander downstairs to see what the first of the remaining 364 days of 1963 might have in store.

After stuffing a couple of slices of burnt cinnamon toast down my gullet and lubricating the internal passageways with a tall glass of fresh squeezed frozen concentrate fake orange juice, I put on my jacket and stepped outside. I immediately spotted Pop thirty feet in the air standing on a narrow plank platform as he painted the upper portion of one of his two wooden spaceships a bright shiny silvery color. It looked great. Like an Ed Valigursky cover painting I remembered seeing on a recent *Amazing Stories*.

In the weeks he'd been working on the ships so far, Pop had made considerable progress. Maybe too much. I was beginning to worry he was neglecting his real work—the kind that bought money into the house. I couldn't remember the last time he'd gone into town to pick up work from Dr. Simon. Still, you had to hand it to him. The ships did indeed look impressive. Almost like the real thing. Like a pair of Atlas rockets waiting to be launched. Seen from a far enough distance, you might even convince yourself they could fly. Until you looked closer and saw they were mostly made out of sheets plywood nailed together.

While painting, Pop wore a long yellow slicker raincoat over top of his work clothes plus the thigh high wading boots he used when fishing. Around his head he'd wrapped a bright red polka-dot bandana, which accentuated the piratical look his eye patch gave him.

Spotting me looking up at him from below, he gave a wave and called down, "Hold on there, Charlie. Don't run away. There's something I need to ask you about while you're here."

He let himself down the side of the ship, using the rope pulleys he'd installed with the plank platform.

"So what do you think so far?" he asked, turning and surveying his work, tilting his head back as far as it'd go. "They look pretty darn good, don't they?"

"Sure, Pop. Almost like the real thing."

He gave me that fierce one-eyed glare that as a boy had always made me tremble in my boots. I was used to it now though

"They *are* the real thing, Charlie."

"If you say so, Pop."

"I finally got your mother to come out here and take a look last night. While you were at your party. I couldn't talk her into riding up top to get a closer look—she's scared of heights as you know—but she did agree they looked gosh darn pretty. What needs to be done next is to get cracking on the interiors. The crew and passenger quarters. We want people to be comfortable, don't we?"

I nodded. "Sure, Pop, sure. That only makes sense."

Whenever he got wound up about his ships, I felt the air going out of my lungs. I kept telling myself he couldn't be crazy. He was my father. I'd known him all my life. Except for the spaceships, he was the same difficult hard-to-like but eminently sane man he'd always been.

"You find out anything new about Hightower yet?" he asked me.

"Well, something maybe. I'm not sure yet."

"Spill it and let me be the judge."

So I told him about Katy Cross having seen Warren Wunderly over at the Hightower home. I explained that Warren was a well-known science fiction fan and very eccentric. "He always wears an Uncle Sam top hat. He's never seen without it."

To my surprise he shrugged it off. "This Katy Cross girl," he said with a distant look. "She's your girlfriend, is she?"

To put it mildly, I was growing weary of having to explain all the time. "No, she's not. She's a girl. She's a friend. But she's not my girlfriend. We're not going steady or anything like that. I've never even kissed her."

"This is the scrawny one with the weird make-up, the clothes that don't match, and drives the car that looks like a poor man's Corvette?"

I had to bite my lip to keep from laughing. "That's Katy all right."

"So what's she doing running around with the Hightower kid?"

I tried explaining that this was all part of the plan some of my friends and I had come up with. To find out more about Hightower.

But again he seemed to lose interest. There was a faraway look in his eye.

He broke in on me: "Did I ever tell you how I first met Clay Hightower?"

"Uh, actually, Pop, you did."

"I did?"

"Sure. With Uncle Phil and the Marines who came to your house to arrest him."

"I told you all that?"

"You did. Just the other night. You said when he took his hat off you saw—"

"Never mind that. I say a lot of things sometimes. Too goddamn many,

I think."

"But, Pop." I stood there staring. "Pop, is something wrong?"

"Wrong? Wrong with what? With me? Hell, no. I never felt better in my life than I do today."

He turned his head and gazed at the ships again. The expression on his face was like that of a proud father contemplating his first-born child. (Not me. I was number two. Slim was there first. By eight years actually.)

I felt a lump in my throat as it sunk in what Pop had been going through. The amount of sheer hard physical work he'd put in building these ships, while trying to keep his family afloat at the same time.

For maybe the first time in my life, I was seeing my father as a person. As a living breathing human being. Another struggling soul, so to speak.

The thought didn't last long though.

"You don't think they'll fly, do you?" He indicated the wooden ships with a wave of the hand.

I couldn't lie to him. Even if I'd wanted to. He knew better. "It doesn't matter if they do or not. They still look beautiful." Like folk art, I could have added. But I didn't.

"I'm not done yet either, you know."

"I know."

"So tell me more about this then." He stuck a hand inside his raincoat and pulled out a creased and wrinkled digest-sized magazine. I recognized it as one of mine. The latest issue of *Serendipity Fact & Science Fiction.* The cover painting by Kelly Freas illustrated a scene from a Poul Anderson novelette I still hadn't got around to reading. One problem with being so involved with science fiction fandom was having so much less time for reading SF. "I found this up in your room the other day."

I suppose I should have been annoyed about him poking around in my private stuff but if the worst he'd come up with was one little science fiction magazine I didn't have much room to whine. Not that my room was packed with illegal contraband but there were a few things tucked under my mattress I wouldn't have wanted my mother to see. (A couple of issues of *Playboy* and *Escapade*, a few soiled black-and-white postcards of Mexican origin, and a recent paperback book entitled *Lust's Bright Lights* by a writer supposedly named Carlos Dickens.)

"Pop, they're just stories is all," I said. "That's why it's called science fiction. It's all made up."

"Not this one." He opened the magazine to the slick paper rotogravure section in the middle where the popular science articles appeared. The piece he wanted me to look at included several pictures showing a chinless little man with a pipe in his mouth standing beside a cluttered workbench with a proud smile on his face.

Pop jabbed a finger at the page. "This Botts Battery thing, it says right here, it's an invention that's going to change the world. This is no made up story either. There's real pictures. You can see them right here."

That much was true. "But, Pop, I don't think—"

"You've read it, have you? You've read the article?"

I had to admit I hadn't. (Nor did I intend to—but that was beside the point.) "No, not yet, no, but—"

"Then come talk to me when you do." He shoved the magazine at me. I had no choice but to take it.

"This fellow Botts," Pop said, "he's invented a battery that can produce infinite quantities of energy. With one of those—no, make it two of them— getting these ships of mine into outer space is going to be easier than shooting off a Roman Candle come the Fourth of July."

With that he spun on a heel and headed back to work, leaving me standing there in the middle of the yard with a worried look on my face.

* * * *

I went up to my room, shut the door, and sat down in front of the big black Royal typewriter Mom had got for me at a Catholic church rummage sale six years earlier when I was first writing short little science fiction stories of my own. (Happily—thank you, God—none still exist.)

I tried getting back to work writing my soon-to-be first fanzine's editorial.

Three words in, I got stuck, not knowing what came next.

What the heck, I thought.

I got back up, flopped down on the bed, and read the whole damn thing. "The Miracle Botts Battery" by Kingsley C.K. Babbitt IV.

The article told about Hari Botts and the amazing astounding fantastic gadget he'd invented in his New Jersey basement laboratory. The Botts Battery that was going to revolutionize science and everything else as well. Because it could produce unlimited quantities of energy at the flip of a lever.

The article written by the magazine's longtime editor stated that the Botts Battery would revolutionize science as it was known today.

Did I buy it?

Did it make any sense to me?

To be honest, I didn't know enough to really say for sure.

I went downstairs and called Tom Powers on the phone.

When he answered he sounded as though he'd just woken up.

I asked him about the Botts article. Had he read it yet?

He said he had. Twice.

"So as somebody with a degree in physics, what did you think of it?"

Tom was still laughing hysterically when I ran out of patience and hung up the phone on him.

FIVE: TIME IS A JET PLANE

i

Here's some pertinent stuff I didn't find out about till later but I'm slipping it in here where it seems to fit best because what follows won't make sense unless you know the rest of it from the start.

May 15, 1945, one week after the German surrender to the Allied forces in Europe, an unmarked C-47 transport aircraft took off from a secret airbase in Britain bound for the captured enemy capital of Berlin, where crack units of the Soviet Red Army were diligently scouring the ruins of the shattered city in search of any stray German women who might somehow have evaded being raped and ravaged by other roving bands of troops.

The lone passenger aboard the plane was a steely-eyed man with a trim Clark Gable moustache wearing the uniform and insignia of a full colonel in the U.S. Army Air Corps.

In truth the man was not a member of any branch of the armed services. He was in fact a civilian official in a highly secret clandestine intelligence agency tasked with overseeing the operations of all the other many intelligence agencies, military and civilian alike.

His name (in case you failed to recognize him from the clues) was Clayton Hightower. Before the war, he had been a successful prosthodontist and frequent contributor of fiction to the magazine *Flabbergasting Science Fiction* under a variety of pennames.

Upon his arrival in Berlin "Colonel" Hightower was met at the airfield by his regular limousine driver, a former ranking heavyweight wrestler, who immediately whisked him to a heavily guarded underground compound where a recently captured prisoner suspected of being a leading figure in German wartime weapons research was being held pending interrogation.

It was Hightower's mission in Berlin to conduct this interrogation.

After first ordering everyone except his driver and the prisoner out of the room, Hightower removed a sheet of note paper from his uniform shirt pocket and read from it a series of eight questions.

The prisoner responded to each question with sincerity and forthrightness. For the record he added that as far as he was concerned the war was over, his work here was done, and he wished nothing other than to be allowed to return to his home and family in war-torn Budapest.

At the conclusion of the interview Hightower shook the prisoner's hand and thanked him for his candid responses. He then nodded to his driver, who stepped forward, struck the prisoner once on the jaw, shackled his wrists and ankles, and carried his unconscious form out to the limousine.

Back at the airfield again, the refueled C-47 stood ready for immediate departure. On landing in Britain, the now-conscious prisoner freed from his shackles was overjoyed to discover his wife and three children waiting for him on the tarmac. Two hours later, the entire family and their escort boarded a troop ship bound across the Atlantic for America.

On the trip over Hightower explained to the prisoner that he and his family would henceforth be living in the borough of Red Bank, New Jersey, some twenty-five nautical miles from the island of Manhattan. Their names from now on would be Hari and Wanda Botts, he a semi-retired research chemist in the frozen food industry, she a former ballroom dance teacher. The ranch-style house where they would be living came with a fully equipped basement laboratory. Here Hari Botts would be expected to continue the research he had been engaged in prior to his capture. Once each month, a certified check in the amount of one thousand dollars would be deposited in a safe deposit box in a nearby bank. When picking up his monthly check, Botts would be expected to replace it with a brief written account of the research work he had accomplished over the previous period.

For nearly the next two decades, Hari Botts carried out these instructions to the letter. In all this time he was never once contacted by government agents of any kind. To any outside observer his life was a simple and ordinary one. His children graduated from public schools, attended college, started lives of their own. His wife Wanda resumed teaching ballroom dancing and eventually opened a studio of her own. In August 1959 she was diagnosed with a rare form of cervical cancer. A year later she died. Hari Botts, now living alone, continued to pursue his research work in his basement laboratory. Once each month he collected his certified check—grown now to five thousand dollars—from the safety deposit box at the same neighborhood bank where he kept his own account. In return, he left a one-page handwritten description of the work he had accomplished over the previous month. Invariably, this could be summed up in only two words: results negative.

In September 1962, however, for the first time his monthly written account concluded with phrase, "Success appears to be close at hand."

The following month in October he wrote: "Experimental data indicates a complete and total success."

The day after his visit to the bank, there came a rare knock on his door.

Opening it, he found himself standing face to face with a man he had last seen in June of 1945. A steely-eyed man with a trim Clark Gable moustache. Today he was wearing civilian clothes: a green polo shirt, khaki trousers, and navy blue boat shoes. Perched on his head was a cloth golf cap with the emblem the United States Marine Corps stitched above the bill.

He was not alone. "Hari," said Clayton Hightower, "I'd like you to meet a good friend of mine, King Babbitt. King, this is Dr. Botts. Hari, we're here to do an interview if you don't mind."

ii

The two county detectives came by the house the afternoon after the day our neighbor down the street, Mrs. Ethel Radke, had been brutally assaulted and slain by what appeared to be a succession of vicious hammer blows to the back of her skull in the bedroom of her home. No murder weapon was recovered at the scene of the crime.

After talking briefly with Mom, who'd answered the door and invited them in, the detectives told her it looked as though they needed to talk to me. Mom came upstairs to my room where I was sitting at the typewriter cutting the last stencil for British fan Alan Dodd's review of a recent Hammer Studio horror film starring Peter Cushing and Christopher Lee.

"They say they need to ask about poor Mrs. Radke," she said.

"But I don't know anything about it."

"Then you need to tell them that," she said.

Through my bedroom window I could hear the sound of Pop working away on his wooden spaceships even as we spoke.

I came downstairs to where the two detectives were seated side by side on the sofa. Each had a small spiral notebook open in his lap and a pencil in his right hand.

I immediately denied knowing anything at all about the murder of Mrs. Radke beyond what I'd seen on the television or read about in the morning *Times-Post*.

The two detectives looked at each other and smiled thinly.

"It's not that you're a suspect or anything, son," the older of the two— presumably the lead detective—assured me. "We just want to ask you a few routine questions."

I smiled back at them, radiating innocence. A clean-faced seventeen-year-old boy with a neat crew cut and horn-rimmed glasses fresh out of school for the day and still munching the remains of his afternoon baloney-on-Wonder-bread snack while wearing ivy-league khakis with a buckle in the back, a buttoned down long sleeve cotton shirt, white gym socks, and tasseled brown loafers.

The kind of lad who wouldn't hurt a fly. (Alfred Hitchcock's latest film *The Birds* had just opened locally but I'd seen his earlier *Psycho* five times in a row the day it came out, refusing to relinquish my seat during the intermission breaks. As a result I could quote lines of dialogue from the film at drop of a hat.)

"Because from what your mother tells us," the other detective said, "you walked right past the murder site at the approximate time the crime was being committed."

A fact that had struck me too. Though I hadn't said anything to anyone about it.

"Gosh, fellows, I guess that's true," I said, with the disarming ingenuousness of Anthony Perkins. "But that happens every day."

"You're saying a murder happens every day?"

"Oh, no." A rueful grin. "I meant I walk home from the school bus the same way every day past the Radke house."

"Ah, then you didn't see anything in particular? Not that day, yesterday?"

"Or hear anything either?" his older partner added.

"You mean like a terrified scream?" I said.

"Yes. Exactly."

I pretended to think. I scrunched up my face, wiped my forehead, stroked my chin, tugged on an ear. Finally I said, "Nope, not a thing."

"You're sure about that?" The older detective scooted forward, in his eagerness almost knocking over the so far untouched tall glass of lemonade Mom had placed on each sofa arm nearest the two men. "Think hard, son. This could be important. Anything out of the normal?"

"Well…" I said, dragging it out.

"Yes?" Both of them in unison.

"It wasn't raining."

The murder of Mrs. Ethel Radke had taken place at right around three-thirty in the afternoon. I'd walked past the house only a few minutes earlier, hurrying because I wanted to reach home in time to catch the latest episode of *The Edge of Night*, the daytime serial Mom watched religiously every day. I'd picked up the habit from her. *The Edge of Night* differed from the usual soap opera because it was basically a crime show. Murders were nearly as regular a feature on *The Edge of Night* as they were on *Perry Mason*. They just took longer than a single hour to solve. Often much longer.

The younger detective admitted that his wife watched the show too. "She loves it," he said. "I try calling her between three-thirty and four to find out what's for dinner and she won't answer the phone."

I chuckled appreciatively, resisting the urge to say something wise and sagacious about women and their foolish ways. (I mean, come on. No use piling it on, right?)

In the end both men gave me their cards, told me to be sure and let them know if I remembered anything else, no matter how trivial it might seem on the surface.

I promised I'd do that. They left, went on to the house next door, and I went back upstairs and resumed typing.

* * * *

Now the reason I bring all this up, apart from the opportunity of boasting about how I was once questioned by the police as a possible suspect in a major homicide investigation, is to show how many different things were going on all at the same time in our quiet little back corner of the universe. Simultaneously. That's always the case of course as the artist Brueghel showed so well in his painting of "The Fall of Icarus" but sometimes when you're reading a story you lose sight of that unless the author reminds you.

So consider yourself reminded.

The Ethel Radke murder case was the biggest news story of 1963 in our local press. A trio of Econoline vans, one from each television station newsroom, sat parked in the driveway next door to the Radke house for a good month afterward, awaiting significant new developments in the investigation that, alas, never happened. (The case is still officially unsolved.) Pop knew the man who lived next door—a tattooed World War II veteran named Donald Sims, who was still suffering from the effects of combat induced battle fatigue and was charging the TV people a flat fifty bucks a day for the use of his driveway. When they finally gave up and left—taking their antenna-toting vans with them—Donald Sims invited Pop over to share a celebratory bottle of the best Templeton Rye to mark the end of his rare good luck. "Here's to dear sweet Ethel Radke," shouted Donald, as he drained the last of the jug, "and to that no-good bastard George Patton who sent us boys out to kill and die without once giving a single hot holy goddamn which it turned out to be!" (I thought of Donald Sims again years later when I saw the movie *Patton* starring George C. Scott, wondering what he might have thought.)

* * * *

The lead suspect in the Radke case right from the start was the husband, Amos Radke. Better known in the Gundy household as "Stinky," the nickname Pop had bestowed on him when Stinky called the sheriff on Pop for using the .22 squirrel rifle he'd borrowed from Aunt Elise—Pop hated hunting, said the only animal he'd ever willingly killed was a bait worm on a fishing hook—to shoot at the pigeons that were nesting—and shitting profusely—under the eaves of the house.

He ended up having to pay a fifty-dollar fine for discharging a firearm within the unincorporated county limits.

My own testimony aside, all that was ever really known for sure was that the presumed murderer had arrived at the Radke home from the airport by taxi at 3:09 that afternoon. The taxi driver described his passenger as a heavy-set, swarthy man with several days' growth of dark beard wearing an inexpensive business suit and a knit cap pulled down over his forehead. He spoke with an east coast accent, the driver said.

Amos (a.k.a. Stinky) was soon cleared after passing a polygraph test. In addition, at the time of the killing he'd been in New York City on business— he was a local executive in a national life insurance firm—and his alibi was ironclad. (Of course he could have hired the killing done, thus the need for the lie detector exam.)

The dead woman's nude and ravaged body, brains and gore splattered everywhere on the walls, the ceiling, the bed, the floor, was found by her son Felix on his return home from school. Even though we both rode the same bus every day, I knew Felix only by sight. He was two classes behind me, a sophomore, and physically resembled a somewhat younger version of the cartoon character Elmer Fudd. He smelled strongly of mothballs and butterscotch pudding and nobody would sit next to him on the bus even when all the other seats were filled. Instead, they stood.

My own favorite theory on the murder was that it must have been a gangland hit. The fact that Stinky had been in New York City at the time of the murder (Mafia Central!) fit right in.

"You've been watching too many episodes of *The Untouchables*," Cisco said as we sat in the Block before class waiting for the final bell to ring.

"That was in Chicago, not New York."

"Same difference."

Then the bell rang.

"A Negro church has been bombed in Birmingham!" cried Mr. Lemon, racing to the front of the room to kick off our daily discussion.

* * * *

Oh. In case anybody is wondering: no, I didn't do it. Dumb as I may have sounded when I talked to the sheriff's detectives, I really didn't know a thing. It wasn't so much that at age seventeen I didn't have a few crazy sick-o thoughts bubbling around in the back recesses of my hormone-addled adolescent brain, but poor Ethel Radke had hips as wide as the battleship *Missouri*, a nose that would have made Rocky Marciano proud, and besides, according to the coroner's report which I recently examined, the sexual assault on Mrs. Radke's corpse (yep, he killed first, then raped) had ended short of climax. (And thus no DNA preserved for future cold case evaluation.)

No way that was going to happen if the assaulter was a healthy, strapping teenage boy like your humble obedient one.

Oh, and one other thing: when the two county detectives stood up to go, the younger one paused with his hand on the doorknob, looking suddenly confused. "What in God's name is all that racket out there about?" he wanted to know. "That hammering?"

"Oh, that's just my husband Bill and the two spaceships he's building in our backyard," said Mom.

They left in a hurry, never touching their lemonade.

* * * *

That same evening after the detectives questioned me Tom Powers came by in his yellow VW to pick me up for our regularly scheduled Thursday Rocketeers meeting at Yul's place in West Seacrest. We'd moved out of the Arcadia Building the summer before when they raised the rent on us. Nobody was less disappointed than Budd. "Does that mean we can finally start bringing beer to the meetings?" he said.

Soon afterward, for the first time in years, our membership ranks began to grow.

I told Tom all about my being questioned by the detectives in connection to the brutal murder of a neighbor woman.

"You admitted nothing, right?" he said. "You didn't let the bulls break you down?"

"Well... no."

"Smart kid."

"But I don't know anything," I protested.

"Never say that. You do and they won't believe a word of it. They'll have you right where they want you, one step from the hangman's noose."

(For what it's worth as a historical note the state of Washington was the last ever to execute a condemned man by hanging by the neck until dead.)

Tom took the long way around reaching the highway and drove past the Radke house. Slowly. There were a half dozen police vehicles, marked and unmarked, parked on the property. In the driveway of the house next door, three Econoline vans sat idling.

"Interesting coincidence that Warren Wunderly happens to be back in town right now, isn't it?" he said.

"You don't think—" I gasped

He laughed. "Warren doesn't slay," he said. "Warren preys."

To be sure I caught his drift, Tom spelled the word out for my benefit.

* * * *

At the meeting that night all anybody wanted to talk about was the Radke murder. So thanks to the fortuitous circumstance of geographical proximity, I got to be the center of attention for the evening, even after Warren Wunderly wandered in at ten o'clock when everybody else was getting ready to leave and tried to spark a serious constructive discussion of whether science fiction fans were intellectually and spiritually superior to mundane people regardless of educational achievement.

"It depends on how many goddamn beers they've had to drink," Budd murmured, as he weaved toward the front door, his elbow braced by Melanie at this side.

"Charlie Gundy is a leading suspect in the Radke murder case," Tom Powers blurted out when Warren blocked his path to the fridge. "So far he's keeping his trap shut. But further revelations are expected momentarily. If I were you, Warren, I'd counsel him."

"Why me?" Warren wanted to know.

"I thought you might have some experience in these matters."

"None at all," Warren huffed, stepping aside. "My police record is as clean as a whistle."

This was the same Warren Wunderly who was known to brag about having an official California State certificate testifying to his own sanity.

Signed by a state psychiatrist of course.

A short time later, once Tom had put away one last beer, the two of us slipped out the door, leaving Yul to figure out a way to get rid of Warren Wunderly. Tom's suggestion: feed him salted potato chips so that he ran out of bottled rainwater and had to leave in search of more.

"As soon as he's out of the door, bolt it," Tom added.

* * * *

The next day at school Katy Cross came up to me in the morning Block moments before the final bell rang and asked if I wanted to add my name to the sign-up sheet or not.

"What sign-up sheet is that?" I innocently asked. It had been a late night even for a bright-eyed young fan like me who was never allowed more than one beer per meeting. I even had a splitting headache to go with it.

"The one for the hike on Saturday."

"There's a hike?"

"Sure. Fifty miles."

I studied the list of names signed up. There had to be a hundred kids on there already. Fifty-mile hikes were a Kennedy family thing. Something they'd popularized and turned into a fad. For your health supposedly.

"We're trying to raise money for the foreign exchange program too," she said.

"Who's we?"

"The John Galtist Group."

I started in surprise. John Galt and John Kennedy? Strange bedfellows indeed. "I thought you were going to quit those creeps."

She lowered her voice. "I can't when I'm undercover. So, look, do you want to sign or not? I'm supposed to ask everybody. It'll look better if you sign."

"All right." I scribbled my name at the bottom of the list. "I can't promise anything though."

"Nobody's asking you to."

After she stalked off, I tried calling after her: "On second thought I—"

But it was too late. She was gone. Now sitting next to Ronnie Hightower with Sue Dietz at his other side.

"Consider the possibilities," murmured Cisco as he went by me to take his seat. "*Ménage a trois.*"

I'd forgotten he was taking French his year.

Just then Mr. Lemon marched to the front of the room.

Our day was on.

* * * *

"Robert Frost died last night," said a solemn voice from behind. I turned and saw it was Nedd. He had a finger between the pages of the book he was reading, a paperback called *Catch-22*. A World War II novel about the Air Force in Europe. "The funniest book I read in my life," he told me.

From his description the book didn't exactly strike me as the height of humor. Anything but. (I changed my mind later when as a member of that same Air Force I actually read the book. I passed it around the barracks. You could always tell who was reading it by the way they were laughing out loud.)

"Robert Frost was the old guy who read the poem at Kennedy's inaugural?" I said, remembering how when they played it live over the school PA system nobody had been able to understand a word.

"That was him, all right. He was in his eighties by then. But he was good—really good. 'Stopping in the Woods on a Snowy Night.'"

Nedd had been reading a lot of odd things lately. *Another Country*, *Catch-22*, lots of poetry too. Getting ready for college in the fall, he said. He showed me the application he'd had to fill out for Oberlin. The essay he wrote was twenty pages long.

I was still having trouble coming up with a three-page editorial for my *Briar Patch #1*.

Before we could say anything else, Mr. Lemon cleared his throat in a leonine roar. "I know all everybody wants to talk about today is our shocking local murder, but we're not here for that, so please try and put it out of your minds for the time being because what I want to talk about instead are civil rights and racial discrimination, what's happening in Alabama—in Birmingham. Any of you want to kick things off with some thoughts?"

Raymond Sung popped to his feet. Jack-in-the-box style. With a thought. Or two. Or ten.

It wasn't that I wasn't sympathetic with much of what Raymond said. Mom had tutored me from an early age on the rightness of equal treatment for all. Regardless of race, color, creed, or national origin. She knew a lot about it too. Her own family—the Sneads—had originally come from Alabama. Her great-grandfather Josiah Snead, a schoolteacher, had moved there from Massachusetts after the Civil War—he'd fought on the Union side and twice been wounded—to work for the newly created Freedman's Bureau.

"What's a creed?" I asked her, barely five years old when she first told me about her family.

"It's a system of belief," she said. "Like a religion. Mine was Methodist. Your father was a Catholic."

"And now you're both nothing," I said. The other kids in kindergarten had already informed me of that after I admitted we never went to church.

"No," she said, "we're everything."

* * * *

Once Raymond Sung finally wound down and dropped back exhausted into his chair, it was time for the mob to pick up their torches and pitchforks and get to waving them in the air.

With Sue Dietz at the head of the pack.

I only half-listened as she rattled on at great length on the highly charged subject of lawns. It seemed to be a significant point of focus among the young conservative crowd.

I'd heard it all before.

"If they'd only learn to keep their yards up, then I could almost understand the whole open housing situation," Sue orated, lips like ripe red plums above her starched white blouse (heaving breasts furtively concealed from view, alas).

Oh, and did I neglect to mention earlier that Sue's father Heinrich Dietz, a dapper little ex-Viennese baker with a bristle moustache who owned the Dietz Delicatessen on Bomber Boulevard, had arrived in America under cloudy circumstances shortly after the conclusion of World War II?

And, yes, folks, if you're thinking I'm hinting at what you think I'm hinting at, you're not that far from the core of the matter. (Hari Botts and Werner von Braun were not the only questionable characters rescued from the ruins of postwar Europe.)

"I'm sorry, Sue, but what exactly do lawns have to do with racial discrimination?" Mr. Lemon managed to break in.

"Have you ever driven around up there in the CD around Jackson Street and looked at their yards?" she demanded. "The houses are awful enough, falling into ruins, broken windows, yards full of trash and garbage. It's a disgrace. How would you like to have people like that move in next door and there's nothing you could do to stop them?"

"Maybe they'd do more if they actually owned their own homes," said a soft voice near my ear.

Nedd?

Like me, Nedd had never uttered a word during classroom discussion.

Funny though, isn't it? Adolescent shyness, I mean. Here comes a bright young lad with a mind like a bowl of steaming lava and a yammering mouth to boot and as soon as he hits age twelve, all that boldness seems to flutter away on a dank breeze, and he (or she) finds him (or, okay, sometimes her) self frozen in abject dread, afraid even to open his (her) mouth in public.

"Afraid of what?" you may inquire. Of other people, for the most part. Of other kids, especially. Afraid of what they might say, afraid of what they might think, their derisive snickers.

The black cloud of self-consciousness. It's something some of us never outgrow till we're finally past an age when it matters a holy damn what others think.

By then it's too damn late.

You'd think the opposite, wouldn't you? That the years of youth, the time when boys (and, yes, girls too) stand at their most open and daring, when growth not only in a physical sense but the intellectual and spiritual as well comes in huge rippling bursts—why the hell should that be the time when so many of us choose to fall idiotically silent?

It's a great overwhelming shame. A pity. And explains how come the I-wish-I-knew-then-what-I-finally-know-now lament remains as common as liver spots and creaky knees among us surviving remnants.

* * * *

So where were we again?

Oh, right—Sue Dietz: "And the public housing projects—they're even worse. Strawberry Park and Elysian Fields. And we pay them with our taxes to live there too. On welfare."

Well, I'd been to Strawberry Park when my junior high rink pal Bobby Parker's big sister lived there with her flock of four bastard kids and bought us pints of white port wine in return for babysitting while she went partying with her latest sailor boyfriend.

(Who sometimes mowed her lawn for her too.)

"And you're a dumb ignorant moron," came another voice whispering in my ear. Not Nedd this time though.

It was me.

I blanched. (Think here of the snake swallowing the elephant.)

But luckily nobody except me heard a word of it. (*Coward!* I thought.)

"You had your hand up, Ronnie?" said Mr. Lemon, as Sue Dietz plopped back down in her chair, skirt billowing up to expose those legendary knee-caps.

"Yes, sir, I did." Ronnie rose to his feet, not a single crewcut hair out of place. (Maybe he spray-painted it on.) Sue Dietz, watching him rise, re-minded me of the wide-eyed extras in the movie *King of Kings* watching Jesus (Jeffrey Hunter!) ascend the mount to deliver his famous sermon of the same name.

Ronnie hooked a casual thumb in the pocket of his white Levi's. "My father, Dr. Hightower, who many of you know, is a colonel in the Air Force Reserve," (*huh—since when?*) "and recently received a letter from a close associate of Senator Goldwater's in which it was explained that the Constitution of the United States leaves it to the discretion of the individual states to deal with such matters as racial discrimination. In other words, federal meddling such as that contemplated by the Kennedys in their so-called civil rights legislation would be a clear violation of the expressed language of the sacred founding document."

Somehow Ronnie managed to get all of this out without pausing to take a breath.

"So what you're saying here, Ronnie," Mr. Lemon helpfully interpreted, "is that it's up to the people of, say, Mississippi to decide what's best for Mississippi—"

Another whisper: "Like lynching for instance."

"—and the people of New York what's best for New York."

"And Washington State for Washington State," Ronnie agreed, his head swiveling as if searching for the source of something he'd just heard. "That's Senator Goldwater's position and mine as well."

"And also the Ku Klux Klan." *That whisper again.*

Other heads were swiveling now, looking, seeking, searching. (Mine not necessarily among them.)

"How many of you agree with Ronnie?" Mr. Lemon was looking around now too. "And if you have something to say, please speak up. We really need to raise our hands here—oh, yes, Charlie Gundy, you had something you wanted to add?"

A miracle had just happened. Me on my feet. (*I could walk I could walk.*) Me with my hand in the air.

And a hundred pairs of eyes staring straight at me.

"Tell us what you think, Charlie," Mr. Lemon demanded.

"I think— I— I, uh—" For a moment I was stuck. My tongue turned numb, my mouth and throat as dry as the sands of the Kalahari. (Or, to give it a science fictional context, the sands of Mars. A world with no breathable atmosphere where you'd die in a minute, never mind what that poet Ray Bradbury said.)

"You did have something to add, right?" Mr. Lemon prodded.

"What Ronnie said—" this was me here—I was talking—speaking in a voice that sounded exactly like my own "—what Ronnie just said is the most asinine pile of drivel I've—"

Mr. Lemon: "Charlie, please, we need to be civil here."

"Then what about the Fourteenth Amendment?" I countered.

"The *what*?" whispered Cisco from beside me

"The Fourteenth Amendment," I repeated. "The one that guarantees everyone equal rights under the law regardless of race, color, creed, or national origin. No matter where they live."

"Ah, yes," said Mr. Lemon and I could have sworn I saw a smile—however fleeting—flicker across his features. "I believe it does say that. Ronnie, your response?"

He had one of course. They always do. Only in books and bad movies does the hero get to strike the villain dumb. Rising again to his penny loafered feet, thumb confidently cocked in pocket, not even deigning to notice me still on my feet, Ronnie said, "I'm afraid that's a rather naïve interpretation. According to Senator Goldwater—"

That was as far as he got.

Because just then the most astonishing thing since my own sudden rise to my feet happened.

Nedd Young stood up too.

You could have heard a cockroach sneeze.

"Okay if I add something real quick, Mr. Lemon?" he asked, in that quiet calm voice of his without even pretending to notice Ronnie Hightower with his mouth hanging open.

"Certainly, Nedd. We'd be glad to hear from you."

"There's one thing all of you seem to have forgotten. None of us ever asked to come here. Nobody asked me if I wanted to be an American or asked my dad or his dad before him. For three hundred years now that's how it's been, so what I'd liked to ask—after all this time—is why can't you just leave us alone?"

"But that's what we...." Ronnie started off. But again he stopped. Sputtering out. He just stood there.

"No," said Nedd. "No, you don't. You don't leave us alone. You won't. Not with your police dogs and burning crosses, your lynching and your church bombings. You don't understand and I'm not sure you ever will."

He sat down.

So did I.

And of course right then the bell had to ring.

I'd love to report that the entire class burst into frenzied applause with people rushing over to shake Nedd's hand and pat me on the back and tell us how right on we all were while Katy Cross led us all in singing, "We Shall Overcome Some Day."

Nothing like that happened. Everybody grabbed up their books the same as always and scurried off to their next scheduled class.

Okay, so none of it was Martin Luther King. But Nedd had said what he felt. And so had I.

Let me tell you one last thing.

We both felt a hell of a lot better for it. Try it yourself sometime. Speak up. It works like magic when you do.

* * * *

Raymond Sung did come running after me as I left class with an unusually silent Cisco at my side—Nedd a few yards ahead of us both—to say how he much appreciated our "bold courage" (his words) in standing up to those two "pickleheads" (Ronnie and Sue presumably) and how it was surely high time somebody did.

"But you disagree with them all the time, Raymond," Cisco pointed out.

"But nobody ever listens to me because I'm just that weird Chinese kid."

Which was sadly true. Though I didn't say so. (Maybe because too often in the past I'd felt that way about Raymond myself.)

* * * *

When I got home that afternoon Mom was sitting at the dining room table with a hand of solitaire laid out in front of her and one of my favorite SF paperbacks of all time—*What Mad Universe* by Fredric Brown—open beside the cards. "Some girl called for you a few minutes ago, Charlie. She said she'd call back later tonight."

"What girl?" I asked.

"She didn't say."

Since with Mom "some girl" could mean anybody from Jackie Kennedy to Mother Theresa I spent the rest of the afternoon and evening waiting for the phone to ring in hopes that the "some girl" turned out to be Katy Cross calling to congratulate me on my daring boldness in speaking up in class and demolishing those two pickleheads, Ronnie and Sue, once and forevermore.

Alas, come eight-fifteen when the call finally came through again it turned out to be a seventy-seven-year-old fan from Goose Creek, Wyoming (my first ever long distance call!), named Myrtle Cassidy wanting to know if I could possibly publish the next issue of the International Fantasy Fan Group of the World official bulletin *Lightbeam*. Somehow she'd found out about my now having a mimeograph and since the club was down to fewer than a dozen members finding people who could actually publish was becoming increasingly difficult. Mrs. Cassidy was the current club president having taken over from her late husband Ezra upon his tragic death in what sounded an awful lot like the explosion of an illicit whiskey still.

Since I wasn't planning to renew my $1.60 annual membership dues in the IFFGW, I begged off, citing how busy I was putting together my own ish of *Briar Patch #1*.

Unable to entirely conceal her disappointment, she thanked me kindly and hung up.

Figuring I'd suffered enough already, I swallowed what remained of my manly pride and dialed Katy Cross's number.

After eleven rings her mom picked up the phone. In an oddly dazed voice—I much later realized she'd likely been stoned out of her everloving gourd on some red dirt marijuana, a habit she'd picked up hanging around Greenwich Village jazz musicians (including the late great Charlie Parker) in the early fifties.

"Katy's not here, my sweet little man," she drawled back at me.

After she hung up, I stood there with the phone in my hand undoubtedly looking like one of the Three Stooges (Shemp, perhaps, my favorite) when the Channel 5 News broke into the latest episode of *Adventures in Paradise* starring Gardner McKay to announce that an arrest had been made in the murder of suburban Seacrest housewife Mrs. Ethel Radke: an airport taxicab driver named Willington Cruise.

A mug shot flashed on the screen.

"Oh, Jesus H. on a popsicle stick!" Pop exploded. (He'd just come inside from the backyard to use the toilet.) "Now watch the proverbial shit hit the electric fan."

Because Willington "Willie" Cruise turned out to be as black as... well, as a Negro.

The phone in my hand started ringing.

iii

Come the next morning as I drifted slowly awake I caught sight of a strange orange-red glow shining through the curtains of my bedroom window.

Now what? I idly wondered lying there.

Was it World War III? An alien invasion from outer space? Or had the sun gone nova at last as predicted in the Arthur C. Clarke story "The Star?"

Eventually, when the glow failed to go away, curiosity got the best of me. I crawled out of bed, stumbled across the room, pulled back the curtains, and looked out the window.

The orange-red glow turned out to be nothing more dramatic than a house on fire.

It was Nedd's house. The shotgun shack on the other side of the backyard fence.

The flames were reaching toward the sky.

* * * *

By the time I threw on enough clothes to make it outside in the late winter chill, Mom was already there in the yard along with Polly and the Dink.

They were all three watching the fire burn.

"Your father was the one who saw it first," Mom reported. "He saved both their lives and then called the fire department."

"Where is he?" I asked, looking around, not seeing him.

"He went over there to help if he can. Dick Wilson is in charge."

Dick Wilson was the Lake Delridge fire chief. He and Pop had been volunteer firemen together when I was a boy before the department went professional. I still retained vague memories of Pop springing up out of bed in the middle of night when the fire siren went off and rushing off to do his part.

I took a step toward the back fence before Mom grabbed hold of me. "Better go around," she suggested. "You might get in the way otherwise."

* * * *

By the time I circled around and stood in front of the burning house, the second of two fire engines was pulling up. I stepped aside, waiting until the fire fighters had leaped off their truck and gone racing toward the flames before joining the growing crowd of on-lookers.

The fire was bad, all right. The flames had already engulfed the entire rear of the little shotgun shack and were now spreading across the roof. Even from the street, I could feel the blistering heat of fire against the skin of my face.

Nedd and his dad were standing off by themselves apart from the rest. Both were in their robes and pajamas. They looked shocked, stunned. Nedd's dad held a blanket folded in his arms but because of the heat neither needed it.

At first as I went over they didn't seem to recognize me. They were both staring at the fire as if transfixed.

"How did it start, Nedd?" I asked.

He didn't look at me. "We don't know for sure, Charlie. It just did. If it hadn't been for your dad, we'd still be in there."

Firemen continued rushing past us, moving like shadows through the dense gray-black smoke that seemed everywhere.

Eventually, I spotted Pop. He was standing by one of the two fire engines, talking to a man I recognized as Dick Wilson.

Leaving Nedd and his dad, I went over to where Pop was.

"You be careful, Charlie, and not get any closer than we already are," Pop warned me. "With a fire like this you never can tell what it's going to do. A lot of the time they seem to have minds of their own."

"How did it start?" I asked. "Mom said you were first to see it."

"I suppose I must've been. Helps if you get up early in the morning." He pointed over to where the nosecones of his two wooden spaceships could be seen above the rising cloud of smoke. "I was inside doing some touch up work on the crew quarters when I smelled it. I knew right away it was a bad one. How did it start? How else? Arson, it's got to be. A fire like that doesn't get started on its own."

"Now just a second there, Bill," Dick Wilson broke in to say. "Let's not go jumping to conclusions. We still have an investigation to conduct."

"Investigate all you want, Dick, but it'll come out the same. Somebody started that fire and they did it right where those two were sleeping. Ten minutes later and they'd never have gotten out alive."

It was beginning to get too busy for any more talk. A third fire engine had driven up and parked crossways slewed across the middle of the street. More fire fighters went running by. Generators thumped, pumps churned, radios could be heard blaring. Dick Wilson told Pop and me to move further back. Then he edged up closer to the fire himself, shielding his eyes against the glowing blaze.

Pop stayed where he was and let out snort. "Something like this happens, everybody puts their brain on hold. Nobody wants to face facts. I say when those bastards come back we need to be ready for them."

"What bastards, Pop?"

"Which ones do you think? The no-good sons of bitches who set this house on fire and tried to kill your friend and his old man. Come on. Let's see how the two of them are getting along."

Pop and I went over to where Mr. Young and Nedd were still watching. The fire was finally beginning to burn out now with all the water that had been sprayed on it. There was very little left to burn anyhow.

I'd spent many an afternoon over here after we'd first moved in. For a time Nedd was the only other boy in the neighborhood my age and we became fast friends almost automatically, even though at school we were in different first grade rooms. Nedd and his dad were almost like a second family for me. Since Mr. Young, unlike Pop, didn't care if the TV was left on during dinner, I ate over there as often as I could. Most of my favorite shows—*Beany & Cecil, Howdy Doody, Kukla, Fran, and Ollie*—came on right around the dinner hour. This way I didn't have to miss them while we ate.

In later years, after I outgrew the other shows, there was always *The Micky Mouse Club* to watch at five o'clock with "Spin and Marty" and "The Hardy Boys." I hadn't been over to Nedd's much in recent years. My TV bingeing days were behind me anyhow. I hardly watched it anymore. I was more a reader. The stories in books were better—longer too. Nedd agreed. About the only TV I ever watched was *Johnny Staccato* or *Peter Gunn* when they happened to coincide with my finishing whatever book I was currently reading. *Twilight Zone* was usually pretty good too. They sometimes did stories I'd read by writers like Ray Bradbury, Richard Matheson or Damon Knight. The famous episode "To Serve Man" was taken straight from a Knight story.

Watching the shotgun shack burn—so named, Pop told me, because if you fired a shotgun blast through the front door it would go straight on through and come out the other side—I couldn't help thinking of the old days.

"Your old man saved our lives, Charlie," Mr. Young said. "If it wasn't for him, Nedd and me would both be roasted like chickens on a spit."

"Just doing my civic duty calling in a fire when I see it," Pop said. "Doesn't mean anything out of the ordinary."

"Lot of people around here might not have done it."

"There I have to contradict you, Earl. People aren't that miserable."

"You may not know them the same way I do, Bill."

As a matter of fact, the whole time we'd lived here—twelve years—I don't think Pop had exchanged more than a dozen words with Earl Young. Not until today. He was always polite to Nedd and never said anything against the two of us becoming such good friends. But that was as far as it went.

"So what are you two fellows planning to do now?" Pop asked them. "If there's nothing else, we've got a spare room free where my oldest, Slim, used to sleep before he went on a spiritual quest. Hell, you can sleep up in one of my ships there if you want. There's room there too."

"My sister Minnie has a house off East Union in the Central District. Nedd can stay with her for the time being. Until fall. Then he's off to college anyhow."

"And yourself, Earl?"

"Don't worry about me, Bill. I'll get by. I always do."

* * * *

By then a pair of sheriff's cars had pulled up beside the fire engines. Two uniformed deputies stepped out of the one car and a plainclothesman out of the other. They went over to where Dick Wilson was watching his men rolling up their fire hoses and spoke to him for a few minutes. Then he pointed over to us and the three men came over.

To my surprise it was Pop the plainclothesman spoke to. "That your place over there on the other side of the fence, sir?"

"It's where I live, yes. What of it?"

"We were wondering about all that construction going on over there. What's that all about?"

"Nothing to do with this fire."

"Nobody said it did," one of the uniformed men broke in. "We were just asking what it was."

"It's spaceships," Pop said. "Like the ones John Glenn goes riding around in."

"Like models you mean?"

"Something like that, yes."

"Awfully big for models."

"I suppose they are, yes. They're big all right."

We watched the firemen rolling up their hoses for a few more minutes, then Pop nodded his head. "Come on, Charlie, we better get you off to school. It's getting late."

"I guess so, sure."

The two of us walked off. As we went around the corner toward home, Pop looked at me and said, "I'll give you a lift but there's one stop I want to make on the way first."

"Where's that?" I asked.

"You'll see when we get there," he said grimly.

SIX: HARI BOTTS

i

Pop and I piled into the Hillman Minx. I sat there waiting patiently, school books stacked in my lap, while Pop pumped the gas pedal, coaxing the little four-cylinder engine to life. The stench of smoke left over from the fire filled the air.

"How come you won't tell me where we're going?" I said, as the engine finally started and the little car chugged and shook.

"Haven't you figured it out yet?" Pop swung his head and gave me a sharp look with his one good eye.

"Am I supposed to?"

"I didn't raise my kids to be morons."

"What about Slim?" I said. A lot of people thought Slim was dumb. I didn't. He was simple but never dumb.

Pop thought so too. "Slim's no dummy. He just found his own path to follow. He's lazy maybe but not dumb."

"I'm lazy too," I said, cheerily.

He cocked an eye. "There I won't argue with you."

My alleged laziness had long been one of Pop's two major complaints concerning his number two son (i.e., me), the other being my admittedly smart alec mouth. The charge of laziness went back to when I was six and seven and first assigned a set of daily chores to accomplish. Being a sensible sort of lad—no moron me either—I couldn't help thinking of the many more valuable things I could be doing with the time I was spending mowing the lawn, feeding the ducks and chickens, hoeing the caked rabbit turds out the back of the hutches. (The rabbits were supposedly Polly's responsibility. Except for their turds—which for some unknown reason belonged to me.) The pay was lousy too. Six measly bits a week in allowance. But what could a boy do? Go on strike? (I considered the possibility but didn't want to risk a trip upstairs to the bathroom for another licking like the ones my fat mouth had already earned me.)

With the engine rumbling, Pop grabbed hold of the gearshift on the steering wheel and gave it a hard jerk. Gears clashed, metal teeth grinding, as we shot backward out of the driveway into the street beyond.

Pop popped the clutch and off we rolled.

As with life, when he drove, Pop never looked back. Seldom to the side either. His attention remained fixed on the road ahead.

At the corner—ignoring the red sign with the word *STOP* emblazoned across the middle—he swung a looping left, downshifted, upshifted, and headed for the Point. I grabbed hold of the bottom of my seat with one hand, the dashboard with the other, and pressed both feet against the floorboards till I was worried they might burst through to the other side.

"Wheeow!" whooped Pop, as he shifted into high gear. "The Lone Ranger rides again!"

Did that make me Tonto?

"School's back the other way, Pop," I said, letting him know that I knew.

Apparently he did too. "I'll get you there, don't worry."

"If I miss class they'll mark me truant."

"Tell them you were helping your friend whose house was burned to ground by racist bigots."

"You're telling me to lie?"

"There's no lying in that, son."

"For real?"

"Absolutely. Hang onto your hat and you'll find out the rest of it when we get there."

With Pop driving there was no need to encourage me to hang on. I was already doing that—in spades. The closer to the water we got, the nicer the houses looked. Newer bigger homes with wider plusher green lawns. Now and then through the treetops a glimpse revealed the gray-green expanse of the Sound below.

Risking letting go of the door handle I'd been clinging to in the event of a need for rapid escape, I clicked on the radio, hoping to catch the morning jazz show on the downtown Negro station, KWRB. But somebody else must have been riding with Pop lately—presumably Polly, who usually avoided it at all costs—because the dial was set to Channel 99, so instead of Miles or Mulligan we got a blast of the Four Seasons' lilting falsetto square in the face.

"Turn that crap off!" Pop snarled.

Agreeing with him totally for a change, I tried another station. This time I got either Frankie Fabian crooning or his cousin from Philadelphia Bobby Avalon moaning.

"I meant all the goddamn way off!" Pop bellowed.

By then I'd managed to figure out where we were headed. There weren't that many possibilities. The Point was definitely not Gundy country.

"We're going to see Dr. Hightower, aren't we?"

He grunted. "So what?"

"So how come?"

"Just keep your eye peeled for that goddamn mutt of theirs," Pop said, as we turned down the narrow winding lane that led to the massive stone house perched on the cliff edge. "Last time I came here it damn near tore my leg off."

The Hightowers' dog—some kind of giant mutant Airedale—was a well-known threat to life and limb. One time it got loose, somehow made it all the way to our place, and killed three of our ducks. Louie, Huey, and Dewey. Pop sent Clay Hightower a bill for the damages and we ate duck remains for dinner the next month.

"The dog's dead," I told Pop, having overheard Ronnie telling Sue Dietz the other day. (She was afraid of the hound too, I gathered.)

He grinned. "Some good goddamn news for a change. First since Nixon gave his last press conference."

"The dog's name was Peaches," I added.

He snorted. "Figures."

* * * *

We pulled into the long crescent shaped drive in front the Hightower house and stopped.

"Let's move it," Pop said, squeezing out from under the wheel. "Son of a bitch better be home too," he added, banging the door knocker. The door swung slowly open.

To my surprise it was Ronnie on the other side.

"Why aren't you in school?" I blurted out.

He gave me a long penetrating look as if he was examining a banana slug that had just crawled up on the doorstep. "What's it to you, bozo?"

Pop saved me the effort of kneeing Ronnie in the balls. "I'm here to see your old man, junior. Fetch him."

"He's rather busy right now, I'm afraid."

"Then you better tell him to unbusy himself right pronto." Lowering his head like a battering ram, Pop charged forward. Left with no other option except getting creamed, Ronnie twisted deftly aside. "I'm not leaving till we get this thing settled once and for all," Pop roared.

"What thing is that, Mr. Gundy?" Ronnie said, as he chased after Pop. Who seemed to know exactly where he was going. He raced up a long twisting flights of stairs and stopped in front of a solid-looking oak door. Using the heel of his hand, Pop pounded on the wood.

"Goddamn it, Clay Hightower, open the door. You and I have matters to settle."

"But, Mr. Gundy, you can't—" an out of breath Ronnie squeaked, as he finally caught up with us.

The door opened. Dr. Clayton Hightower stood on the other side. As usual he was wearing a hat. A dark blue baseball cap this time. Printed on the front above the bill it read:

USAF Academy
The Fightin' Falcons

"Well, Gundy," Hightower said, stepping aside, "this is an unexpected pleasure. I don't recall having sent you any dental work recently. I'd heard you were busy doing other things."

"Never mind that," Pop said, as he pushed his way in. I followed, Ronnie at my heels. "I've here to tell you your pals have gone too goddamn far this time."

The room we were in—Clayton Hightower's private den—was huge. The kind of room where in the game of Clue Colonel Mustard would have bumped off Mr. Body with the lead pipe or perhaps Miss Scarlet with the more ladylike rope.

One of the fancy new electric IBM typewriters that let you switch between typefaces by inserting different metal balls sat in the middle of the big desk. The Champions owned one like it too—Selectrics, they were called. Sitting beside it were three lead cases. The odd thing about them was if you looked at them too long they seemed to glow.

I made myself look away.

There were two other men in the room. I recognized them both from photographs. One was Kingsley C.K. Babbitt IV, the editor of *Serendipity Fact & Science Fiction*. The other man was Hari Botts.

What they were doing here I couldn't begin to guess.

At first Pop paid neither of them the slightest mind. He remained where he was in the open doorway, arms crossed, glowering at Hightower, waiting for him to speak in response.

Finally, he did: "I'm afraid I don't know what you're talking about, Gundy. You must have me confused with someone else."

"The hell you say." Pop looked mad enough to spit. He didn't—though I wished he had.

"I haven't left this house all day. Ask these two gentlemen. They'll attest to that."

"I don't give a—" Pop stopped as his eyes lit on the two men. His jaw dropped open in recognition.

"I'm dreadfully sorry to hear about the fire," Hightower went on smoothly, "and about your poor Negro neighbors. If there's anything I can do to help, please let me know."

"I have your word on that, Clay?" Pop said. He fixed him with a glare again.

"You do, Bill, yes."

"Good. So how about introducing me to your guests then?"

Dr. Hightower proceeded to introduce Pop to King Babbitt and Hari Botts in turn. Pop stepped forward and shook hands with both of them.

"Then you are the same man who is building those wooden spacecraft in his backyard," Botts said.

Pop nodded. "That's me, yes. My two wooden spaceships. You don't have a problem with that, do you?"

"Oh, no. Not in the least. On the contrary in fact. Though I think, more accurately, they should be described as starships. Surely that's your ultimate goal, is it not? To reach the stars."

Pop thought it over for a minute, then grinned. "I think you nailed it right on the head there, friend. My boy tells me the nearby planets—the Moon and Mars—don't have enough air for people to breathe. We'll have to find us a place where there is."

"Yes, quite sensible," said Botts.

He then went over and whispered something into Clayton Hightower's ear. Hightower nodded.

"Dr. Botts just reminded me, Bill. Before you go, I have something for you."

He then went over to the desk, sat down behind it, and took out what looked like a checkbook. He wrote a check, tore it out of the book, and beckoned Pop over.

"Here's something for you, Bill. Consider it a contribution if you would. Or an investment."

Pop took the check, looked at it, and whistled. He put it away in his wallet.

"Charlie," he said, "I think it's time for us to go. We need to get you to school."

"But, Pop, I—"

"Glad to meet you, Mr. Barrett." He meant King Babbitt. "And you too, Dr. Boots. It's been a privilege."

"No, sir, the privilege is mine," Hari Botts said.

Grabbing me by the arm, Pop led me out of the room.

* * * *

On the drive back up the hill toward home I asked Pop what the heck was going on back there. What was the check Dr. Hightower gave him supposed to be for?

"Nothing important," he said.

"But, Pop, I—"

"You did see what I saw, didn't you?' He jerked on the gearshift, dropping it into low as we climbed the hill.

"You mean those things on the desk? In the cases?"

"The ones that glowed, yes."

"I saw them, yes, but I don't—"

"They're our ticket out of here, son. They're what I've been waiting for the whole damn time. Our ticket to the stars."

Then he tromped on the gas pedal one more time and to my amazement the little Minx responded by surging forward like the tortoise overtaking the hare.

ii

I talked Pop into letting me stop off at the house by telling him there was a book I'd forgotten to bring along. The real reason, I'm ashamed to admit, was because I was wearing the same red shirt I'd had on the day before, but today being Thursday meant it was National Fairy Day (as recognized at Lake Delridge High) and any poor boy caught wearing red on Thursday was immediately branded a fairy in front of all his friends. (No, I'm not making this up. You think the early sixties weren't sometimes dumb as mud, you weren't there.) While there were undoubtedly more than a few actual gay kids among Lake Del's nearly two thousand students, I had no idea who they were and cared even less. In case you missed it, I had definite real problems of my own.

But in spite of all this I took the cowardly way out and changed into a baby blue shirt. On the way out, to keep Pop happy, I grabbed a book at random off the shelf—it was the new Heinlein, *Glory Road*, which I hadn't had a chance to read yet—and hurried downstairs. Mom was in dining room reading another new book of mine, *The Man in the High Castle* by Philip K. Dick, and didn't even glance up as I sped past in my new safely heterosexual shirt. Must be a good book, I thought. She hadn't even dealt herself a hand of her favorite five-card solitaire.

* * * *

I made it to school just in time for the third and final lunch bell to ring. Since I hadn't packed anything from home to eat and the cafeteria was serving Turkey ala disgusting King again, I decided to do without. I dropped by the lunchroom anyway, hoping to spot a familiar face—Katy Cross my top choice, Cisco Cordova a distant first runner up. I didn't see her but he was there sitting with a clutch of other senior dorks. Going past, I flashed him the high sign and he soon joined me at an empty table, bringing his half eaten lunch along. I took one of his two tuna salad sandwiches—his mom used too much mayonnaise as far as I was concerned—and while I ate I filled him in on the fire at Nedd's house.

It turned out he'd already heard most of the details. Funny how things like that get around places like high school faster than you can ever say Jackie Robinson plays third base. I explained that Nedd would likely be staying with his aunt in the CD for the time being.

"I'll have to call him when I get home tonight."

"You have the number?"

"They've got this new thing now called a phone book. I'll try finding the aunt there. You should call him too."

I told him I would. More than a little ashamed at having to be reminded there were other people in the world with problems too. Like not having a home of their own to live in. Unlike my own cozy household— with or without the two half-built wooden spaceships—or, as Pop was now calling them, *star*ships—in the backyard.

After first stopping off at the office for a permission slip to let me into class—they knew about the fire too and accepted my excuse for being late. They asked how Nedd was doing. I told them the same things I'd told Cisco.

I got to algebra class just in time to hear the bell ring and see everybody getting up to leave.

Perfect timing, I thought. I still hadn't done the homework that was due today.

My sixth and final period was a study hall. Putting my head on the desk with my arms for a pillow, I was sound asleep inside of ten minutes. I wasn't the only one. There were more than a few of us who took a nap here more days than we didn't.

* * * *

When I got home Mom was still at the dining room table reading *The Man in the High Castle*. The bus had run late and *The Edge of Night* was already on. To my amazement, Mom had neglected to switch on the TV. I had to do it for her. She barely looked up when I did and went right back to reading.

I watched the show play out while munching my usual afterschool white bread and baloney. It was a good episode too. There'd been another mysterious arsenic murder in Monticello and criminal lawyer Mike Carr was hot on the case.

When it was over I turned the TV off and looked at Mom. Her face was still buried in her book.

"It's really that good, is it?" I said. I'd seen some early reviews in fanzines, all of them favorable. I'd read only one other Philip K. Dick book before, though he'd written a bunch. *Eye in the Sky*. I'd enjoyed its satirical portrait of an alternate world where there really was an Old Testament God running things down here on earth from up in heaven.

Budd Champion, who read everything SF as soon as it came out, said *The Man in the High Castle* was so far the leading contender for this year's Hugo Award for Best SF Novel to be handed out at the World Convention in Washington D.C. in September.

I was still hoping to somehow make it to the convention but practically speaking it didn't seem likely. As little as I liked to think about it, the fact remained I'd be graduating from high school in June and after that...

Well, that was the problem. After that I didn't know.

And strictly between you and me, that was scary. But only when I thought about it. Which was why, for the most part, I didn't. (Picture here an ostrich with knobby knees like mine and a head buried in the sand.)

"It's wonderful," Mom said, looking up from her book. "Not at all far-fetched." Being farfetched was Mom's major complaint with science fiction she disliked. She preferred her stories to take place no later than, say, the day after tomorrow. Her all-time favorite books though—even more so than *Gone with the Wind*, which she'd read as a teenager—were *The Lord of the Rings* trilogy. I'd never heard of them until I got involved in fandom where everybody was raving madly about them. There was even a fanzine published in Los Angeles, *I Palantir*, devoted to nothing else. To my surprise, I found all three books on a dusty shelf of the town library. I was only the third person to check them out in a year. As soon as I finished each volume, I passed it on to Mom. She went through them even faster than I did.

Mom said what she liked about *The Man in the High Castle* was the way it made her think, see things differently, how it expanded her mind. The book was another alternative timestream story set in a world where the Axis powers, Germany and Japan, won World war II.

"It makes you think differently about the war," she said. "Maybe it wasn't as simple as we all thought at the time. It's gives you a different perspective."

"You mean about Hitler and the Nazis?"

"Oh, no. They're as horrible in the book as they were in life. Like if the Ku Klux Klan had ever come to power here. But the Japanese, at least in the book, they try to be kind. Like Polly's little friend Karen Oishi. Her parents are the nicest people you'd ever want to meet."

The Oishi family had lived here in Seacrest since before the war. After Pearl Harbor, the entire family had been rounded up and sent to a relocation camp in Idaho. Both aged grandparents had died soon after arriving at the camp.

For a change I hadn't heard any noise coming from the backyard since I'd got home, so I asked Mom where Pop was. She said he was down in the basement finishing up a rush job for Dr. Simon that was already several days overdue.

I decided to go down and see him.

"Tell him Becky called again—" Dr. Simon's wife, who worked in his office as a nurse "—and the lady is still waiting for her new teeth."

As I went down the basement stairs, I noticed the lights weren't on. Taking care where I stepped, I fumbled around in the dark searching for a light switch. When I finally found something that felt like one, I gave it a click.

The lights flickered on.

And there was Pop. Crouched on the floor. Squatting on the floor. Underneath his work bench. Sitting in a puddle of dirty water. (Like most basements in Seacrest, ours leaked like a sieve all winter long.) There was a bottle of Thunderbird—his favorite cheap fortified wine—cradled in his lap. He looked to be asleep.

I went over and shook him by the shoulder. "Pop, wake up. What are you doing down there?"

No response.

I tried again—louder: "Pop, you have to wake up!"

Still, nothing.

"*Pop, can you hear me?*"

This time he raised a hand to his head. The left hand. He rubbed his forehead, scratched the tip of his nose, then let the hand fall into his lap again.

With his right hand, he raised the green T-Bird bottle to his mouth and took a long thirsty swallow. The whole time his good right eye never opened. The black patch covering the other had come askew.

I watched as his Adam's apple bobbed up and down.

"Pop," I said softly. "Pop, for God's sake, what are you doing?"

The eye opened. He stared at me. But said nothing.

"Why do you have to do this, Pop? Why can't you just... *stop*?"

For a second I thought he was going to say something. I saw his mouth open, his lips move, his tongue quiver. But nothing came out. Not a sound. He just sat there, drunk on his ass, gazing at me, staring...

Not knowing what else to do, I tried edging him out from under the bench. I managed to get an arm around his shoulders and pulled hard. He grabbed my shirt and held on. After several long minutes, I got him far enough out from under the bench that he was able to stand up.

He did. But then he couldn't walk.

When he tried to take a first step, his knee gave out under him as if it were made of water. I caught him around the waist and held him up. He tried another step. With me holding onto him, this one went better.

Somehow together we managed to stumble up the stairs. "Your mother doesn't need to know about this," he murmured as we came through the door into the kitchen.

"Put him in the bedroom," I heard Mom call from the dining room. "Let him sleep. I'll wake him for dinner."

I put Pop to bed in what had once been Slim's room. It was the closest—the only bedroom on the bottom floor. As soon as his head hit the pillow, he began to snore. I reached down carefully, pried the Thunderbird bottle out of his hand, and took it with me back into the kitchen. I emptied it out in the sink and tossed it in the garbage.

Back in the dining room, Mom had dealt herself a hand of solitaire. The TV was back on too. *The Secret Storm*. Another daytime soap.

It looked like she'd finished *The Man in the High Castle*.

"Did you ask him about Dr. Simon's teeth?" she said.

I shook my head. "I tried to but he wouldn't say."

"Then I guess I'd better give Becky a call." She reached for the phone. By now Mom was well used to making excuses for Pop being late with work. The reasons she gave were seldom believable but since Pop's was the only local dental lab—and his work was always top notch—so far the dentists were putting up with the delays.

I sat down across the table from her, picked up *The Man in the High Castle*, and started flipping pages.

"It almost makes you feel sorry we won the war," she said as she dialed. "And the atom bombs. Those were simply terrible."

"Then they shouldn't have started it, should they?" I said. "They shouldn't have bombed Pearl Harbor."

"No," she said with a sigh. "No, I suppose you're right. They shouldn't have done that."

I picked up the book, carried it with me upstairs to my room, and lay down to read.

* * * *

Pop slept all the rest of the day and into the night, finally getting up just after midnight as I was heading back up to my room, too beat to watch any more of the syndicated Steve Allen show from Los Angeles that I generally preferred over Jack Parr's *Tonight Show*. Steve Allen was not only funnier, many of his regular guests like Louis Nye, Bill Dana, Mel Brooks and Carl Reiner with their running 2000-year-old-man gag, were even funnier yet. The music was better too. One night Dizzy Gillespie showed up and played a set with the studio band. You never saw people like Dizzy on the Parr show.

I was already half-asleep when I heard the first muffled sounds of hammering coming from the backyard.

* * * *

Unlike Thursdays, Fridays were officially dress-up days at Lake Del High, so I wore as I usually did one of Pop's old dress shirts from when he'd worked downtown, a pair of black slacks, and a leftover necktie, also one of his. As soon as I got to the Block, Cisco pulled me aside and asked if I'd heard anything yet from Nedd. I hadn't since I'd forgotten completely about calling him. Cisco said he'd tried calling the aunt's number but nobody answered the phone.

"Maybe they went out to eat," I said.

"In that neighborhood?" He chuckled.

"Maybe they went downtown or to Ballard or something."

"That's possible, sure."

Tomorrow, Saturday, was the day of the big fifty-mile hike. Cisco wanted to know if I was planning on going. I lied and told him I'd try to make it. It was easier that way. Everybody else seemed really excited about the whole idiotic thing. I liked the Kennedys well enough but not enough to waste a whole Saturday. Even Miss Hunt with her artificial leg said she'd be there for the start even if she couldn't do much of the walk.

"Not me," Cisco said, surprising me. "Not after what happened to Nedd."

"What's that got to do with it?"

He made a face. "Haven't you figured it out?"

The bell rang before I could find out what he meant by that. For unexplained reasons, there was no Contemporary Problems discussion period with Mr. Lemon today. Instead we went right into English with Miss Hunt, Mr. Myerson, and the English Romantic poets of the early nineteenth century. My favorites. Coleridge, Byron, Shelley, and the great John Keats.

One of the poems Mr. Myerson recited aloud that day stuck with me ever since. It was by Keats:

> *When I have fears that I may cease to be*
> *Before my pen has glean'd my teeming brain,*
> *Before high piled books, in charact'ry*
> *Hold like rich garners the full-ripen'd grain;*

I looked it up later. Keats died at age twenty-five from tuberculous. (Mom's mother had also died from TB. In search of cleaner mountain air she'd moved from Texas to Adobe, Colorado, which is how Mom ended up meeting Pop. Her mother died a few years before I was born.)

Not that I had any real worries about that. About dying from TB, I mean. The way I figured as long as we didn't blow ourselves up over something stupid like missiles in Cuba my chances of living to a ripe old age were pretty good.

I still like the Keats poem though.

* * * *

A few weeks later as spring was about ready to burst forth in bloom the phone rang. Polly, who'd just gotten home from ninth grade, sprinted to grab it. "It's for you again, Dork," she said, looking annoyed. She stuck out her tongue at me as I grabbed the phone out of her hand.

iii

It was Tom Powers.

"How come you're home this time of day?" he demanded, as if only just now noticing the hour.

I explained that we got out of school at two-thirty every day. I was almost always home by three-thirty. "When *The Edge of Night* comes on."

He pretended not to know what I was talking about. "Kind of like working the day shift at Cantrell Air," he mused. "But I'm glad I caught you, pal. I wanted to know if you'd like to go for a drive this Saturday."

"Where to?"

"Visit a friend who wants desperately to see you again."

"What friend is that?"

"Can't say. That would be telling."

"Then… I don't really know. There's a big fifty-mile hike at school that day."

"You're kidding."

"No there is."

"I meant about you going along. Look, what if I said Warren Wunderly's involved?"

"He's still in town?"

"So the rumors say."

"Where? At Yul's?"

"Not this time, no. The specifics must remain confidential for the time being."

"But why would Warren want to see me? We've hardly exchanged twenty words."

"That's also classified."

I thought it over for another moment. "So why are you all of a sudden interested in Warren Wunderly? I thought you and Budd agreed he's a kook."

"He is. But he's also an interesting kook. Make a great character to slip into my book when it gets boring. So you want to go along or not?"

"Sure. Okay. Why not?" It made a good excuse for missing the hike. In case somebody—Katy Cross for instance—wondered why I wasn't there. "Speaking of your book though, how's that coming along? When are you ever going to finish?"

"Got me. I guess when it's done."

I thought about quoting a line from Keats to him. The one about the pen and full ripen'd grain. "So when do I get to read this opus?"

"When you buy a copy of the finished book. At your favorite bookstore. After it's published. You won't like it anyhow. It's not SF."

"I read things that aren't SF."

"It's not *Catcher in the Hay* either. Or that other godawful thing he wrote: *Franny and the Zoo*."

I'd once made the mistake of telling him that J.D. Salinger was my favorite writer. "I liked it."

"Your problem, not mine. I'll pick you up at noon. Be sure and wear your propeller beanie. You'll need it."

* * * *

I was sitting on the front steps, thumbing through the new May issue of *Serendipity F&SF* when Tom pulled up in his yellow VW bug. He hopped out and stood waiting for me, shading his eyes against the sun, peering into the backyard. "Your dad's still working on those things of his, I see."

"Yeah, I guess."

"They're looking more and more like real spaceships by the day."

"Starships, he's calling them now. That's where he says he's going. He's finishing up the insides now. The crew quarters, he says."

"When's he planning to be done?"

That was another thing I'd never asked. Figuring I wouldn't like the answer. (And what then? I wondered. What came next?) "About the same time you finish that book you're writing."

"Touché," he said, as he hopped back in the car. "You forgot your propeller beanie"

"I don't have a propeller beanie."

"Don't be ridiculous. Every young fan has a propeller beanie. It goes with the territory."

* * * *

We headed down into the Lower Valley, a strip of fertile farm land dotted with dairy farms and horse ranches that lay between the Cascade foothills and the Seacrest city limits A pair of rivers—the Green and the Puyallup—often flooded much of the valley in the spring when the snows of winter melted in the mountains

"What's Warren Wunderly doing way out here with the milk cows and the hayseeds?" I asked, as we chugged along a twisting highway nearly empty of other traffic in spite of it being a rare clear and sunny Saturday afternoon, the first I could recall in a long while.

"You'll see when we get there."

"When's that going to be?"

"When it happens."

Tom drove another five or so miles while we chatted about various topics—school, fandom, what it was like working in an aerospace munitions factory—Tom's term for Cantrell Air, though they actually built plenty of commercial aircraft too—before he swung a hard right onto a narrow dirt road full of ruts, potholes, and puddles of ankle-deep mud. We bounced along for another mile until Tom pulled up in front of a broken-down relic of a farmhouse.

"Dis must be de place, boss," he said, cutting the engine.

I looked around. Besides the farmhouse there was a dilapidated red barn sorely in need of major repair and an empty corral, half its wooden slats on the ground. The outlying fields stretched into the distance, grown over with tangles of pussy willow and goldenrod, nothing in the way of crops to be seen. Surrounding the main house the wild grass grew tall and lush, still green from the winter rains but sorely in need of cutting. A few scattered early spring dandelions rose here and there among the weeds.

The house was three stories high, gray shingled and surrounded by a white picket fence missing as many pickets as it contained. Standing by the broken gate, holding onto a picket for support, loomed Warren Wunderly, dressed as always in his ragged denim suit, sandals, and mad hatter's top hat.

He didn't look especially happy seeing us as we emerged from the car.

"I don't think he's expecting us," I said.

"Damn. I must've forgotten to phone ahead."

Through the big front window partly covered behind a dank gray bedsheet I could see furtive shadowy shapes moving inside. A pair of chubby pink-faced children squatted in the tall grass, playing some kind of game with a red rubber ball and a set of metal jacks. One of them, the smallest and presumably youngest, wore nothing but a droopy, yellow-stained diaper while the other, a frizzy-haired blond girl of eight or nine, was as naked as Eve the day she emerged from Adam's rib.

"Cute little tykes, aren't they?" Tom said. "Part of Warren's brood, I believe."

As we approached the house, a stringy-haired woman in an ankle-length smock emerged from inside, scooped up the diapered toddler in the crook of a bony arm, and led the naked little girl inside by the hand. The woman paused briefly on the doorstep, glaring suspiciously at Tom and me and then, kids in tow, disappeared inside.

"Is she Warren's wife?" I asked.

"God, no. That's Nellie. Warren picked her up somewhere down in Mexico, I believe."

"Then they're not really his children either."

"Depends on what you mean by his. In the Cosmic Kingdom all God's children belong to God."

I had no idea what that was supposed to mean.

Warren, hurrying now, intercepted us as we reached the broken gate. He stood blocking our way. "I wasn't expecting you again today, Powers."

"I know. I should've called ahead. I couldn't find your number in the book."

"We don't have a phone here. You know that. It's not permitted. No phones, no radios, no television. We here in the Kingdom have no need for artificial diversions that interfere with the cosmic connections."

"What? No *Gilligan's Island*? Say it ain't so, little buddy." Tom was looking around as he spoke, as if searching for something he hadn't so far seen. "Where's the rest of the gang, Warren? You're not hiding them, are you? We're not the fuzz, man. Your secrets are safe with us."

Whatever Tom was talking about, Warren ignored him. He was looking at me instead. Staring. "I know who you are now," he said. "You're young Charlie Gundy, are you?"

I didn't bother mentioning that we'd met before. A couples of time in fact. "That's me, yes."

"You're a former subscriber of mine, I believe."

That was true enough. Early in my fannish career I'd mailed Warren Wunderly two quarters scotch-taped to a blank sheet of typing paper for a six-issue subscription to *Fanacdotes*.

"You haven't put out a new issue in a while," I said.

"Too busy, I'm afraid. Too much involved." He opened both arms in an expansive gesture encompassing everything around us. "This is my dream come to life. This is what I've been working toward my entire life."

"The Cosmic Kingdom," Tom whispered from behind a hand.

"Don't mock," Warren said.

"Me?" Tom backed up a step as if offended. "Mock you, Warren? Pray tell, never. Mind if we come inside for a piece, get some of the dust off us from the long ride?"

Warren's initial reluctance changed as he continued to look at me. "No, not at all," he said, with a sudden warm smile. "Do come in and meet the others. I must warn you in advance though." He was talking strictly to me now, ignoring Tom. "We're not all fans here in the strictest sense of the term. Fandom was where I began my work, seeing that as a fertile field for tilling. Fans are slans, I continue to believe. A superior intellectual breed. But I soon encountered an unexpected resistance among some. I grew disillusioned and expanded my efforts to encompass a wider range of people. The results you'll see inside."

Stepping closer, he draped an arm around my shoulders and led me off toward the house.

"We have lemonade and various fruit and vegetable juices inside," he said. "And water fresh from a nearby stream. You're more than welcome to quench your thirst." He looked back over his shoulder at Tom following. "Both of you are welcome."

As we stepped up on the porch and went inside, I glanced back at Tom. He gave me a wry grin, shook his head, and shrugged as if to say don't mind me, I'm only along for the ride.

Once out of the light and inside the dark cavern of the house, it was difficult at first to make out much of anything clearly. Gradually, I began to discern certain shapes. At first it was just the furnishings. A broken sofa leaning against one wall, much of the fabric torn away, metal springs poking through the cushions. There were three rickety chairs set beside an old card table, the broken stub of one leg propped up on a brick. Magazines, books, newspapers, and even a few fanzines were strewn everywhere. On the table, on the floor. Dust covered everything. The air was thick with it too.

Then I began to notice the people. The stringy haired woman Nell occupied a corner with a baby nestled in her arms. Her head was bent low, her hair falling across the child as she nursed it. There were others here too scattered around the room. Maybe a dozen in all. Children, kids, most of them boys. The oldest were my age. The youngest, the naked girl I'd seen outside. They were all squatting or lying on the floor. They were wide-eyed and blank-faced. Looking nowhere, seeing nothing, their faces as expressionless as painted masks.

I shuddered looking at them.

Tom suddenly stepped past me, spread his arms wide, and called out in a loud voice, "Welcome to the Cosmic Kingdom!"

None of the children in the room—or the woman Nell with the baby for that matter—took the slightest notice.

* * * *

Warren led us into the kitchen in the back and had us sit down at a table. Unlike the other room there was enough light coming through the windows so that you could actually see things in front of your face. Everything was filthy though. Unwashed plates and dishes were heaped in the sink and adjoining countertops. The stench of rotting food was overwhelming. There were grocery sacks stuffed with garbage and trash blocking the doorway leading outside.

Warren Wunderly seemed totally oblivious to all this. He kept chattering on about his Cosmic Kingdom. My disciples, he called the children. There appeared to be many more of them. Upstairs, out in the barn, in the fields too. From what I gathered he'd picked them up one or two at a time in his travels around the country. They were the lost, the homeless, the runaways. "My sweet urchins," he called them.

That was when Tom rose to his feet. "All right, Warren, you've had your fun. I've let you run on. But enough is enough. It's time for Charlie and me to head back to the home planet for dinner and ice cream."

Warren stood up too. "But I'm not through yet. We haven't yet discussed the possibility of Charlie here joining us. I want to start expanding the Kingdom, bringing in the fans who should have been with me from the beginning. Charlie here could be the first of—"

"Enough," Tom said. "This is nuts. We're leaving, Warren."

He pulled me up on my feet. It wasn't that difficult. I was more than ready to go. As I went past, Warren tried once more to grab hold of me by the arm. This time I pushed him back. He fell against the table, lost his balance, and tumbled to the floor.

That's when I reached down and in a quick gesture knocked the top hat off his head. It wasn't something I'd planned in advance. It just happened. I reached out, gave a swing, opened my hand, and off it flew.

Underneath where the hat had been his head was as bald as a shaven cue ball.

Not a single hair grew.

No tendrils either.

* * * *

As we hurried out the gate toward the car, I asked Tom, "What's wrong with all of them anyway? The kids. They act like they're on drugs or something."

"Maybe they are," he said as he got in the car.

I climbed in beside him. "Shouldn't we do something about it?"

"That's what I've been trying to decide."

"How long have you known about this?"

"Since last Tuesday. Yul brought me out here. He didn't know what to do either."

"Isn't it obvious?"

He looked at me, surprised. "You may be right," he said.

He started the car and drove off.

* * * *

On the way Tom stopped at the first phone booth we went past and got out to make a call. "I don't know if they'll toss him in jail or what," he said, when he came back. "A mental hospital is where he belongs, I suppose. As for all those poor kids, Jesus, who can say?"

* * * *

As to how it turned out, Tom drove back to the site a few days later and found it empty. The dirty dishes were still in the sink, the dust and filth hadn't changed, the magazines and books were still strewn all over the floor. But there was nobody there.

As far as Warren Wunderly and his connection with SF fandom was concerned, that seemed to be over too. This was such a common phenomenon among fans there was even a fannish acronym for it. GAFIA—Getting Away From It All. In this case getting away from fandom.

When Warren Wunderly went Gafia, few people took note of it.

Eventually, there'd be a brief sequel. Stay tuned.

iv

Oh—and about the rest of that day and night. After we left the Cosmic Kingdom behind.

"So what do you want to do now?" Tom said, as we headed up the curving two lane blacktop that would eventually carry us out of the valley. "How about a movie?"

"You're kidding," I said.

"No, why should I be?"

"Because, I mean, after all that's happened I need some time to think."

"Thinking won't get you anywhere, buddy boy. Not where Warren Wunderly is concerned. The night's young, the air's sweet, there's a cool double bill playing at the Sasquatch Drive-in. You've got Hitchcock's *The Birds* on the one hand and Jerry Lewis as *The Nutty Professor* on the other. Both for a slim buck and a quarter. Plus all the fine eats you can afford. Foot-long hot dogs, popcorn slathered in fake butter, Milk Duds, Crackerjacks. Can't beat that for wholesome grub. So how about it? Heck, son, I'm buying the tickets. You get the food."

"It's a drive-in theater?"

"No better place to see a movie."

"I've never been to one before."

"Even better." He stepped on the gas pedal. "Get ready to lose one key part of your virginity. As Henry Miller once wrote, virginity is a condition created solely to be shed."

* * * *

I'd already finished wolfing down the first of two foot-long hot dogs as Tom pulled into a vacant slot in the back row of cars. "I prefer the view from back here," he explained. "When the movie gets boring, I can always watch the people in their cars. You'd be amazed at the things that go on in a place like this. Whole lotta shakin' goin' on, as the preacher once sang."

It was becoming dark enough now for the screen to take on an eerie glow. While I wiped dabs of spilt mustard off the front of my jacket, Tom lit up a cigarette. He let his hand dangle out the window and blew smoke into the open air around it.

"I didn't know you smoked," I said.

"I just started today."

"Really? Why?" I'd never heard of anyone starting to smoke at Tom's age.

"Does my smoking bother you?"

"Not especially. My mom used to smoke when I was little. My brother Slim did too. Before he went back to Alaska."

"Good. Then I'll finish this one." He brought his hand back inside and took another deep drag. "I'm surprised more people don't start. It's an amazing habit. So utterly and totally pointless and yet it can kill you."

"You believe that?"

"Sure. Don't you?"

"Yes. That's why I don't smoke."

"Oh, and I thought it had something to do with the phallic imagery of it all. But you're right of course. Smoking really is idiotic." He tossed the cigarette out the window, fanned the air, and leaned back with a big wide grin on his face. "Let the show begin," he said.

* * * *

I was just finishing up hot dog number two when the big rectangular silver screen exploded in a burst of Technicolor imagery.

After several trailers previewing coming attractions—the new James Bond picture *Goldfinger* looked especially neat to me—and a Road Runner cartoon in which Wylie Coyote should have been dead at least seven times over (Tom and I counted along), the first of the two features came on.

The Nutty Professor. Jerry Lewis's personal take on the Dr. Jekyll and Mr. Hyde story. There had been a time earlier in my life—say, when I was nine and ten—when I'd been a huge Jerry Lewis fan. I'd even convinced myself that I looked like him. (Though in retrospect it would have been far better for my emotional development if I'd looked more like Dean Martin.)

I cultivated a talent for being able to chew and swallow an entire fried egg sandwich in a single gulp. I practiced sticking my foot behind my ear and wiggling my toes at the same time. I slobbered strawberry soda pop over all my clean shirts. (I nearly got a licking for that till Pop decided I was too big to be spanked and instead docked my seventy-five-cent weekly allowance for a month. I'd rather have had the licking.) Every chance I got I gave out a screeching *"Hey lady!"* designed to shatter glass at twenty paces. (A phrase, by the way, Jerry Lewis himself never once uttered.)

The Nutty Professor turned out surprisingly good. Jerry played both roles of course. The good Dr. Jekyll in the person of nerdy chemistry professor Julius Kelp and the evil Hyde, a brilliantined lounge singer named Buddy Love. I found myself laughing out loud any number of times and when I sneaked a look at Tom slumped behind the wheel saw that he was grinning like a cat named Cheshire. During the sweet love scene between Jerry and the luscious Stella Stevens (yum-yum) high in the hills over Los Angeles while "Stella By Starlight" (as Tom informed me) played on the soundtrack, I swear a tear went sliding down my cheek.

Partway through *Nutty Professor*, my returning hunger pangs got the better of me and I ducked out to the concession stand for one of their signature corn dogs on a stick.

As a result I half-missed (no sound) the big scene where Professor Kelp as his Buddy Love alter ego visits the Purple Pit nightclub where all the college kids he teaches chemistry to (as Kelp) hang out after school. But I could follow the action clearly enough through pantomime and it made me think of asking Tom if night spots like the Purple Pit really were where college kids hung out. Since he'd been to college himself back east at Cornell and ought to know. It marked the first hint I'd had that made college seem like something worth seriously considering, that it wasn't just high school with more books and teachers who actually knew something about the subjects they taught.

When the *Nutty Professor* ended and the screen went blank, Tom looked over at me and said, "So, Mr. Hitchcock, how do you plan to top that one? Hugo nomination, anyone?"

The second movie, Alfred Hitchcock's *The Birds*, started on a slow note with some dull romantic fencing between the leads—Rod Taylor and Tippi Hedren—in various San Francisco locales. "My second favorite town," Tom remarked, "after Seacrest."

Me, I'd never been farther away than Tacoma.

When the storyline finally shifted to the oceanside village of Bodega Bay, Tom said, *"Psycho* this sure ain't."

"I heard the Bloch book was better." *Psycho*'s author—Robert Bloch—was well known in SF circles. He'd been a regular writer for the magazines since the 1930's and sometimes wrote for fanzines too. I'd added his name to my mailing list for the first issue of *Briar Patch*.

"Have you read it?"

"Not yet, no."

"Then be quiet until you do."

Soon after that, the bird attacks started coming one after the other and the movie got a lot better. I quickly became engrossed and all thoughts of Warren Wunderly and his Cosmic Kingdom were pushed as far from my mind as the other side of the moon.

"Another Hugo nominee, eh, little buddy?" Tom said, as he turned the key and waited his chance to enter the steady stream of traffic headed for the exits.

"It's not really science fiction, is it?"

"Sure it is. If ornithology's not a science, what is it?"

He finally found a gap in the line of cars heading out and slipped deftly into it. We were about to exit through the gate when all of a sudden Tom jerked the wheel hard to the left and slammed on the brakes. "Good God," he said, "look who's here."

I turned and looked and immediately recognized the two men standing by the concession stand eating popcorn out of matching paper bags.

"King Babbitt I saw in Pittsburgh," Tom said, "at that panel where he called fandom a small uniformed minority and barely escaped with his life. But the other guy—he looks familiar too."

"That," I said, "is Hari Botts."

I have to admit I got a charge and a half at the look that passed over Tom's face when I told him that.

SEVEN: LIGHT IS FASTER THAN SOUND

i

The first issue of *Flabbergasting Tales of Wonder and Mystery* appeared on the newsstands of Depression America on the tenth day of January, 1931. The editor-in-chief listed on the magazine's masthead was Leonard Bloodstone Brodsky, a thirty-six-year-old veteran writer of hack pulp fiction. For much of the next decade, Leonard Bloodstone Brodsky would continue to edit the magazine from his sparsely furnished one-room office on the ground floor of the Rex Hotel on West Eighth Street in Greenwich Village, a notorious haven for gangsters, gun molls, and hophead Negro jazz musicians.

The unsigned cover painting on that first March, 1931 issue—now a collector's item worth several hundred dollars—depicted a squad of heavily armed soldiers battling a gigantic multi-armed beetle-like creature clutching in its thrashing mandibles a nubile young woman in a badly torn gown exposing her large, heaving, melon-like breasts to view.

These large, heaving, melon-like breasts would remain a staple of the magazine's cover art for some years to come.

"Tits sell," a long-retired Leonard Bloodstone Brodsky told fan journalist Warren Wunderly in an interview conducted in his Kingston, Arizona, nursing home room in August, 1959. "Always have, always will. You want to get some traveling shoe salesman to buy your lousy twenty-cent magazine when he's got maybe six bits left in his pocket after shelling out for his nightly half pint of hooch, you gotta grab him by the balls and never let go."

In truth, sales had little to do with the magazine's ultimate success or failure. Its owner, hidden under the cover of the Amsterdam Printing & Development Company, was in reality Otto "Abbadabba" Berman, wizard accountant in the employ of Arthur Flegenheimer, better known as Dutch Schultz. *Flabbergasting Tales* was one of several shady enterprises used by Berman to conceal and launder the vast profits of the various illicit enterprises of the Schultz mob.

To avoid unnecessary paperwork, the entire contents of each issue of *Flabbergasting Tales* (as the title was soon shortened to)—including covers and interior artwork—were the work of Leonard Bloodstone Brodsky. "I paid myself a flat penny a word for the fiction, two hundred bucks for a cover painting. When Otto found out what I was doing, he checked around and saw those were fair rates and let me live. He told me later he liked a man who showed initiative and so did the Dutchman. They were good guys, the both of them, and what that lousy dago did to them was a real tragedy."

The tragedy that befell the two good guys occurred on October 23, 1935, in a Newark, New Jersey tavern, when Dutch Schultz and Otto Berman were both gunned down and killed by assailants thought to be in the employ of rival gangster, Charles "Lucky" Luciano.

For the next several years Leonard Bloodstone Brodsky struggled to keep his magazine afloat. "The funny part was," he told interviewer Wunderly, "the more I got into it the more I got to really liking that crazy Buck Rodgers stuff. It gets into your blood, I don't really know why. I think it must be the sense of wonder it imparts."

By the fall of 1939, however, as war in Europe threatened, the end of *Flabbergasting Stories* appeared near. There was not enough money in reserve to pay both the magazine's contributors—all of them still Brodsky —and its printer.

It was at this point that there came a knock on the hotel room office door.

Standing on the other side was man with a trim Clark Gable moustache wearing a broad brimmed Panama hat. He held in his hand a certified check in the amount of fifteen thousand dollars. "I wish to purchase full rights and title to your magazine," he told Leonard Bloodstone Brodsky, "assuming, that is, it's for sale."

"Sold to the American!" cried Leonard Bloodstone Brodsky.

Twenty minutes later, certified check in one hand, cardboard suitcase in the other, Leonard Bloodstone Brodsky raced through the lobby of the Rex Hotel. As he went past the desk clerk, he shouted, "Hollywood or bust!" (As a matter of fact Leonard Bloodstone Brodsky later enjoyed a long and lucrative career as a film and television producer.)

Three months later saw the first issue of the totally redesigned magazine now known as *Flabbergasting Science Fiction* (the first word printed in type so miniscule it could barely be seen from a distance greater than six inches). The cover by Hubert Rodgers featured an astronomical view of Saturn and its moons—no large, heaving, melon-like breasts in sight. Fiction included new work by Robert Heinlein, L. Sprague de Camp, Lester de Rey, and A.E. van Vogt. There were two science fact articles, one by the German refugee scientist Willy Ley and the other by Dr. Irving Greysmith of the Harvard

Observatory. Directly below the magazine's title appeared the slogan: *The World of Tomorrow Today!*

The magazine's new editor as listed on the masthead was Kingsley C.K. Babbitt IV.

ii

The moment I walked into the Rocketeers meeting that night at Yul's place in West Seacrest, I couldn't help noticing the funny looking little man trapped in a corner of the living room by a rapidly gesticulating Mrs. Eva Jones.

I tugged at Tom's sleeve and drew him back. "Look who's here," I said.

He turned and gaped. "The man with the popcorn," he said. "The Einstein of Jersey City."

It was Hari Botts all right.

"And alone too," Tom said. "No sign of King Babbitt that's for sure. He'd have to be a brave man to come here after what he said about fandom. I wonder what Botts is up to."

"Maybe we should ask."

Tom thought it over. "Nah. Never mind. Later on maybe. Right now I want a beer. Come along. I'm buying."

Since I needed to see Budd Champion about the *Howl of the Rocketeers* mailing list he'd promised to let me use in sending out my own first *Briar Patch*, I let Tom lead the way into the kitchen. As expected, we found Budd standing guard by the fridge, charging twenty-five cents for each bottle of Satan's Brew he let out. Collecting club dues, he called it. "Don't want the revenuers after us for bootlegging," he explained.

The Rocketeers had been undergoing a renaissance of sorts in recent months. Our membership rolls having grown from the usual same eight to ten regulars to as many as thirty and forty attendees per meeting. Budd credited our moving out of the old Arcadia Building with its ever-clinging odor of moldering wheat germ and holding meetings instead in member's homes. With that went the freedom to serve beer and soft drinks. Yul had happily retired his coffee maker for the duration.

"What's Hari Botts doing here?" Tom asked, once he'd handed over his half-dollar for two beers.

"Botts?" Budd said. "King Babbitt's latest crackpot? He's here? You're kidding me."

Tom told of us seeing both Botts and King Babbitt at the drive-in movie. "Botts is out there right now trying not to get run over by Mrs. Jones. If you want we can go out and try and rescue him."

"I'll pass on that. I gave up crackpot science when Hubbard decided to turn Dianetics into a church. Besides, I have dues to collect." He reached out and grabbed hold of a longhaired college-student-looking guy with a guitar hanging around his neck. "That'll be two bits for the beer, my friend, and the folk singing is strictly limited to the back bedroom. Down the hall, last door at the end. You can't miss it for the moaning and wailing and gnashing of guitar strings going on."

* * * *

Tom and I wandered back toward the living room. It was packed. Not a big room to begin with, it was definitely standing room only. Two college age girls in sweaters and black tights who I'd bet anything had come with the folk singing guitar player stood in the doorway. Tom stopped squeezing past to talk to them—not that I was blaming him in the least—and as he did a hand came down and grabbed me by the shoulder.

It was Yul Borensen with a bottle of green soda pop in his other hand. He pointed across the room to where I could make out Mrs. Eva Jones still blocking the corner. "For some weird reason our distinguished guest over there wants to meet you."

"Hari Botts does?"

"That's what he said. I think he just wants to escape the clutches of the dread Mrs. Jones. He showed up here at five when I was still cooking dinner and said he didn't want to miss the meeting. So I shared my tuna and noodle casserole with him. He kept asking if I was sure you were going to be here tonight. I said you hadn't missed a meeting since you turned sweet sixteen." A slight exaggeration—but who was I to argue? "Come along and we'll see if we can fight our way over. I'll introduce you."

But there was no need for us to move because by then Hari Botts was coming our way. Having somehow pulled off an intricate maneuver and slipped past Mrs. Jones, he was heading straight toward me with a hand extended.

"We need to talk, young man," Botts murmured, as we shook. His head swiveling, he looked around the room as if searching for someone or something.

"But you don't know me, Mr. Botts," I blurted out.

"I know of you. And your father."

"You do?"

"Oh, yes. Most definitely. This way, please."

He tried to lead me off toward the kitchen but by then the crowd had grown so dense that it was hard to find even a few square feet of empty space to maneuver in.

"Let's go outside," he suggested. "There's something out there I need to give you."

By then his nervousness was making me nervous too. He continued looking around the room as he talked.

"Please," he said, grabbing me by the arm. "Let's go now. I don't want to wait."

Seeing no way to resist, I let him lead me outside onto the porch. He made sure the door was firmly closed behind us and only then seemed to relax. It was still early enough in the year—summer never really gets going in Seacrest till after the Fourth of July—I wished I'd brought my jacket along. It was chilly.

"Stay here, please," he said. "I'll be right back."

While I waited on the porch, shivering, he went down the steps, out into the yard, and knelt down beside a large rhododendron bush. Reaching underneath, he emerged holding two of the lead carrying cases I'd seen on the desk in Dr. Hightower's den. Stepping cautiously due to the weight he was carrying, he brought them over and set them both at my feet.

He wiped the perspiration off his face with a handkerchief.

I started: "Aren't these your—?"

He raised a finger to his lips and hushed me. "Please. Let's get them to your car. They're meant for your father. He'll need them where he's going."

He picked up one of the cases again and set off across the street to where Tom had parked the VW. He must have seen us when we drove up.

Bending down, I picked up the other case and followed him across the street. It wasn't as heavy as it looked. Twenty pounds at most. As for its glow, it didn't feel noticeably warm to the touch either.

I carried it across to the car. With each step I could feel something moving around inside, rattling as it did. It sounded like a cylindrical object rolling back and forth.

As usual—"there's nothing worth stealing in this car"—Tom hadn't bothered to lock the doors. We put both cases down behind the front seat where they couldn't be easily seen from without. By the time we were done I was sweating too.

"Thank you, young man," he said. "Now don't forget. They're for your father."

"How do you know my dad?" I asked, as we went back across the street. "I don't."

"But then how can you be sure he'll want these things of yours?"

"He does. He may not know it yet. But he does."

As we came up the porch steps, the front door opened and Tom Powers poked his head outside. "So there you are." He pointed a finger at Botts. "You just kidnapped the president of the club right when we were about to have an official meeting."

Tom was right about that. Not about the official meeting. About me being the current president of the Rocketeers. Elected in February to a six-month term. By acclamation. (And without opposition.)

I'd hadn't presided over an actual meeting yet. I couldn't remember the last one we'd had.

"We need to hold a quick vote," Tom said. "To reimburse Budd for the beer he's been supplying."

It was at this point when a car came squealing around the corner from the intersection below. It headed straight toward us, headlights burning like angry eyes.

As the car swept past, two shots blazed out.

The first bullet passed over the top of my head by inches and struck the door, scattering wood chips like daggers. The second shot caught Hari Botts in the throat. Even as I ducked my head in automatic reaction, I saw blood spurting from the wound.

Botts reached up, grabbed hold of his neck, and looked over me.

His lips moved but no sound came out.

He crumpled in a heap.

Tom bent down over him as I swiveled my gaze in time to see two red tail lights vanish around the next corner.

"Ford Fairlane," Tom mumbled. "1962 hardtop convertible. Eight-cylinder engine, blue with white trim, license number 643640A."

While Tom droned on, I could hear shouting and yelling from inside the house. The door was hurled open and Budd raced out. A small crowd of people looked on from behind. I saw both Yul and Mrs. Eva Jones among them. Budd had a gun in his hand—a .22 pistol. It belonged to Yul, I later learned. Fortunately—or otherwise—it wasn't loaded. "I'm not goofy enough to keep a loaded gun in the house," Yul explained to the police. "Not with all the crazy people I know." Because of that remark, Yul ended up having to explain to the detectives what science fiction fandom was all about. No wonder none of us made it home till after daybreak the next morning.

With poor Hari Botts's head and shoulders swaddled in his lap, Tom looked up at Budd. He shook his head. "I'm afraid the poor man's dead as a stone," he said.

* * * *

What with the ambulances, the flashing lights, the police detectives and reporters—a Channel Five TV crew showed up just before the eleven o'clock news—-it was five a.m. before Tom and I and the rest were allowed to go home. Unlike on shows like *M-Squad* or *Naked City*—my two favorite TV cop programs—nobody warned us not to leave town. (Not that any of us intended to. I had high school to graduate from first.) They did tell us they'd be in touch later if they needed to ask further questions. (As with the Ethel

Radke case, I never heard from them again.)

As soon as we got in the car, since the sun was already half up over the eastern horizon, Tom spotted the lead carrying cases in the back.

"What are those things, may I ask?" he said.

"Oh, just something somebody gave me. They're for my dad."

"They're glowing."

"It only looks that way. An optical illusion. Touch one and you'll see. They're not even warm."

He turned in his seat and laid a finger tentatively on top of the nearest case. He let it stay for maybe fifteen seconds.

"Okay, so they're not hot. But that still doesn't tell me what they are or where you got them from."

"I'll tell you while we drive."

"You're sure about that?"

"Sure I'm sure. Why would I lie?"

He hesitated only briefly, then started the car and drove off. At the end of the street we made a U-turn and headed back down the hill.

"So okay," he said. "Now spill it. What's this all about?"

I explained: "Those are two of the Botts Batteries. There's at least one other." I told him about seeing the three of them on the desk at the Hightowers' that one time. "Mr. Botts said he wanted my wanted my father to have them."

"Correct me if I'm wrong but I don't believe you mentioned any of this to the police."

"I didn't, no. Should I have?"

He thought about it for a minute before finally shaking his head. "No, you did the right thing."

"You're sure about that?"

"Nope. But if you did the wrong thing, I imagine we'll find out soon enough."

* * * *

When we got to my place Tom volunteered to help cart the two lead cases up to the house. He carried one, I took the other. We left both of them out in the backyard near the wooden starships.

As we turned to go, the sound of hammering could be heard from above. "That your old man up there at work already?" Tom said.

It was a bit past six a.m. "It's like that every day now. He says he's near to being done. Finishing up on the interiors. The crew quarters and the galley."

"Have you been inside yet?"

"He hasn't asked me."

"You're not curious?"

"I said he hasn't asked me."

"Then do me a favor, will you?"

"What's that?"

"When he does ask, put in a word for me. I'd love a guided tour. I'm as curious as you are, brother."

iii

Needless to say, I didn't make it to school that day. It was a Friday anyhow. Nothing much ever happened on Fridays and I didn't feel at all like a dress-up day. I went to bed and stayed there until dinnertime catching up as well as I could on lost sleep.

The headline on page B1 of the afternoon *Seacrest Daily Star* seemed to sum it up well:

Murder at Science Fiction Club
Famed Author Shot Dead While Shocked Fans Look On

Hey, that's me, I thought, seeing the headline. The accompanying story named only Yul Borensen, however—unavoidable since it was his house where the shooting occurred—describing him as a Cantrell Air Design Engineer instead of a mere draftsman. They also managed to misspell "Harry" Botts's name as well as calling him a "famous science fiction writer," which he wasn't.

The police detectives quoted in the story seemed convinced the shooting was a case of mistaken identity. The suspected shooters— "neighborhood hoodlums," they were referred to—had apparently mistaken our club meeting for a gathering of a rival gang and had opened fire at random. There was no mention of the license plate number Tom had given the police or of any arrests.

The Sunday papers—we got both the *Star* and the *Times-Post*—said nothing more about the shooting.

Yesterday's news, I suppose.

* * * *

Come Monday when my alarm went off at six, I crawled up out of bed, tossed on a few school clothes—white Levi's, long-sleeve button-down shirt, brown loafers, white gym socks—and padded downstairs. The kitchen was empty. I could hear somebody—Mom presumably—moving around in the adjacent bedroom but she hadn't yet emerged. I fixed myself a bowl of Wheaties, ladled on some canned peaches, gulped down three glasses of lemonade for the quick energy, and headed for the door.

On the way out, I grabbed my school books and pee-chee as well as the paperback I was reading, *The Long Goodbye* by Raymond Chandler. A detective story. I was still branching out in my reading. I hadn't read an SF novel since *The Man in the High Castle*.

The reason for my hurry was that I wanted to try and walk to school today. It wasn't all that far—three miles at most—plus it was a rare Seacrest April spring morning. No rain, no chill, no drizzle. The sun was already up and shining over the peaked roof of the house where I could see the nose cones of the two starships painted in shimmering shades of metallic silver rising through the blue of the morning.

I'd only gone half-a-block when a familiar voice called out to me from behind: "Hey there, Charlie, hold up, man."

If it had been anyone but Nedd Young emerging from the small house trailer his dad had been living in next to the burnt-out ruins of their former home, I might well have ignored him.

But it was Nedd. So I held up.

"Mind if I tag along?" he asked, when he caught up with me.

"If you want, sure. I'm not taking the bus though. I don't think I could handle that today. I'm walking."

"Cool. I'm early too."

We walked the rest of the block in silence until we'd passed out of sight of both his place and mine.

"Does this mean you're back for good?" I asked.

He nodded. "Does look that way. It took me a while but I finally wore them down. My dad and Aunt Minnie both. They kept saying there wasn't room in the trailer for two. I kept saying I wanted to graduate with my class. Finally they got sick of hearing me whine. They were right though. There isn't enough room. But there's only a couple more months of school and there's the senior prom and graduation day and everything that goes with it. I worked too hard to get this far to let it go now."

"You could graduate from another school."

"Not the same though, is it?"

"I suppose not. And there's the prom." I said it with a slight sneer since I'd never planned on going. And still didn't.

"Wouldn't miss it for the world," he said, with all due sincerity.

I let it go by, just happy to have him back.

"Hey," I said, reaching out and punching him gently on the arm. "I missed you too. There's only so much Cisco Cordova a guy can take."

"I know. I went over there last night to say hi. And Katy Cross? How's she doing? Cisco said she hasn't been around much."

"She's fine," I said. Perhaps a little too quickly. Nedd gave me a quizzical look but didn't say anything.

We went another block in silence.

Then I asked the question that had been preying on me ever since he brought it up: "So if you're really going to the prom, who are you taking?"

"Her name's Gloria Davies. She's a junior at Garfield. Her mom's a friend of my aunt's. They thought we should get to know each other and we did."

"Cute?"

"Beautiful. Smart too. She wants to go to Stanford."

"I'm jealous."

"You are? Of her?"

"No, you."

"You shouldn't be."

"Why not?"

"Don't you know?"

I pretended I didn't. I asked him about his own college plans for the fall instead.

It turned out he'd been accepted into Oberlin with a full scholarship. He said he could hardly wait.

He asked me what my own plans were.

"I don't have any," I said.

"But it's April, Charlie. We graduate in June. Two months from now. Then what?"

"Then it's July. My birthday. I'm eighteen. Maybe I'll throw a party."

"I'm serious."

"Me too."

"You really don't know?"

"I guess I'll have to find a dumb job. What else is there?"

"College?"

"With my grades?"

"You could go Delridge JC, get your GPA up, and then transfer."

"Still no good. Pop's broke. We're lucky we can eat. And I don't want to go Delridge JC. Too much like high school with all the smart kids gone. I'd rather—I don't know—I'd rather bag groceries at the IGA."

"No, you wouldn't."

"Yes, actually I would."

This time he let me off the hook and dropped the subject of college.

"What I'd really like to do," I mused, "is go someplace else. Like California maybe. San Francisco. Or LA. Both have big fan communities. People I already know. On paper anyhow. Or New York City. Greenwich Village. That's the place to be."

"So why don't you?"

"Money," I said. "I don't have any, remember."

"You could save up."

"That's a lot of groceries to bag."

"Try it and see."

"Maybe I will," I said. "I don't see anything else."

By then we'd reached the first stoplight announcing we were about to enter the Delridge Drive business district.

While we waited at the corner for the light to change, Nedd said, "I heard about what happened to you the other night. It was on the radio."

"They said my name?"

"No. But it was a science fiction club. There can't be two of them in Seacrest, can there?"

"What else did they say?"

"Just that there was a shooting at a science fiction meeting and a man was killed. They thought it was some kind of case of mistaken identity. A writer, they said."

"He wasn't a writer. More of a—I don't know—a crackpot, a crank." Like certain family members, I thought. "My friend Tom Powers who was there too—he's an engineer at Cantrell Air—he got the license number of the car. So they should be able to catch whoever did it."

"They said on the radio the police were investigating."

"I suppose so, sure."

The light turned green. We went across. This early in the morning, pretty much everything was closed. Elmo's Famous Pancake House was doing its usual steady business as were the three filling stations, one on each corner. The fourth corner was occupied by Clem & Clyde's Burgerland and a block farther on the red brick edifice of Lake Delridge Senior High School loomed.

As we crossed the street, Nedd said: "Do you ever get the feeling that all of this—the way things are now—that it's all about to change? That something big is about to happen and it's going to be so—I don't know—so important that everything afterward will seem completely different."

I turned my head and looked at him. I'd never heard him talk like that before. "You mean like a war? We already went through that, didn't we? With Cuba? Now there isn't going to be one."

"No, not a war. But something else. Something almost as big. Maybe not as bad but not good either. Something that will make everything change whether we want it to or not. It's like it's in the air. You can feel it coming."

"Maybe so," I said.

"You can feel it too?"

"Sometimes," I said. "Sometimes I can feel it too."

"Does it scare you?"

"Yes and no. Both, I think. Sometimes I'm scared, sometimes I'm not."

"Me too."

By then we were there. At school.

* * * *

Nedd and I stood out by the flagpole watching the busloads of kids arriving out front, the many hundreds of sophomores milling around like ants as they scurried to get inside.

"They act like they're happy to be here," I observed.

"Maybe they are," Nedd said. "Not everyone hates high school like you do, Charlie."

"Ah, but they should."

"I don't know about that. I think I'm going to miss the old brick barnyard when I'm gone."

"Then you're out of your head. When they hold the first Class of '63 reunion, don't look for me there. I'll be the guy three thousand miles away laughing my head off."

We headed around toward the Block. Nedd took a book out of the shoulder bag he carried and showed me the cover. "You know who this is, don't you?"

"Sure. It's the Buddha."

"That's what the book is about. It's called *Siddhartha*. By a German writer named Hesse. It was on one of the college reading lists I got from the counselors up there. It's about the early life of the Buddha. How he came to achieve his state of enlightenment. I think you'd like it, if you want it."

"Sure," I said. I took the book from him.

On the way Cisco fell into step and joined us. After punching each of us in the arm in turn, he said, "I read in the paper some writer got killed at your science fiction club the other night, Charlie."

"I know," I said. "I was standing right next to him when it happened. The first shot missed my head by inches."

"That's something I wanted to ask you about," he said.

"What's that?" To tell the truth, I was getting tired of talking about it. There was only so much you could say. I'd already said most of it too many times.

"How do you know they weren't shooting at you?"

I thought it over for a moment. "I guess don't."

Then the three of us all burst out laughing, attracting curious stares as we sped through the doors.

As we headed for our seats, I decided not to hold back any longer.

"After graduation I'm going to enlist in the army," I announced.

With perfect timing too, as the final bell clanged.

Later on while we sat huddled in the football bleachers waiting for the fire department to give the okay for us to file back inside after the fourteenth false bomb scare of the school year—they never did find out for sure who was calling them in from the pay phone by the office, though most of us had a pretty fair idea from watching to see who was laughing the hardest every time it happened. That was a weird kid named Bob Lane, who later ended up in the reformatory at Monroe for supposedly molesting his twelve-year-old stepsister. Cisco wrote me with the details.

"Do me a favor, Charlie," he said as we sat out there in the morning chill, "don't join the stupid army."

"Why not?"

"Because I don't want to see my best childhood friend get blown to smithereens in Vietnam."

"There's nothing that serious happening over there. *Time* magazine says it'll be over by next summer. Kennedy and McNamara have a plan to get us out."

"Do me the favor anyhow."

"Then how else am I going to get out of here? At least Vietnam would be different."

"So join the navy like my brothers. It's way safer. They have to sink the whole boat to kill you."

"I thought about the navy but no. For one thing I can't swim a lick. For another their uniforms make you look like Donald Duck."

At that point our beloved vice-principal Mortimer Washburn stepped out on the football field and announced that we could all now file safely back to our classes in a quiet and orderly manner. "Third period!" he called out. "Go to your third period classes."

"Just think," Cisco said. "You won't have to put up with dumb crap like this in the army."

I never could figure out whether he was kidding or not.

iv

You're no doubt wondering by now whatever happened to Katy Cross. If I needed a date for the senior prom, why not ask her?

Two reasons. First of all, ever since Katy had taken up sitting among the John Galtists, opportunities for interacting with her were severely limited. (Was she still acting as an undercover agent for us Comancheros? I have to admit to having my doubts.)

Reason number two: Katy was dating Tom Powers. They'd been going out ever since I brought her to the Champions' New Year's party. They went to movies and shows, hung out together at a couple of U-District coffeehouses that served European espresso in tiny china cups. I didn't find out about it until later when Tom tried telling me it was no big deal. She was just a fun kid to go places with. So what if he was twenty-two and she was eighteen? It wasn't like he was sneaking into dive bars underage. He laughed and asked if I was jealous?

I told him, "Anything but."

At that he laughed some more.

* * * *

The Saturday morning after the senior class prom—from which I'd steadfastly absented myself as vowed—Pop came barging into my room the way he almost never did without bothering to knock and shook me awake.

"What's up, Pop?" I said blearily

I noticed the black patch covering his missing left eye was askew again. You could see the shadow of the hollow underneath. "I wanted to know if you were doing anything special today."

"No, not really. How come? What's up?"

"How'd you like to go for a ride with your old man?"

"You're kidding." It wasn't as if we'd ever done much of anything together before. Pop was always either busy working or fixing something broken around the house or lately building wooden starships in the backyard. When I was younger Pop and Slim were always going off fishing together but the couple times they tried dragging me along I never could get the hang of it. To me fishing was just plain boring. I mean, you dip your line in the water with the poor worm squirming in agony on the hook and then wait endlessly around for a fish to swim by. I mean, wow, what a thrill. I guess you could say I missed the point of it.

I didn't like eating fish anyhow. Too much trouble picking out the bones.

Apart from that, the only other time I could remember doing something with Pop was a single Pacific Coast League baseball game on my ninth birthday—I was already a huge ball fan—pitting our Seacrest Coastal Indians against the rival Oakland Oaks at Cantrell Fields. Pop made us get up and leave in the middle of the seventh inning with the score tied two-to-two saying he had to get up early in the morning for work. When I left for school at 8:45 he was still in bed.

"A ride where?" I asked him.

"Not far. Just down the road a piece. I thought you might want to tag along."

The look on Pop's face as he stood looming over me reminded me of our cat Pickles the time she ate Mom's yellow canary Sammy.

"Sure," I said. "Let's go."

He reached up and adjusted his eye patch, grinning. He had on his red-and-white polka dot bandana again today too, giving him that piratical look. "I thought you might say that, my boy."

* * * *

I tossed on some clothes and followed him downstairs. By the time I grabbed my jacket and slipped into some shoes, Pop had the Minx revved up and ready to roll. As I slid into the seat beside him, I asked, "So what's this really all about?"

"Call it a surveillance mission. There's things going on down there that I want to have a look-see at."

"Like what and where?"

"You'll find out."

Pop jerked the Minx into reverse and we sailed out the driveway narrowly missing weird old Mrs. Garrison from down the street as she went pedaling past on her bicycle, the one with the basket attached to the handlebars where her dog rode along.

Letting out the clutch, Pop sent us chugging around the corner and loping downhill toward the Point below.

"We're going to see Dr. Hightower, aren't we?" I said.

His grin grew even wider. "Smart boy," he said. "I knew you'd turn out to be a chip off the old block after all."

* * * *

It was another dank, sullen, gloomy, typically gray springtime Seacrest day, the short weekend before the long weekend for Memorial Day, after which, as inexorable as Death rendezvousing with the condemned man in Samara, would come the joyful days of my final two weeks of high school.

By now I'd pretty much decided to go into the Air Force rather than the army. The Air Force was four years rather than three but likely worth it for the diminished chance of getting my head blown off. In four more years I'd be twenty-one and ready to take on life on my own terms. So I kept telling myself.

And I'd always liked airplanes. Built plastic scale models as a kid. Blew them up with firecrackers on the Fourth of July. Read *Thirty Seconds Over Tokyo* and watched the movie version with Van Johnson and Spencer Tracy when it showed on TV. Sunday afternoons Pop would sometimes drive us all out to the airport to watch the planes take off and land. One every fifteen minutes. Afterward we'd stop at the old man's ice cream store on Bomber Boulevard for double dip cones.

In a way I guess you could say it was in my blood. The Air Force was.

Pop's brother Uncle Horace had been a B-17 bombardier during World War II. On his next to last mission he'd been shot down over Germany and spent two years in a prisoner of war camp. He never liked to talk about it though. What I knew I'd learned from Mom.

* * * *

Pop pulled into the Hightowers' crescent shaped driveway and stopped directly in line with the front door. He cut the engine, slid the key out of the ignition, and dropped it in his pocket.

Then he sat back, linking his fingers behind his neck, and gave me his best Long John Silver grin.

"Aren't we getting out?" I asked.

"We can see what we came to see better from here."

"Doesn't look like there's anyone home anyhow." The curtains were drawn. The house was dark.

"Oh, they're in there, all right."

"How do you know?"

"Because this won't work otherwise."

"What won't work?"

"You'll see. Trust me. When it happens you'll know."

From years of past experience I knew there was little point in arguing with him when he got like this. Still, I decided to give it one more shot. "So what are we supposed to do now? Twiddle our thumbs?"

"Patience is a virtue, my lad."

If there was any old saw deliberately designed to drive a healthy teenage boy into a raging fit of rage it had to be—

That was as far as my thought got.

Because right then the whole world split open like the shell of a cracked egg and everything around me exploded in my face.

I grabbed at my skull, covered my ears, trying to blot out the raging burning fire that seemed to be everywhere. It was as if a giant hand had come reaching down from the heavens, grabbed up our dorky little car in its grasp with us still in it, and tossed us in the air as if we were as light as the wind. I watched it all happening as if from a distance. The car, the giant hand, Pop. And me. I saw us hopelessly tumbling. And then we hit the ground on all four wheels and the tires burst open and the searing redness of the flames and the howling wind and then—

I think that was when I finally lost consciousness.

An overwhelming stillness filled the air.

* * * *

When I came awake again—slowly, gradually—I forced my eyelids open.

I took a look around. Shards of broken glass were everywhere. Splinters of metal coated my face. I reached up with my fingertips and delicately removed pieces from my skin.

I was bleeding. In several places. Patches of bare skin showed through what was left of my clothes. The sleeves of my shirt had been burned away. My white Levi's were torn and ragged. I'd lost one shoe and its accompanying sock.

There was a taste in my mouth like foam and salt.

I spit blood.

Then I looked over at Pop. He lay beside me, his head and shoulders tucked under the twisted lump of what had once been the steering wheel. He wasn't moving. I touched him, felt his forehead. The skin was warm. I could hear him breathing now.

He was alive.

I tried pulling him up and out of the trap he was caught in. But I lacked the strength.

"Hey, knock it off," I heard him say. "That hurts like the dickens."

"You can talk?"

"Yes. But knock off the pulling and tugging. Let the firemen do their job when they get here."

I sat back, gaping at him. "Pop, what just happened?"

"Looks like something blew up." He was moving his head back and forth, stretching the neck muscles. "I think one arm's broken but the rest of me seems okay. That was one hell of a bang, wasn't it?"

I said yes.

"Somewhere, sure as hell not in heaven, that little Nazi son-of-a-bitch Hari Botts has to be laughing his fool head off." He licked his lips, wincing as he tasted his own blood.

"Careful, Pop," I said.

"You too, son."

"I think I'm all right."

"Hell, maybe we both are." I could see him flexing his free hand, moving the fingers. It must be the other arm that was broken. "Try doing this," he said.

I tried, first clenching the right fist, then the left. All the fingers seemed to be functioning. I wiggled my thumbs. Them too.

"Now can you feel your toes?"

It took me a moment to decide. "Yes."

"Now kick with your feet."

I did that.

"Both of them."

I did it again.

"Now remember to take it slow and easy," he said, sliding his hand up and clutching what remained of the steering wheel. "Looks like we're going to need to see if we can't get out of here on our own. Think you can do it?"

I tried to nod. I said, "Yes."

"Then let's do it. On the count of three. One… two…"

That must be when I lost consciousness again.

* * * *

When I came to the second time I was lying flat on my back on the damp ground with a child's quilt decorated with pictures of Indians galloping on horseback covering me to the chin. The sun was shining overhead like a gleaming eyeball and a face hung suspended in the air above me like a puffed-up balloon.

I recognized Ronnie Hightower.

"Hey," I somehow managed.

"Charlie," he said.

"Ronnie, how you doing, man?"

"You want a drink of water?"

I felt myself nodding. The chin and jaw muscles seemed to be in working order too.

"You better sit up or you'll spill it all over yourself."

To my considerable astonishment, I managed to do just that. I sat up.

Ronnie held the cup to my lips as I drank.

When I started choking, he took it cup away.

"Want some more?" he said, when I stopped gagging.

"No, that's all right."

"The lady across the street says she's making coffee too."

"Coffee would be good right now."

"Give it a few more minutes."

Past his shoulders, I could see the rubble and ruin. Where the great stone house had once stood nothing remained but a twisted tangle of wood, glass, steel, wire, and rock. The big Douglas fir in the backyard lay toppled full length across the remnants of the roof. Clouds of drifting black smoke swam past overhead.

All in all it seemed utterly impossible anyone could have survived the blast.

"Your dad's over there," Ronnie said, pointing.

There he was too. Pop on his feet standing in the middle of the road, a hand raised to his forehead shielding his eye against the glare, blood dripping from several facial cuts and wounds. A crowd of people stood nearby. Neighbors, I assumed. The sound of their voices was muted. The words reached me in fragments and half phrases.

"How did you ever make it out of there alive?" I asked Ronnie.

"I was in the yard when it happened. My dad sent me to get you. He saw your car parked out here. He said I should go and invite you in for coffee."

"And then it all blew up?"

"I guess it did." He shook his head slowly. "It must have, right?"

"Then who—?" But I stopped. It seemed a futile question. One to which I may not have wanted an answer. I managed to pull myself out from under the quilt and staggered to my feet. I went over to where Pop was standing, skirting around the heaped wreck of our car, wondering idly if the insurance would cover an explosion. I was sure we couldn't afford a new car without it.

There was a woman with Pop standing in the street wearing a cotton housecoat and bedroom slippers. A thin, pallid, fleshless woman who looked vaguely familiar.

"Hello, Mrs. Hightower," I said, when I reached them.

"Hello…. Charlie." She had to think to come up with the name. But she knew it.

I noticed to my surprise that Pop was holding her hand.

"Nora here was asleep on the porch when it happened," he explained to me. "The explosion must have passed right over her—the main force of the blast."

"It was most fortunate," she said. "When the furnace blew."

"It was a furnace?" I said.

"Oh, it must have been. My poor husband and his old friend Mr. Babbitt both died instantly."

She was looking at the wreckage as she spoke.

"I was very fortunate," she repeated, turning her head back and gazing at me.

"We were all fortunate, dear," Pop said.

In the distance sirens were howling.

"Took them damn long enough," Pop said. He put an arm around my shoulders and drew me close. He'd never done anything like that before that I could remember.

We stood out in the road waiting for the fire engines to arrive.

v

Come graduation day, 1963, there I sat, bored as a hibernating grizzly bear, shoulders slumped, dressed in the obligatory black gown and mortar board hat, Mom on my one side, Pop on the other, both nattily attired, Pop's left arm propped in a sling, hand and wrist encased in a plaster cast smelling of pine liniment, wearing his one remaining good pinstriped double-breasted blue suit, silver tie speckled with azure polka dots, black shoes shined to a gleaming tint, Mom resplendent in pearly white, neck wreathed by the same precious white fox stole worn by her own mother the day Mom graduated from Centennial High, Adobe, Colorado, class of 1933.

I thought she looked quite divine. (If not in exactly those precise words.)

Oh, and us too, I guess. Us 496 Lake Delridge High School graduating seniors. All of us also looking quite divine.

Like lambs heading for the slaughter.

Oops, an errant bit of foreshadowing there. Though not—thank Ghu—my own. *Hot damn, Vietnam!* (And, besides, lambs don't wear black robes or mortar board hats, do they?)

Meanwhile, our class valedictorian, Ronald Hightower, orated on: "Blah-blah much etcetera blah. The Will of the STRONG MAN sanctified. Much further blah-blah-blah."

I was barely listening. Same old Ayn Rand slinging shit crap. Even having your own beloved father blown to pieces in a mysterious explosion changed nothing.

In the crisp cool June early evening we sat slumped in our metal folding chairs as dusk curled around us. I gave a throaty yawn. Earlier on during the endless recitation of names from Amundson, Cheryl (better known as "Razor Tits") through Ziegler, Wilmer (a.k.a. "Weiner Butt"), as each graduate pranced forward to receive his or her official scroll, I numbed my mind by meditating on the riddle at the heart of the Zen koan of Mokugen's smile. I'd just gotten a letter from Slim setting it out for me. He added at the end that he and his Aleut wife and her many children were on their way south for a family visit.

The class valedictorian cleared his throat in a Mississippi mud-like rumble and proceeded in his oration: "Blah-blah-blah."

"And so soon after that dreadful freakish gas explosion," said a pinched female voice from somewhere past my shoulder.

"Such courage," chimed in another motherly voice.

"Such big fat wagging balls," came a guttural masculine assent.

"Like in wartime," said another.

"Or the World Series."

"Like Iwo Jima, 1945."

"Or Ebbets Field, 1955."

The back-up singers wailed in rhythm: "It's a miracle… it's a miracle… it's a miracle."

I looked over at Pop. Except for his broken arm in the sling and a scratch or two on the fleshy parts of his neck and chin, he looked pretty well recovered. His good right eye shined brightly attentive. I even caught him nodding in agreement as the valedictorian droned on.

And yet for me Pop represented in body, mind, and spirit everything contrary to the stupid, shallow, hateful philosophy of the Hightowers, man and boy.

And that's without even getting into the part about the tendrils.

I suddenly came to my feet.

"Where do you think you're going?" Pop growled *sotto voce*.

"Out," I said.

"But the boy's not finished talking yet."

"He's finished for me"

"Charlie, be gracious now," Mom said.

Earlier, Principal Carl T. Whalen, head bowed, solemnly dedicated tonight's ceremony to the two fine upstanding men who'd given their lives to God in the freakish furnace explosion which had so tragically wounded two others of our own.

Pop, listening attentively, wiped a tear from under his good eye.

"I need to pee," I lied.

"You can't hold it?"

"Not if you don't want to have me piss my gown." (It was rented.)

Pop, still glaring, pulled in his knees and let me slip past.

Mom, more knowing as always, gave me a lingering sorrowful look.

* * * *

As I made my way down the row toward the freedom of the center aisle, I kept my head bowed, glancing down at the passing assortment of footwear: black oxfords, tan loafers, a pair of white tennis sneakers, high heels, low heels, stiletto-heeled riding boots, thigh-high rubber waders. (Okay, I made the last one up.)

When I reached the aisle, I lifted my head, cocked my chin, tossed my shoulders, and hurled my mortar board hat high in the air. Catching it one-handed, I ran as if my life depended on it.

I never looked back.

* * * *

A voice called out to me as I crossed the parking lot: "Hey there, sailor, got a match?"

I skidded to a halt. There stood a black-gowned Katy Cross, arms folded on her chest, chin tilted at an equally cocky angle. Her lips curled in a smile of invitation.

"What are you doing out here?" I managed.

"Same as you, Charlie-O—bored out of my scrawny butt."

"I thought he was your boyfriend."

"Ronnie Hightower? You have to be kidding."

"I only thought…"

"Don't. It's not your strong point." She winked. "Didn't your sister tell you I called?"

"When?"

"Every day for the last month. Come on, let's go grab a smoke."

"I don't smoke."

"This you will." She took hold of my arm. "It's a Tom Powers special treat."

* * * *

As we crossed the lawn in front of the red brick building, I noticed she had a wad of chewing gum jammed in her cheek that made her look like Chip 'n' Dale both.

"So where's a good place where we can't be seen? The heat must be out in strength tonight, looking to grab teenage drunks and shake down their daddies for fat fines."

"That's not going to be me though?" Not that I wouldn't have minded a hefty swallow of Budd Champion's Satan's Brew right then. But still no driver's license.

"We can do better."

"How so?"

"Pot, my dear. Grass. Devil weed. Red dirt marijuana. Tom just got in a shipment from an old college chum down Guadalajara way. He was good enough to share."

"You mean reefers, tea?"

She giggled. "Nobody calls it that anymore. I thought you were supposed to be a Kerouac fan. I seem to remember spotting a copy of *The Dharma Bums* sticking out of your hip pocket one day when you were ignoring me in the hall."

I'd read the book. Twice. *On the Road* and *The Subterraneans* too.

"Good. Then you know what you're getting into."

From behind us the roar of the crowd rumbled. There were cheers punctuated by shouts, whoops, and hollers.

We stopped briefly and listened.

"Appears as though it's now official," she said. "We're graduated."

"Sounds like it, yes."

"You feel any older?"

"Ancient as dirt."

"Me too. Then I guess it's time for one great big last *whoopee*. Kiss me, Charlie. We're all grown up now."

She spat out her gum, tossed both arms around my neck, and kissed me square on the lips. We didn't hold it long. When we broke, I could still taste her minty breath on my mouth.

"Jesus," I said, grinning.

She spun her head. "Where? I don't see Him."

It wasn't my first kiss by any means. There was a girl in junior high named Bonnie who once gave me two dollars in cigarette money to go out in the woods with her one day. We necked and after that neither one of us knew what to do next. So we kissed again a few times and let it go at that. My sexual history up until then.

* * * *

Then a sudden shrill whoop drilled us from behind: "Hands up, the both of you! What's going on here? You're under arrest for desertion in the face of enemy fire!"

I swallowed hard, having recognized Cisco Cordova's familiar war whoop.

Behind him, black gown flapping at his heels, came Nedd Young. I can't say I was delirious with joy at seeing them, considering the timing.

"So what are you two boys up to?" Katy asked them.

"Same as you," Cisco said. "Getting away from what was going on back there. We saw Charlie making his escape and decided to follow his lead. When he met up with you, it was too good to resist. The Four Comancheros reunited at last!" He leered. "So where's my kiss?"

"Too late. The moment's gone."

"Damn. Always my luck."

By then the first wave of graduating seniors, parents, family, and friends had reached us. I gazed haplessly around, anxious that if we hung around much longer my own family would wander by and spoil everything.

"Look," I said to the three of them, "why don't we all get out of here? That was the idea in the first place, wasn't it?"

"Like where to?" said Cisco.

"How about the old fieldhouse?" I said. "Nobody'll think to look for us there." The onetime town ballfield and grandstand demolished years earlier to make room for a giant new shopping center that never got built. Now it was just empty lot. But the remnants of the grandstand behind home plate still stood on the other side of a chain link fence any kid with hands and feet could climb over in ten seconds flat. It was a familiar place of refuge for me and presumably others. I'd smoked my first stolen cigarette back there, had my first sip of Pop's whiskey. From the occasional pair of torn cotton panties, others had gone even farther.

"No, forget about us, Charlie," Nedd cut in to say, as Cisco was eagerly nodding. "I've got family here and so does Cisco. You two go on and do what you want to do. We'd better wait."

"But—" Cisco began. Nedd silenced him with a glare.

"Besides," he said, "somebody has to see that these outfits are turned in. Cisco and I will take care of that too."

I looked at Katy and she looked at me. We threw off our caps and gowns in record time and handed them to Nedd.

"We'll catch up with you guys later on," she said. "There's supposed to be a party somewhere."

"Sure," Nedd said. "We'll see you then."

Cisco, who might be slower than some on the uptake but who nevertheless got there eventually, just grinned. "We'll have us a real party someday," he said as he turned away. He gave me a sly wink. "Hey, here comes Mom and Dad with half of Hispanic Yakima in tow. Better hurry off you two while you can."

* * * *

Katy and I headed on down toward the old fieldhouse, skirting the schoolyard grounds. It was a warm, brisk, wonderful evening as far as I was concerned. Perfect as the full yellow moon shining above. I hadn't felt this good—this *free*—since any time I could remember. It wouldn't last of course. Nothing does. My years of reading science fiction—with its vast scope of centuries turning into millennia—had taught me that much.

Katy grabbed hold of my hand and drew me on.

"So," I said, as we hurried, "do you really have that stuff you were talking about?"

"That I do indeed."

"And it's safe, right? I mean, I don't want to die from an overdose or something."

"You won't. The high only lasts about an hour. You'll be able to get back home in time for the eleven o'clock news, no problem."

Even I had to giggle at that one.

* * * *

Overhead at the intersection of First Avenue South and Delridge Drive a banner reading *Congratulations Lake Delridge Senior High School Class of 1963* waved in the wind. As Katy and I waited to cross, cars packed with former classmates began to gather in the parking lot of Clem & Clyde's Burgerland across the street.

"I heard an ugly story you're planning on joining the army," she said. "You sure that's a wise idea?"

Cisco must have blabbed. He and Nedd were the only ones outside my family who knew. "It's the Air Force actually. It's my ticket out of here."

"I'd rather wish you wouldn't."

"I'm not going to get killed if that's what's worrying you."

"No, not especially. I just don't think you'll like it. You're not the trained killer type."

"Maybe not. But what else is there if I want to get out of here? And I do. It's all I think about. I can't wait any longer. There's a whole world out there and I want to start seeing it now."

The light changed and we hurried across. Just as a big Chevy station wagon went roaring past, horn honking. Cisco and family. The car was packed.

* * * *

When we reached the old fieldhouse grounds, Katy found a place where the fence was loose. Holding it up in my hands while she slipped through, I followed. On the other side we both stood still listening to be sure no one else was there ahead of us.

Hearing only silence, we went on. It was incredibly dark back here. Even with the full moon. Katy lit a match. Then another.

"You could always just run away from home," she said to me. "Hop a freight or something like that. What about all the people you know in California? Your science fiction friends. Ride the rails and go see them. The Air Force is for what? Two years, three? That's a long time, kiddo."

"It's four years actually."

"God, even worse."

"That other stuff only works in books anyhow," I said. "Riding the rails or hitching rides. Life isn't a Kerouac story. I need to do this on my own. I have to find my own way."

"You've thought it over, have you?"

"I think so, yes."

"Well… okay. Good luck then." She still didn't sound convinced. I didn't know what else to tell her. Admit that the Air Force was just a way of killing time until I felt ready to take on the world?

We found a place to sit on a slab of concrete that might once have been part of the dugout floor. Way back here you could barely hear the noise of passing street traffic. The loudest sounds were the occasional croak of a bullfrog.

"And anyhow," I found myself saying, "maybe the Air Force will send me someplace interesting. Like you said, New York or California. I start off in Texas. San Antonio for basic training. I've never been there before either. I haven't really been anywhere."

"What about Europe? Or Japan? Could you end up there?"

"It's possible, sure." She hadn't mentioned Vietnam.

"If they send you to Paris, I'd say go over the wall. Live the life of Henry Miller. Become an expatriate."

I'd read *Tropic of Cancer* too. Banned for thirty years and now in paperback. I shook my head. "Too many cockroaches. Besides, they shoot deserters."

"I thought they hung them."

"Both, probably." I made a gagging noise, tried putting a strangled look on my face.

"You know something, Charlie boy," she said, "I'm going to miss you when you're gone."

"We haven't seen much of each other lately."

"Not necessarily my idea."

I could have argued that. But let it go. "We can write each other letters."

"You know where to find me, do you?"

That's when it hit me. All the stuff about me joining the Air Force and I didn't have the first clue what Katy's plans were. What a self-centered jerk. I assumed she was going on to college. She was smart. Her grades were excellent. But we'd never talked about it.

Before I could ask though, she reached down inside her sweater and came out holding a cellophane packet, inside of which were two hand rolled cigarettes.

"You ready for this?"

My mouth was dry. "Sure. Why not? Let's do it."

She handed me the matches. "Light me up," she said.

* * * *

We smoked only one of them. Based on many later experiences—another story, oh yes—it wasn't especially potent. But it did the trick.

The birth of the sixties, as I later came to think of it.

From that point on further events proceeded as you might anticipate.

Henry Miller and D.H. Lawrence aside, I can't stand to read sex scenes in literature. Movies are bad enough—books worse. No matter how good the writer, the prose always seems to end up in the same fluttering place with legs akimbo and the earth turning somersaults while three invisible violinists play gypsy sonatas in the background. So I'll spare you. Paint your own mental picture. While keeping in mind that we were both young and inexperienced. It was my first time. And Katy? I never asked. (How dumb do you think I am?)

As for the weed, I did a lot of coughing and wheezing while Katy tried teaching me how you were supposed to hold the smoke in your lungs as long as you could before letting it ease gently out around the corners of your mouth. Otherwise, all I remember is my head spinning on my shoulders like

Jupiter on its axis—a science fictional metaphor that seemed wildly appropriate at the time.

We both had a good giggle over it.

For what seemed a long while afterward we lay curled up together in the darkness and dankness, smelling the rotting boards, the damp night air, our discarded garments strewn underneath us in lieu of a blanket. We talked and whispered and groped a bit more and painted word pictures of sand castles floating magically aloft in the sky.

If you catch my drift.

Strangely, of the two of us, Katy was the one who didn't have all that much to say. I was the one who turned into a babbling motormouth. She said her head on her shoulders was bouncing like a rubber ball with a rock inside and all she wanted for the remainder of her life was to laugh and giggle and eat till she burst. She was starving half to death, she said, and could have consumed a thousand Hostess cream-filled cupcakes on the spot.

She also said at one point if recollection serves: "The stars tell the stories of what's to come before God even thinks of it."

And, no, don't ask me what she meant.

As for my own babbling spree, I didn't listen. So you're spared. Again.

We stayed huddled there until we both dropped off to sleep and by the time we woke up—Katy first and when she was dressed rousing me as well—it was some absurd time like three o'clock in the morning. And it was cold. Bitterly so. We were both shivering. Even after we were dressed.

The good part being that we now were graduated and grown up and we couldn't get into any trouble over it.

Right?

Though I'm sure we both intended to spout the same unbelievable set of lies about where we'd been and who with and how it had gotten to be so godawful late. When we got home. When and if challenged...

Katy drove. Her mother's car. I didn't ask where she was or if her father (whoever he was) had attended the ceremony or if—

There was a lot I never asked her. I still haven't.

As I stepped out of the car and mouthed a sleepy good-bye, I could hear Pop in the backyard, pounding furiously away with hammer and nails. I briefly considered going out there and saying hi and telling a few dumb lies and maybe even talking seriously about the coming heat death of the universe. But it was late and I was beat and my brain was still reeling kaleidoscopically out of control.

So I went upstairs and crawled into bed and immediately began to bawl my eyes out. It was the first time I could remember crying since my last licking when I was eight and I inadvertently (I swear) clubbed poor sister Polly on the noggin with a croquet mallet—it slipped out of my hand, I'm telling you!—and no, Pop didn't believe me either, thus the licking.

Eventually, I must have conked out. I slept till noon.

When I woke up, everything was quiet. No hammering, no sawing, no Mom puttering around in the kitchen, no TV blaring, nothing.

I felt as if I were totally and completely alone.

I got up, dressed, and went downstairs.

There was nobody there.

I went out in the backyard and looked around.

They weren't there either.

The two wooden starships—both were gone.

vi

After that—to nobody's surprise—all hell broke loose.

Everybody had their own theory to explain what had happened to my entire family. The most popular—the one that ended up in the papers—centered around the fact that Pop was broke. Busted. Bankrupt. His dental lab business kaput. After he vanished, the bank account he'd left behind totaled something like fifteen dollars. (Though you'd think, broke as he was, he'd have taken that along too. In 1963 dollars fifteen bucks, while nobody's idea of a fortune, wasn't chicken feed either. You could buy a decent dinner for two with it—and not at any Clem & Clyde's Burgerland either.

So the consensus of popular opinion went, Pop had ducked out. Gone fishing. Skedaddled. Lit out for the territory. Taken the wife and kids along too. (With one key exception.)

Ah, but where had he gone?

A goodly number of possibilities were raised. There was always Canada. (Close by.) There was Mexico too. (Not so close but warmer.) Australia was mentioned. (Eager for immigrants.) Or Sweden. (Family roots.)

For a time Alaska was also a popular destination frequently mentioned. Since it was now an official part of the USA (a state since 1959), there'd be no hassle getting there via the AlCan Highway. Plus, the eldest son was thought to be already up there in a remote location hard to reach with no telephone or other means of communication. There was mail flown in once a week via ski-plane. That was it.

But then word came back from Alaska that Alfred J. "Slim" Gundy, William Gundy's oldest son, had along with his wife and seventeen or so stepchildren been recently reported missing and feared dead when last seen (by one of his many brothers-in-law) headed in the direction of the Arctic Circle by dog sled while being closely pursued by a supposedly rabid polar bear.

There were skeptics who found this tale a bit hard to swallow but since no crime had been committed and no official missing person's complaint filed, the apparent disappearance of Slim Gundy and his family was never formally investigated.

Me, I knew he'd been on his way to Seacrest in hopes of arriving in time for my high school graduation ceremony. (And maybe he had.) But I kept the knowledge to myself. No use spoiling a good cover story. Especially one complete with a rabid polar bear.

* * * *

In the meantime while speculation ran madly rampant, I stood mute. Even when for a brief time I was the leading suspect in a multiple homicide investigation. (Eventually closed when even the sheriff had to admit there was no evidence of foul play of any kind.)

On the advice of my attorney (another old college chum of Tom Powers), I declined to take a polygraph test.

As for the simultaneous disappearance of the two wooden starships, the funny part was how nobody wanted to talk about that part. (Or about the two burnt places in the tall grass in the backyard.)

It was just too absurd. Wooden starships could not possibly fly. You didn't need to be a rocket scientist to know that. And besides, even if they had somehow left the earth (but how?), why had no one noticed? No radar, no DEW line, nothing. No, what clearly must have happened was that William Gundy, in a fit of angry frustration, had dismantled his makeshift starships before taking his family (minus one) and running away to God only knew where.

Made sense, didn't it? No other explanation possible. Case closed. Shut your mouth. Say no more.

After a few days on my own, the big empty house spooking me worse than I would have expected, I collected my few belongings—SF books, jazz records, clothes, fanzines, typewriter, mimeograph—and moved into the small spare room over the garage at Uncle Horace and Aunt Martha's place. They said they were happy to have me. I went to work at first at the Dietz Family Viennese Delicatessen & Bakery on Bomber Boulevard bussing tables at a dollar and a quarter an hour, saving my money until late July when I turned eighteen and could enlist in the Air Force without the need of parental approval.

At the airport the day I left for basic training in Texas along with Horace, Martha, Cisco, Nedd, Katy Cross, and Sue Dietz (the two of us had become, um, close after I'd gone to work for her dad, the fascist, at his deli), all of the Rocketeers showed up to see me off with the sole exception of Mrs. Eva Jones who was home in mourning over the rumored death by police gunfire (in Mexico) of Warren Wunderly.

I was touched. Deeply. It was all I could do not to bawl my eyes out.

* * * *

Now you may well ask: what did I think? What was my theory to explain the disappearance of my father, mother, and three beloved siblings? (Plus numerous step nieces and nephews.)

Do I really need to draw a picture?

There were three known Botts Batteries. One had exploded in the home of Dr. Clayton Hightower, killing both him and his house guest, New York magazine editor Kingsley C.K. Babbitt IV.

The other two—well, what do you think? Unlimited power, baby. Energy sufficient to—

Well, why not?

To the stars!

As to why I alone got left behind, let me just quote from the letter I found inside my copy of *The Man in the High Castle* when I went to reread it several years ago.

I quote herewith the text in full:

Dear Son,

    I pen these words with unsteady hand and tearful eye to bid you a fond adieu from all of us who today are leaving this world in your better hands.

    You alone among us are the rightful one to remain behind. You alone among us have good work yet to be done. Stay, do your best, and know that somewhere up above someone is watching over you hoping and knowing that you will do him (and all of us) proud.

    Remember to be kind, good, and generous. Live your life with love and all will be turn out fine.

    Your friend and father,

William Gundy

Yes, I know. The letter could easily be interpreted as a suicide note. That's why I've never shown it to anyone else before now. I suspect the tone was deliberate. But I never believed it for an instant. (Besides, if so, whatever happened to the dead bodies?)

Oh, and one other thing I forgot to mention because they covered their tracks so well nobody even noticed they were gone.

Nora Hightower and her son Ronnie were never seen again either after the night 496 young men and women graduated from Lake Delridge Senior High School, Seacrest, Washington. (One of them being me.)

Consider the possibilities.

EIGHT: WOODEN STARSHIPS

(Letters from Home)

A/B Charles Gundy
Flight 919,
3502nd Air Training Squadron
Lackland AFB, Texas

August 6, 1963

Dear Aunt Martha & Uncle Horace,

Big day in my life today as you two ought to remember since you're the ones who signed the early enlistment papers allowing me to be here to celebrate my glorious 18th birthday and while I don't know about the "glorious" part it certainly is a day I'm not going to forget anytime soon.

Since today was also the day we got to run the obstacle course for the first time. We do it two times total before basic's over. The main difference between the first and second times is the first time if you fall in one of the water traps off the swinging rope or the monkey bars you get to bring along a change of fatigues to put on but the 2nd time you go through it and fall you're stuck wearing the wet stuff all the rest of the day till lights out. Happily for me I didn't fall in this time. Five guys did and the TI's rode them all the rest of the day, yelling and screaming in their ears, sometimes both doing it at the same time—you wouldn't want to hear the words they use—but at least that kept them from yelling and screaming at the rest of us including me. It was another boiling hot day too. Like a hundred degrees on up. Us NW guys definitely aren't used to that. They say it's a dry heat but it's still hot as a baked oven like how my mom used to warm up the newborn baby kittens right after they were born, funniest thing you ever saw but she swore by it. I still miss her of course. Wherever it was she and Pop went. I know you still think they may be back but I've surrendered hope.

Well, I better close for now because they only give us the mandatory thirty minutes before lights out to write letters in. Say hi to any of the kids I know if you run into them while shopping. Tell them it could be worse. I got a letter yesterday from my friend Cisco Cordova that I haven't answered yet and also one from a girl I knew at school named Katy Cross who I don't think you guys ever met. I've also been writing to Tom Powers from the Rocketeers science fiction club I belonged to. Letters are the only form of entertainment we get. We're not allowed newspapers or magazines and they took away the two books I brought with me and tore them to shreds. One was a Raymond Chandler mystery I read on the plane down and now I won't find out who the killer was until I buy another copy.

Love to all & apologies for the awful handwriting but they don't let us use typewriters—

Charlie

* * * *

AB Charles Gundy
Flight 919
3502nd Air Tng Sq
Lackland AFB, Texas

August 7, 1963

Dear Tom,

Oops, so now I get it. You were right. Me joining the USAF really was a dumb fool move. Not that I had much choice in the matter as I tried to explain at the time if I wanted to get going on my brand new life. But you did warn me tho, didn't you? At least that's what I was remembering that terrible first day here in Utter Holy Happy Hell (as we call it) when we crawled off the plane at 5 in the morning without sleep—I tried phoning a couple of fans when we laid over in LA 6 hours changing planes but nobody was home—it must have been meeting night—and they herded us like cattle—longhorns, I suppose, this being Texas—into this concrete windowless barn right off the bus from the airport & started going through everything we'd brought with us and throwing away anything we'd brought other than a toothbrush and a razor. I lost 2 books that way, 1 by Ayn Rand who you'd think they'd be too scared to mess with. The guy in front of me in line had his box of rubbers confiscated & then bitched about it the whole rest of the week tho even Don Juan couldn't find a way to use one around here. (They put saltpeter in the drinking water too, one of the guys claims he saw them doing it.) Then they told us to march straight out and meet our new daddy, TSgt Malloy, who I hope isn't reading this. He looks like Alan Shepherd the astronaut tho squatter and with a flatter head and barely any neck. He showed us right off what it's like to be screamed at by a beet-faced man with bad breath and a purple forehead 24 hours a day, 7 days a week, for the next 5 weeks. So welcome to the USAF, I guess. It didn't get any better the 2nd day either & that's not even talking about how they marched us down a line and gave us four shots, two in each arm, one of them for the bubonic plague believe it or not, and your whole arm—both arms!—swollen up like a balloon. Jesus, what fun. We march around all day in formation going nowhere & the food's not getting any better but I sure am eating a lot more of it than I did to start with. Anyway, let me just tell you about this Arkansas kid named Klute with buck teeth and a beer gut who woke up in the middle of the night in the second week and started screaming about being cornholed (no, I'm not kidding here) by giant spiders coming out of the rafters in the barracks. The medics finally came after about two hours of this and carted him off in a strait jacket. The rumor is he later hung himself in the base hospital but that's the kind of thing rumors always seem to say. Me, I was hearing voices for a while too—loud ones, yelling at me, surprise surprise!—as I was drifting off to sleep but am over that part now & doing as well as can be expected, keeping a low profile. So, yeah, I probably was nuts when I joined up. But here I am! The daily grind, besides the marching part, includes PT (physical training) in the morning right after breakfast—puke time!—and also in the early evening because it's too damn hot in the middle of the day to be doing jumping jacks and/or fifty pushups or running a mile without killing yourself from the heat. It's only rained once since I've been here and that was Noah's flood (oh, yeah, and they force march you to church every Sunday, even the Jews know enough not to complain) & for a while it looked like the barracks was going to float away. So what else? you ask. Well, in the daytime when it's too hot to do anything else we go to classes in an air-conditioned building (nice!) taught by the TI's and other sergeants (boo!) & there we learn how to fight a nuclear war with the Russians or Red Chinese—it's like World War II except you wear a radiation suit—-and about what to do when taken prisoner by the enemy. I am an American fighting man I will tell the enemy nothing but my name rank serial number and date of birth. One idiot asks what if you're tortured and the TI makes him stand on a chair outside the chow hall shouting I'm a yellow-bellied coward and piss in my pants for twenty or so minutes while everybody else files by. Fun. Builds character. Me, I ask no questions, tell no lies, pee no pants.

So what's new back there? Has Warren Wunderly been around again? (I heard a rumor he was dead.) And what about that sailor they nabbed for shooting Hari Botts—what happened there? I heard it was all an accident. Don't bother mailing me any fanzines or books either anything not a letter because they won't let me have it. Have you heard from Katy Cross at all? I forget what school's she going to in the fall. I wrote to her but no reply so far unless they confiscated it.

This is the longest letter written since I've been stuck her in Utter Hell. Jeez, am I sick of this place, believe you me. Say hi to Yul and Budd and

Melanie and the rest. Even nutty Mrs. Eva Jones. I miss you all.

Faaannishly yrs,

Charlie G

* * * *

Dearest Bubblebrain:

So how come you ran out on me without saying good-bye? I had to call and talk to your dear sweet aunt (how'd a nice lady like that ever end up related to you?) to get your official govt address down there. Then that same day your letter finally shows up. Marvelous to hear from you, my golden boy, even if coherence under pressure doesn't appear to be in your nature. Love you anyhow, darling dear, even if you dare not say that I did not warn you what you were getting yourself in for, soldier boy. Hey, I don't mean to sound like a pacifist CND (Committee for Nuclear Disarmament—mostly English) type but you do not appear to understand that the people around you are all prospective mass murderers in their heart of hearts. So when are you coming home again? Do I get to see you in your cool blue uniform? I don't suppose there's much chance it'll be before Sept, which is when I depart for college. In California. Mills College. In Oakland. Next door to Berkeley and across the bay from San Francisco. So yep, I made it in. With a decent scholarship. Now I'm scared. Well, nervous. They're mostly rich bitches at Mills so how does little Katy Cross from the Great Northwest Woods fit in with that kind of crowd? (Yes, I know: the "bitch" part is me all over.) By the way, sometimes I can't help thinking of graduation night down by the fieldhouse. Bet you do too. You have my express written permission to tell all the other air boys everything that happened only please omitting my name since one never knows whom one might meet at the crossroads of life and I don't want anybody getting the wrong first impression. And be kind. So how about you? I saw Cisco and Nedd one day and they say hi and they miss you. Cisco's got your old job bussing tables for Herr Dietz. Also I hear they caught the sailor who shot your science fiction friend at the party that night. It turns out it was a dumb accident when they were playing around with a gun driving by in the car and it went off. That's their story anyway and they're sticking to it.

Write me, lazy brain. And hurry. Because I'll soon be gone away.

Kisses & hugs,

Katy Cross

****

A/B Charles Gundy
Flt 919
3502nd Air Tng Sq
Lackland AFB, Texas

August 12, 1963

Dear Aunt Martha & Uncle Horace,

Another hot day but not the kind of day a person's going to want to remember. One thing about this place is how every day is just like every other day except when they're worse, the good part being that now that I'm over the hump it doesn't bother me as much. I could sail through the rest of it if I wanted. But it's not easy, no. If anything, it's tougher than I thought it would be. But I've learned some things about myself too. For one thing that I'm a lot tougher than I thought I was. Bet that would surprise Pop. I know it surprised me. I'm exhausted every day from the time we get up at 5 and in the middle of the night they pull surprise fire drills and you'd better get outside fast because if you don't you have to stand out there the rest of the night in your undershorts and get screamed at by the TI's that you're a stupid burned up imbecile. Some can't take the stress. They snap. One overweight guy in the upper bay got taken out in a strait jacket when he started seeing giant bugs. Later on he hung himself by a bed sheet in the base hospital. So you either take it or you don't and not taking it turns out to be worse than taking it.

So I guess everybody at home is doing fine. I know I wish all of you well. The idea that you might seriously be thinking of selling our old house came as a great shock to me tho. We lived there so long I can hardly remember the other places we lived in before. But I suppose it doesn't make sense leaving it empty. If you happen to run into either Nedd Young or his dad or Cisco Cordova tell them hi from me. Cisco sent me one letter and another friend from school too, a girl I know, did too. Letters are the one bright spot in our lives down here. We're still not allowed books or magazines or even newspapers and you must know how tough that is for me. I don't even know who's in first place in the American League. (I'll bet it's the Yankees tho.) Whenever you get a letter at mail call everybody else yells out or groans or whistles especially if they didn't get one. One day I got two letters, the one from you and the one from the girl at school and you should have heard the noise. To be honest many of the other guys have steady girlfriends back home who write every day and you have to wonder how long that's going to last. We've all changed so much—and in just four weeks. The others in my flight are from Pittsburgh and a few, mostly Negroes, from Arkansas and

South Carolina. Tomorrow we go into San Antonio for the first time. I want to see the Alamo of course. I'll say howdy to Davy Crockett or his ghost.

Well, that should do it for now. They're flashing the lights before turning them off for good at 9.

All my love,
Charlie

* * * *

August 13, 1963

Howdy partner,

News from the home front: the war is over. The good guys won. Victory lies nestled within our clutching grasp like a naked woman with heaving melon-like breasts panting for seduction. In plain words, Charles me lad, the mountain's been peaked; my novel's finished at long last. It'll be published by Viking Press next May but so far that's a secret as dark and mistily mysterious as the dankest dungeon in Denmark, so please say nothing to your fellow Rocketeers should you happen to write one or all, lips sealed with manure-tinged beeswax, please, all violators subject to a lifetime's damnation rereading old King Babbitt editorials and the collected erotic musings of Ayn Rand. Not that any would likely be able to decipher your penmanship— have you thought seriously of entering the medical profession in some non-surgical capacity following the conclusion of your military obligation?—a sane mind bobbles at the prospect. At any event I'll ensure that you're sent an advance copy hot off the presses once the baby is truly birthed. My resignation at Cantrell Air Corp effective in some three weeks time or until the drugs they've given me to blot all classified information kicks in, whichever comes first, has been gracefully tendered and gratefully accepted. My current intention is to invest in a sports car of swank European design and head due south for Mexico. Again, this needs to remain top secret info and I hereby swear you to silence. Am I now rich? you ask. No, I am not now rich, I reply, but the publisher's advance is sufficient to allow me a year's leave of absence from the vicissitudes of the mortal struggle to earn a decent living and I can't think of any better place to expend my idleness than the sunbaked land of Zapata, Villa, Malcolm Lowry, John Huston, Fred C. Dobbs, and B. Traven. And I can write. A second novel bubbles expectantly in the nether recesses of my creative subconscious, one exposing the science fictional microcosm perhaps. Future sales will determine future plans. Meanwhile in Mexico I live an improper bohemian life in the village called Mesquite not far from the teeming adobe metropolis of Durango. Send all postcards, telegrams, birthday greetings to an address to be supplied later. So far as your Air Force term of enlistment is concerned, please keep in mind that all things being equal, then all things must bear a finite duration. So someday the bastards are going to have to set you free. As for that lovely child Katy Cross, please be assured that I never once laid an untoward hand on her. Her beauteous mind alone captivated me like an Oriental fragrance. Honest. Injun. When you receive your copy of my book, check the dedication page. Then be sure to let the boys in the barracks read it too. Any who can read, that is.

YHOS,

T. Powers, esq.

* * * *

Aug 15

Fellow Comanchero—

So what gives, pal? We want to hear from you. What's up? Nedd says he's written you one letter already without an answer. Think you're too good for your old civilian pals? Spending all your free time with the local girlies or what? Let's not forget us sad sacks you grew up with back before you turned into a trained killer for the good old USA. Jesus (pronounced by the way hey-*sus*) I hardly know where to start in telling you what's been going on here. Our lady of the flowerbeds Katy Cross is going off to college in crazy California, land of the fruits and nuts, and you already know about Nedd and Oberlin Ohio. He made it too. So guess who's left holding the bag? Me myself & I, Cisco Cordova. Speaking of bags, you may as well hear it from the horse's trap because I now have a new job working at the IGA stuffing groceries into paper bags five nights a week and Saturday and Sundays all day. Whoopee! After six months they'll train me to start doing actual checkout. But I have to be bonded first. Anyway it beats working for a living for Mr. Dietz, the bigot, and with the $ I'm thinking of buying a car like there's one guy at work with a cherry red '55 Chevy he wants to unload so when you finally haul your ass back here and still don't have a license I can chauffer you around town. We'll go cruising for burgers. Want me to wear a little chauffer's cap or not? Your aunt and uncle came thru the line about a week ago and she said they hardly hear a peep out of you but you did ask about me and said to say hi. So hi back at you. Why not do it in person, buddy? They can't keep you down there forever.

Yr friend & fellow COMANCHERO

Cisco Cordova (& Nedd Young reading over his shoulder & telling him how to spel rite)

* * * *

A3C Charles Gundy
641st Tech Tng Sq
Greenbrier AFB, Mississippi

August 21, 1963

Dear Aunt Martha & Uncle Horace,

Well, the one good thing about getting sent down here is I've finally learned how to spell the word "Mississippi." Except for that lone saving grace you would not believe this horrible place. The bugs are bigger than the people. (Smarter too, hee-haw.) The air's so full of dampness it's like you could chop it with an axe & here you don't perspire you take a bath in your own sweat. One night I was on barracks guard duty and a bug flew in by the light bulb so huge it scared me into spending the rest of my shift at the top of the stairs where if they'd caught me I could of been court-martialed as a coward in the face of the enemy. How'd that look on my future record? But luckily it just buzzed the light bulb for a while and then flew off to go fight with a cat or something else its own size.

I start tech school classes on Monday which turns out way better than waiting around doing nothing which is basically all I'm doing now. Most of the guys here just play cards all day. I read books, even found the new *Serendipity* science fiction magazine at the BX with all the stuff about the late King Babbitt, the editor who was killed along with Dr. Hightower in that furnace explosion. Actually it's going to be a pretty good life here since classes are only six hours a day—not counting lunch at the mess hall—and the rest of the time is pretty much on your own. I went into the base library yesterday and came out with two books, Grapes of Wrath by Steinbeck and For Whom the Bells Toll by Hemingway. I figure if I can't make it through them, I'll go back to science fiction if I can find some in the library to read. Otherwise the usual USAF stuff goes on like scrubbing the commodes and spit polishing your shoes and no spitting on the floor while you're doing it. The barracks I'm in has won Honor Barracks inspection six weeks running so everyone takes great pride in winning again. Also we get to march into lunch ahead of the rest. The inspections are every Friday and so Thursday nights are spent cleaning and polishing everything to a gleam where you can see your face in the toilet water. And the toilets (we airmen call them "commodes") like everything here are about forty years old. Antiques. You don't want to be the guy who causes us to lose the Honor Barracks plaque. The town of Greenbrier is a fascinating place to visit for somebody like me from the North. I went in two weekends in a row and now I don't care if I ever go again. I won't mention the drinking age in Mississippi being only 18 so I'm actually legal but they only sell beer in the state. Hard liquor is illegal—but you can get it across the river in Arkansas but over there the drinking age is

21 again. Complicated. As I'm sure you know everything here is segregated by race. And I do mean everything. Even the rest rooms and water fountains. One says "white" and one says "colored." The movie show where a bunch of us went Saturday night to see a nutty Jerry Lewis movie called Disorderly Orderly has a "colored" entrance and a "white" entrance too but the white people have to sit in the balcony which I actually hate because I can't see much from up there if I'm not wearing my glasses. And I wasn't that night. Leo, a friend of mine from New York City, said that was probably why I liked the movie so much. Because I couldn't see it. The Negro airmen all go to a different part of town and we never see them once they get off the bus. Well, I guess it's what they call a "learning experience" in school but I want you to know I'm more than ready to head back home to the cold rainy North. Mississippi is like an alien planet to me. And not just because of the giant man-eating bugs in the air either. It was strange hearing about the sale of the house going through. It won't be the same for me when I get home that's for sure. I was in the 1st grade when we first moved in. Anyway right now it looks like it'll be just before Xmas when I get out of here. By then I'll know where I'm going next—my permanent base assignment as a personnel specialist. We get to pick our assignments depending on class standing so I'm going to try hard to get top grades. If you wash out they turn you into a cook. Scary thought there. But I'm not too worried because I can already type fast and I got all straight A's in school last year.

Charlie

* * * *

A3c Charles Gundy
641st Tech Tang Sq.
Greenbrier AFB, Miss.

Aug 22, 1963

Dear Tom,

Jesus, man, Mexico. That's some news from you. Congratulations too on the book sale for sure. Viking Press is one of the top mainstream publishers, right? Hey, maybe you can talk them into publishing more SF. So I guess that means your book isn't SF either which is what you always insisted anyhow. I'll go ahead & nominate it for a Hugo anyway. Can't hurt, right? Too bad all this couldn't have happened sooner. Then you could have swung on by San Antonio on your way to Mexico and we could have had us one of those "good old times" they're always talking about in Texas. You could have seen me in my uniform. But now as you can tell I'm ensconced here in the hot & humid environs of the Confederate State of Mississippi. Yep, that's right—they still think the Civil War's going on and they're going to win in the end. What a hell hole this is. Don't suppose I can talk you into swinging by this way. But the people are actually pretty nice though I don't suppose the NAACP would necessarily agree. The first question out of everybody's mouth is what church do you belong to. I always say "Protestant" as it's easier. My dogtags say "Unitarian" but I figure nobody down here would know what that means anyway. Two weekends ago I was coming back from town with a guy in the barracks from NYC & we were too broke for the bus—you try living on $89 a month—and a man & woman all dressed up for Sunday stopped & gave us a lift out to the base. They asked us what church and I said Protestant and he said, "I'm Jewish." It was hilarious. "We don't have many of your congregation here in Greenbrier." No shit, thought I. Anyway, man, your book *QZ* sounds interesting and I'm looking forward to reading it when I get my copy whenever that's going to be. I tried reading some things by Hemingway and Steinbeck and guess what. It's hard to do in an open barracks with 60 other people. Then I found a new paperback Cat's Cradle by Vonnegut. Best thing I never read. And Game Players of Titan by Dick. He's done better like Man in the High Castle. When the permanent base assignments come out I'm hoping for California or maybe NY. There's a base on Long Island. Everybody else wants to get close to home. The opposite of my choice. Why would I want to be close to home? It's the one place I've already been to. Wish I was going to Mexico with you tho.

Got to go,
Charlie

* * * *

2052 19th West
Seacrest 9, Wash.

Aug 25

Dear Charlie,

The way I look at it, now that the more odiferous portion of the bullshit sandwich they're feeding you is over & done with, this might be an appropriate moment for yrs truly, who's been through it before and made it back alive, to let loose with a few quick and, one hopes, sagacious insights into the whole goddamnably stupid military routine. At the same time maybe I can also fill you in to some degree on the latest local upheavals. So to start with, speaking purely as a grizzled vet myself—twice, actually—1940 as a wetnose National Guardsman called up to face the "emergency" and again from 1942-45 in the Reg. Army—I can tell you, my boy, the worst of the shitstorm really is behind you because try as they might none of the bastards has yet come up with a means of making the basic training/boot camp shtick look like anything resembling what comes later. In other words, as you maybe have by now noticed, it ain't nothing like what they try to con you into thinking it's going to be. And you're smarter—and tougher—and one whole of a hell lot more cunning, if I know my people, and by now you've got it pretty much figured, which is to say you don't take it seriously, which is the footpath that leads straight to the loony bin, trust me, thus there's damn little left for them to get at you with. So don't—and you won't. Let it roll off your shell like a wise & resourceful Northwest geoduck and besides which from here on out the crap they've been tossing at you head & shoulders since day one is going to turn into more like a slow steady shit drizzle. Trust me on this one; you can handle it. The worst part is going to be learning to deal with how goddamn boring it'll soon get without going stark raving batshit in the process. So roll with it, live with it, keep grinning that monkey grin, and as time goes by let me know if something comes up that looks tougher than you need it to be and maybe I can help out with some more of my patented grizzled wisdom. In other words, son, stay sane and don't let the small shite bite you in the ass.

So where the hell was I standing before the damn lecture began? The local news. Jeez, where does one begin? I assume they've been letting you get your newszines down there in old man Miss Issip and if you're not, holler, and I'll shoot a recent Starspinkle your way. Then comes the strange saga of one Warren Goddamn Wunderly and I bring this up assuming the sonovabitch has not managed to make bail on his latest rap. This is DNQ (that is, **D**o **N**ot **Q**uote—with or without attribution) but the County fuzz busted him over the weekend on an indecent exposure rap supposedly involving him walking around some small berg out there in the woods with his credentials hanging out for all the local folk to gawk at. A bad scene, all in all. And from there it spread like the proverbial pox to include the latest version of the love camp/chicken ranch thing he's been running out there in the valley. Another abandoned farmhouse. This time multiple arrests soon followed. And that's his version anyhow—least ways according to those who've been contacted from the county calaboose in his quest (so far minus fruit) to raise bail. Anyway let's keep a temporary lid on this one till we see how it plays out in or out of court. The other good news on that front is that so far none of the local newsrags has spotted the connection between him and his love camp and the local SF scene. So far he's being pictured as just another religious cuckoo with an eye for lean young tail—most of them boys. So let's hope it remains that way. Ignorance may not be the bliss it's hyped up as but sometimes it's near enough to call the horseshoe a leaner with fingers crossed throughout the SF community and the best we can hope for is he goes away for a good long stint in the Happy Acres State Rest Home and continues to keep his trap shut. The rest of his gang, by the way, are either locked up with him or, in the case of the damn poor kids, getting placed in foster homes.

And that, as I said, is today's good news. The less good is they also grabbed some punk kid of a sailor off a destroyer and charged him with shooting the lights out on Yul's porch that miserable memorable evening, potting poor old Botts in the process. It apparently wasn't even a matter of mistaken identity. Just dumb luck—all of it rotten. The boy was playing with a loaded pistol and lo and behold the SOB went off and Botts just happened to be standing in the exact wrong place in the spacetime nexus. I wouldn't necessarily buy one word of this but the gentlemen in blue appear convinced and I know enuf about firearms to know putting one together with a certified idiot is a recipe for all hell busting loose. The goddamn things *shoot*. Bullets. They *kill*.

The rest of the kids in the club say hi. Tom Powers is walking around with an even bigger than usual ear-to-ear shit-eating grin plastered on his puss over the apparent huge success of the mainstream novel he's been hiding under his bib. Seems as how he's got a major NYC publishing house lined up to deal some significant dollars and other than that the boy ain't talking. Yul sez Tom handed Cantrell Air his official notice of impending sayonara and is in the meantime talking of a sojourn south of the border complete with hot-and-cold running margaritas and senoritas similarly to boot. Stay tuned.

Now Melanie wants to stick in her two cents worth as well, so over to her & you do take care…

Charlie—I do most sincerely hope this finds you well. Your presence locally is deeply missed by many, certainly including one's self. Your steadiness, steadfastness, and all around good sense should see you through all life's travails. There was an article in the paper two mornings ago—we can send a clipping if you haven't otherwise seen it—concerning your poor missing father and some wooden sculptures he once erected in the back of your family house. Folk art, they're calling it, and quite fascinating from what I can tell. Odd that you never mentioned any of this to us but Tom says he'd seen it going up but that you were reluctant to divulge details. Speaking of which and whom, I imagine you've heard by now Tom's splendid news regarding his novel. Yul says Tom's become quite the celebrity at Cantrell Air but now intends to quit and move to Mexico to live the Bohemian life and perhaps write a second novel. A sensible choice for a man of his youth and lack of deep human attachments. Please continue to keep in touch. We sincerely hope to see you back here safely with us sooner rather than later….

Melanie Champion

* * * *

Box 99
Mills College
Oakland 24, Calif.

Sep 8, '63

Bubblehead my darling,

So here I am a sweet young college girl (not a co-ed, please, as Mills is purely an institution for ladies only) and I'm already fitting right in by having dyed my hair a deeper shade of shoe polish black and taken to ironing it overnight on the communal board. Then I smear on the deadly nightshade also known as eye shadow, slip into my midnight black leotards and ballet slippers, and head out for a night on the town in San Fran. But I jest. Sort of. One part of Mills is definitely Saucy Female Beatnik Central, as we say, except for the other part which contains the Snooty Rich Bitch Brigade. The disconcerting factor for me is that all of them—beat and bitch alike—are smarter than whips and for this trembling girl-child from the rustic northwest woods that can be a tad on the intimidating side of the ledger. But I persevere.

My roommate is one Dolores Valdez who you would definitely not like, I'm sure, though her bangs and moustache are both cute. Meow-meow. Her family, as she'll gladly tell you within ten seconds of meeting, were original Spanish land grant California settlers, never Mexican, and she knows Gov. Brown personally and even once went out on a date with his son who is now studying to be a priest who can blame him after that. Oh, and about half of young Hollywood too, she says—all on a strictly first name basis. Tab, Rock, Sal. "I never bother with American movies," I counter, with my famous archly casual sneer. I got a letter from your science fiction friend Tom Powers the other day saying he's already started writing another book—a shorter one this time and both you and I are central characters—I bet he tells that to all the girls—and then he's off to Mexico any day now and wants me to come along. (No, don't hold your breath on that.)

So, lover doll, please do let me knows what's going on with you? Mississippi, huh? Jesus but you're sure finding all the fabulous spots to visit. Well, Korea would be worse or, I guess, Laos or Vietnam where they shoot people like you. A recommendation: try reading some Thomas Wolfe. I'm 2/3's through Look Homeward Angel for a class and last night started bawling and couldn't make myself stop. Hard to read a book that way. Little ol' sentimental me.

Well, a couple of beatnik babes from down the hall just charged in and want to know if I want to run over to SF (never ever say "Frisco") to a coffeehouse in North Beach to hear a folksinger. One of them, the Peter, Paul & Mary dishwater blonde, has her daddy's Fiat Spider for the weekend.

Zip, I'm out the door. (By the bye, that "marijuana" we smoked that famous graduation night was pretty weak tea compared to the Real Stuff available down here. Some guy named Tom back in Seacrest swore me to absolute secrecy where I got it from but now that he's a famous author maybe a little jail time would serve him right.) More later, my sweet angel, my love, my glorious first love—hey, don't get shot in some stupid idiot war. There's so much else in life right now…

Love, yes!
Katy C.

* * * *

Benjamin Wade Dormitory
Oberlin Univ.
Oberlin, Ohio

October 19, 1963

Dear Charlie,

Today marks my third full day as a resident student here at Oberlin and I must inform you that it remains for me as strange and alien an environment as it did when I first arrived, as if I had somehow accidentally stumbled upon a separate and distinct existential plane from the one in which I lived my first eighteen years of life. Which is not to say that I am either unhappy or displeased. It's just that the differences between there (Lake Delridge, Seacrest) and here (Oberlin) are stark—and enormous. (The only words I can think of that fit.) Before proceeding further, however, I do wish to first express my deep abiding appreciation to you and your entire family for the support you provided over the years since my father and I first moved in next to your home. It's certainly queer now feeling as I do a stranger in a strange land and remembering that once upon a time not terribly long ago I felt exactly the same in yet another place, another time. In the end, however, I remain convinced that I am going to like it here. The people are decent, they treat me with respect and dignity—perhaps at times too much respect, too much dignity, but that remains another topic for another time. The classes, by the way, are superb. You would surely appreciate them equally.

Now, I am afraid, I must draw to a close as it is near time for yet another group orientation session with our class counselors. Before going, let me express one more thought which I have been unable to shake in recent days and which I feel I must share. Is a new epoch truly dawning? Can you also sense a surge of sudden new energy carried as if on the wind? Everyone here is talking about how each dawning day brings with it some new and wondrous revelation never seen or felt before. It's nothing as simple as the March on Washington—though seeing that on TV and listening to Dr.

King's oration brought both my father and I to genuine tears or President Kennedy and the recent signing of the Nuclear Test Ban Treaty (at long last!) or the people of all races who flocked to the South (your bailiwick, my comrade) to help register voters this past summer. (Many of them from right here at Oberlin.) Is this truly the dawning of a time of hope, a time of goodness, a time of possibility and vast dramatic change? I am convinced there is no better moment to be alive—and young. I wish you could be here to share this with me.

But I am making speeches which is not something one should do in front of friends.

Your comrade for life
Edward T. Young

* * * *

A3C Charles Gundy
641st Tech Tng Sq
Greenbrier AFB, Miss.

Nov 1, 1963

Dear Aunt Martha & Uncle Horace,

Well, you're right about how I felt hearing the new people already moved into the house after all these years. *SIGH* It's really not going to be the same when I get home which now looks to be the first week of December for sure since they've gone ahead & merged the two data processing units into one week so that we can get an earlier start heading home for the holidays. My permanent base assignment—we choose next week, keep your fingers crossed for me to get something good since I'm still #1 in the class and get first pick!—reporting date won't be till after the first of the year so I should have a full month at home. Which is fine with me except that it'll use up all my leave for a while. It's turned cold the last couple days too, a big change from what I was telling you about in August with the heat & the humidity and the giant man-eating bugs. There was even a coat of white frost on the ground this morning (at 5 am!—when they make us fall out for PT and then breakfast).

I don't have much of anything else to write about but wanted to get off my chest how I felt about the old house. Too bad I'm not going to be around to help you with the packing and moving. (Ha-ha.) All that stuff (ok, junk) Mom and Pop collected over all those years. I'm hearing from more people back home now than I did in Basic. It's a good feeling being more connected with the outside world and I also have more free time of my own to write back in. In fact except for classes and the Friday morning Honor Barracks inspections and the practicing for the parade we're having in 3 more Saturdays—the reason I need to practice is that I'm going to be the "guide-on bearer," believe it or not, that's the person who marches in front with the officers and carries the squadron flag—our time is pretty much our own. Mostly though I stick around the barracks with some of the guys who've become good friends, better than most of the ones I had in high school for what that's worth. We play a lot of "Hearts" for pennies a point. I'm getting pretty good at memorizing cards and win more than I lose. (Twenty dollars total.) Last Friday we went into town for a local high school football game. Kind of funny because I hardly ever went to any games at Lake Delridge High. Anyway as I've said before Mississippi sure can be a strange place. Everyone seems to hate the Kennedys because of the civil rights movement. In my opinion, the way the Negroes are treated here is a disgrace and this is supposed to be one of the more enlightened parts of the State. Nedd Young who sent me a letter from Ohio where he's going to college and doing well would be sick to his stomach to have to see it. I hope he never does.

Anyway, gotta run now and study for a test tomorrow as I'm still trying to keep up my 94 point average tops in my class. They say there's next to no chance of any of us going overseas, by the way, so what I'm hoping for is a base assignment somewhere on the West Coast or even New England which would be different. Anywhere except Texas and the South since I've already seen enough of those places to last me a lifetime. And also before I forget I heard from Cisco Cordova again who said he saw you shopping at the IGA where he's now working. I bet the poor guy has to be feeling low with all his old friends gone away. It honestly wouldn't surprise me to see him join the Air Force or Army or even the Marines. I can't see him working in a grocery store for long. He's not that kind of person. If you see him again though say hi for me but please don't say anything about what I just wrote. I might be wrong about it anyhow.

Well, guess I ended up having more to say than I first thought.
All my love,
Charlie

* * * *

99-23
General Postal Office
Ciudad de Mesquite,
Durango, Mexico

Nov 16, '63

Hola, Señor Charles—
Do my eyes dare deceive me?
Do my senses spout lies?

Have I not now found the promised land of paradise?

And me a boy-child of a mere 20-odd years.

In other words, Charlie, me lad, I like it mighty fine down here south of the border.

It's one cool paddock, daddy-o.

And I'm settling in, even as we speak. The address above, actually belonging to a crusty former chum-in-arms from Cornell, will serve fine in reaching me for the time being. Share it—though with due caution, por favor (already the local argot creepth into my consciousness)—no Warren Wunderlys or fanzine lettercols, please—& give me the excuse for daily visits to the local postal station where I serenely bat eyes back & forth with the lovely bronzed goddess of a señorita who passes out the gringo mail. I think I may well be in love, Charlie, O muse, as her English equals my non-existent Spanish, and our mutual incoherence strikes a perfect recipe for long term ecstatic bliss. (Unfortunately, someone—either a husband or brother lurking in the background—seems less taken with our burgeoning romance. I keep in mind that under Mexican law potting a horny Americano rates a mere ten-peso fine. If that.)

On the drive down here, I stopped to dally briefly in first Dallas and then Laredo—did you receive my picture post cards?—sorry for the "Free Cuba" natterings on the back of the one—did your sergeant read it aloud to the troops before handing it over?—visiting with (yes, yet another) Cornell chum (love that word!) in the former town and stocking up with some final & vital American provisions in the latter—such as good typing paper & coal black ribbons, some ink in which to dip my fountain pin, several gallon jugs of bottled water, vials of rattlesnake anti-venom. The college chum in Dallas —oh, hell, let's give him a name, "V"—came this close (insert here mental picture of sweaty fingers being rubbed) to dropping wife, embryo, job, 1956 Plymouth sedan, twostoryramblerhouse, and running off in companionship with yrs truly to the land of scorpions and mescal. In the end it was the wife (call her Mrs. V) who did the running off—of rather than with, alas, me—and this despite her six-month pregnancy and the fact that in our mutual college years we had once shared a bed (as I attempted in vain to remind her of before the skillet flew, whistling as it sailed through the fierce Texan night like a Clifford Brown staccato trumpet burst, though both of us fully garbed at the time, me in my gorilla costume.) (Another long college story, yes, complete with drunken vomiting. A slightly fictionalized version appears on pp 462-78 of my upcoming novel.) Dallas looms darkly as the archetypal American horror city writ large through our shared mutual history of barbarism, racism, genocide, and rape. V mentioned in passing that one K (the President) would soon be visiting. I silently wish him well and give a shudder.

Then onward to Laredo & its legendary streets of dust, its loping cow-pokes & sun-seared brown folk who couldn't speak the language (mine). Fun though in a cool bleak way, wandering through skeletal saloons, spitting in sawdust puddles, etc., and someday I may set down the scene in a novel but it will perforce end badly—in steamy death, blood aflow like water, murder most rotting, corpse foul, etc.

Then across the border—the plunge to the good side, as I now think of it. Local friends speak in hushed tones of a peculiar mushroom plant native to the slopes of the Yucatan which, when ingested, produces visions of earthly paradise. Ah, what comes next in this brave new pharmaceutical world of ours? I wonder. God Himself imprisoned in a vial? There's also something in the wind about LSD-25.

In any event, later,
Big Tom (alias "P")

* * * *

A3C Charles Gundy
641st Tech Tng Sq
Greenbrier AFB, Miss

Nov 22, 1963

Darling Katy (you don't mind, I hope?):
The cold has truly hit. Snowflakes falling this morning as we shivered in the five a.m. darkness doing our push-ups and jumping jacks. Last night a bunch of us went to the base movie theater to see Lawrence of Arabia. We were given special permission to stay up past the usual 9:30 lights out time since the movie runs four hours. I think it must be the greatest movie I've seen in centuries which you probably won't like hearing me say since there are no women in it at all. I'm writing this during our lunch break here in the barracks. Somebody just came running in and said on the radio shots were fired at Kennedy in Dallas. I guess I better go find out what the heck's going on.

www.ingramcontent.com/pod-product-compliance
Lightning Source LLC
Chambersburg PA
CBHW050732250626
47155CB00005B/1762

9 781479 441075